CONJUGAL
RITES

Also by Ellen Feldman:

a.k.a. Katherine Walden

CONJUGAL
RITES

Ellen Feldman

WILLIAM MORROW AND COMPANY, INC.
NEW YORK

Library of Congress Cataloging-in-Publication Data

Conjugal rites.

I. Title.
PS3572.I38C6   1986   813'.54   85-15247
ISBN 0-688-04739-4

Printed in the United States of America

First Edition

1 2 3 4 5 6 7 8 9 10

BOOK DESIGN BY PATRICE FODERO

for Judith and JoAnn

I

"I have never understood," Emily Brandt said, "why people who couldn't get along in marriage expect to become the best of friends during divorce." As Emily's legal practice had grown over the years, her professional ethics had shrunk or at least kept pace with the changing laws of the state. She no longer felt obliged to try to save the marriage, only her client's sense of humor.

"I wasn't talking about friendship," Laura said, though she supposed that was what she'd meant. For seventeen years she'd thought of Ezra as her best friend. The habit died hard. "All I meant was amicable. Ezra said the divorce would be amicable. He said he wanted to be fair. He said he'd see that Isabel and I were taken care of. And now he won't even pay her tuition."

At the other end of the phone Emily turned her swivel chair to face the window behind her desk. Her office was small, cluttered, and lacking in any redeeming aesthetic value, but the view of the Chrysler Building provided a spectacular escape. It spoke of earlier times, sturdier values, and enduring romance. It lied, but Emily didn't want to think about that now. She wanted only momentary respite. It wasn't that she didn't sympathize with her clients' problems in general and her sister Laura's in particular. It wasn't that she hadn't been there herself. It was only that in the unhappy family department Tolstoy had been way off base.

"Listen, Laura, you're my older sister, but for once I'm going to give the advice. There are two circumstances in which you must never trust a man, and the second is when he's trying to get out of what the first got him into."

"God, are you cynical."

"It has been my experience that the minute a woman begins to make sense, someone tells her she's cynical."

Laura looked at the bare floor of what had once been her estranged husband's consultation room. Erza had done a thorough job. He'd taken the Chinese rug, the big old partners' desk she'd found for him at an auction years ago, the two club chairs, and the red plush chaise that looked as if Freud himself had cut his teeth on it. He'd left a bereft space waiting to become something. She dropped her voice, as if she were afraid it might echo off the bare walls and come back to haunt her. "I feel so damn helpless. For seventeen years I've been running my own life. Managing a house, raising Isabel, paying bills, making my own decisions. Now, all of a sudden, I'm a ward of you and Ezra and Ezra's attorney and God knows who else. I can't stand feeling so dependent. So helpless."

Emily went on staring at the view. For seventeen years Laura had had the trappings of independence. Now it was Emily's job to get her the real thing. This was no time to start questioning that job. At fifteen she'd fallen in love with Clarence Darrow. At twenty-two she'd aspired to be Oliver Wendell Holmes and Learned Hand. Pushing thirty-five, she was beginning to feel an alarming kinship with ambulance chasers.

"I'm sorry," Laura went on. "I don't mean to whine. It's just that this is uncharted territory for me. I don't know what to expect."

"Madness. Everyone goes a little crazy during a divorce. I've seen men and women do things they couldn't have conceived of a few months earlier and were deeply ashamed of a year later. The only thing I can promise you is that it'll pass. It's insanity, but fortunately it's temporary insanity."

Laura was not encouraged. After she had hung up the phone, she sat in the single chair in Ezra's empty office with her hand still on the receiver. She was constantly wanting to call people these days, though when she did, she found she had little to say to them. Or else she said too much and regretted it. She looked at her hand on the instrument. Her fingers were naked, marked only by a band of pale skin that the sun had not touched in seventeen years. The band was like a white flag, a symbol of her defeat, a sign to the world that she was a nation conquered, easy prey for marauding bands, open to rape and pillage. Laura was not only uncertain of the future, she was terrified of it.

After Emily had got off the phone with Laura, she sat staring at the Chrysler Building for a few minutes longer. The hard October sunlight glancing off its surface like steel spears lent it an unreal quality. The building looked as phony as a set for a thirties movie. It looked as false as Laura's assumptions. Emily ran through the angry litany again. Why hadn't Laura looked beyond the final clinch that was no more than a backdrop for the closing credits? Why had she assumed her life could be sewn up as predictably and blissfully as a screwball comedy? And why had she allowed herself to become dependent upon the kindness of strangers, for a stranger was what Ezra had turned into? The questions were worn smooth with use, but Emily's impatience and frustration were still sharp as the flash of guilty pride that at least she, reared on the same fantasies, hadn't fallen for them.

She turned back to her desk, dialed the number of Ezra's attorney, and learned he'd already left for the day. Then she closed the mental file on her family, only to have her younger sister, Hallie, reopen it half an hour later. "I have a crucial meeting first thing in the morning, and I absolutely must pick your brain tonight."

Emily told her to turn up around six-thirty. In this decade you no more refused a woman's demand to pick your brain than in the last you declined a man's to use your body. Revolutions, sexual, feminist, or otherwise, might be liberating for society, but they had a nasty effect on the individual.

She dialed Peter's number. She could tell from the way he said hello that he was not alone. She explained her plight succinctly. Peter outdid her. "Quite," he answered, and she knew he was with the visiting professor of English history. For a man whose opinions were written in stone, Peter had the voice, or at least accent, of a chameleon. When he talked to the British, he sounded like Noel Coward. When he sat on student-faculty committees to discuss open admission, she caught cadences of the street and even, once, the word *funky*. A year ago, when he'd given a series of lectures on the Confederate generals, he'd shuffled around the apartment drawling orders like Massa Robert himself—and condescending to Emily as if she were his old but, as he repeatedly told her, much-loved mammy.

"We were supposed to stop at that party," he said.

"Faculty parties," she pleaded. "I stand around like an extra on a Cecil B. De Mille set while you move academic mountains and part the sea of red tape."

There was a moment's silence, while Peter, who wouldn't argue in public, let her wage both sides of the battle in the privacy of her own mind. He didn't really need her at those departmental receptions, but that didn't mean he didn't want her along.

"Hallie's in a bind," Emily said.

"The whole world's in a bind," Peter answered, and mumbled something that might have been "good-bye." She was sure of one thing. It wasn't "cheerio."

Several hours later, when the evening shadows had climbed almost to the top of the pale limestone façades across Park Avenue, Laura heard the bell, not the buzzer from the lobby downstairs but the bell from outside the apartment door. She knew that the man who had signed on seventeen years ago to be her guide to all uncharted territories, the man who had, impossible as it seemed now, urged and pleaded and schemed and fought for the position, was back, at least temporarily. This was Thursday night, and on Thursday night Ezra took his daughter to dinner. There was a time when he'd taken his wife and daughter to dinner, but though that time was little more than half a year ago, it seemed much more distant to Laura.

As she glanced in the hall mirror, she managed to miss the thick honey-streaked hair, not entirely natural but still sweet, high forehead, and good bones and go straight to the point. Her eyes, she decided, looked like FDR's at Yalta. She leaned closer to the mirror. So, come to think of it, did her skin.

The bell rang again. Patience had never been one of Ezra's virtues. Laura went to the door.

In the suit he'd had made two years ago in London and the Turnbull and Asser tie she'd bought him to go with it, Ezra was a walking testimonial to good materials properly cut. She'd married a gaunt, rawboned youth. She was divorcing an ersatz English squire. His milky gray eyes were shadowless as a baby's. His skin looked buffed. She tried to concentrate on his hair, or rather lack thereof. His head looked like a field after the thresher had gone through. Only a few sparse patches had been overlooked. The sight should have made her feel superior or at least immune, but it only reminded her that no one else in the world would know how much Ezra had grieved for the loss of his hair.

"Hello, Ezra. You're looking well."

His smile wasn't smug, only confident, as if he knew the truth of her statement. "So are you." She could always tell when Ezra was lying, just as she could tell when he'd had too much to drink. She was as attuned to a white lie or an extra two ounces of vodka in his voice as she'd once been to Isabel's crying in the night. Then she remembered that evening last winter when she'd spotted the extra drink and he'd told that absurd but carefully unverifiable lie to cover it. "I wish you'd have the doorman ring from downstairs," she said.

"I always mean to, but he never offers, and I don't like to

ask. There's no point in involving the staff in our private lives."
He took several steps into the apartment. "I thought I'd come
up to get Isabel. There are a few books I need."

His proprietary manner and the memory of that lie last
winter, which hadn't turned out to be so white after all, did
what the sight of those sweet, vulnerable tufts of hair had been
unable to. "I didn't know you'd left any. Your consultation
room looks like the Louvre under the occupation."

He started down the hall, giving her the same wide berth
she gave the neighborhood bag men asking for handouts. But
like them, Laura could be persistent, especially when she had
good cause. She followed him to his consultation room and
stood in the doorway while he rummaged around in the closet.
"Isabel's school called today. They said they still haven't gotten
the check for the rest of her tuition."

The dark closet yawned in silence. Laura felt as if she were
waiting for the oracle to speak.

"I talked to Emily about it."

"And what did Emily say?" This oracle had trained at the
New York Psychoanalytic Institute. He spoke not in tongues
but in questions.

She thought of the strategy Emily had outlined. First we'll
threaten to go to court. Then we'll threaten to go to court for a
lot more money. If necessary, we'll threaten to go to court and
sue on grounds of adultery. But Emily had also said she'd make
the threats.

"I'm the heavy in this. You play a cross between Melanie
Wilkes and Stella Dallas."

"She said you're responsible."

The oracle revealed himself. He was wearing the expression
he reserved for stockbrokers, real estate salesmen, and psycho-
therapists without benefit of medical degree. "Of course, I'm
responsible. Laura," he said in his reasonable voice. "Laura,"
he repeated. "Have I ever let you down?"

Yes, Ezra, you let me down. That Sunday morning you sat

down on the side of the bed and said you no longer believed marriage was a viable institution you let me down. Correction, you didn't sit down. You sat up. That's one thing I'll never forgive you for. Funny how viable marriage had looked twenty minutes earlier. Yes, Ezra, you let me down. With a bang.

"I mean financially," he went on as if she'd actually spoken. Either he knew her as well as she did him, or all those years of sitting in silence staring at the tops of blocked patients' heads had given him rare intuitive powers. "Haven't I always provided for you and Isabel? Do you really think I'm going to let them throw her out of school?" He smiled his I-have-seen-humanity's-suffering-and-alleviated-it smile. The damnable thing was that not only did it still touch her, but it still converted her. "Give me a break, Laura, as the kids say. I'll take care of it."

"I'd appreciate it if you would," she answered, and went into the kitchen because these days she didn't know where else to go when Ezra was in the apartment.

When she heard him walk back down the hall to Isabel's room, she turned on the water, but Isabel's voice carried over it. "Wow," she cried, and Laura knew that her daughter, made in her mold, had noticed the suit. "Are we going to Lutèce?"

"Lutèce, c'est passé."

How had she managed to marry the only native-born American who spoke French with a Middle European accent, as if he'd learned the language in Vienna at the turn of the century? But the thought was no armor against the memory of that August in the south of France. It was the first time they'd gone abroad together, like children bravely holding hands on their way out into the world, and Ezra had spoken only French, worn espadrilles and neckerchiefs, and called it their Gerald and Sara summer. The Middle European accent not withstanding, the French memories hurt a lot.

Isabel came dancing into the kitchen. Her translucent skin, a legacy from Laura, was dramatically pale against the mass of curly black hair she'd inherited from Ezra. The full mouth, also

Laura's, was smiling. Laura caught a whiff of her own perfume. "*Très chic, n'est-ce pas?*" Isabel asked in imitation of either her father or one of the Gabor sisters.

"How you say? Very," Laura agreed.

Isabel did another turn around her mother before the tug of white tablecloths, surly waiters, and trendy restaurants pulled her back to Ezra.

"I'll bring you a truffle," Isabel called from the hall. "A doggy bag full of truffles."

Laura opened the refrigerator door and bent as if she were examining its contents. In that position her face was not visible from the hall. "Just have one for me," she called. "And a good time."

After her husband and daughter had left, Laura stood staring at the inside of the refrigerator for several minutes. Finally she closed the door without taking anything from it. You could say one thing for divorce. It was less fanatic than Weight Watchers, cheaper than the Golden Door, and more effective than Pritikin, Atkins, et al. Of course, the same could be said of an affair, or so Laura had heard.

Hallie appeared in the door to Emily's office promptly at six-thirty. She was wearing a gray pinstripe suit that was destined to grow up to be chairman of the board, a foulard bow tie straight off her husband's tie rack, and a pair of shoes that cost an arm and a leg and looked as if they'd been wrestled from the feet of a dead WREN during the blitz. The look was severe. The wearer was anything but. Emily thought of the old movie line "But, Miss Smith, you're beautiful without your glasses." Hallie was beautiful with them. Her eyes, huge and sooty behind the no-nonsense frames, dared you to betray their trust. Her hair, even fairer than Laura's, fell in a neat page's cap. Her full mouth looked as if she were about to take a good bite of life. Some twenty years ago a smooth-faced adolescent who had slipped Emily contraband editions of D. H. Lawrence had said that it was okay that Hallie was the pretty one because Emily was the smart one. The adolescent had been wrong. Hallie was smart, or at least successful, as well as pretty, and at the moment she looked too elegant for Emily's office. She must have known as much because she insisted they do whatever brain picking was in order over a drink at the Helmsley Palace.

Emily stood, saw the look on Hallie's face, and sat again. She took a hand mirror from her desk drawer. The least she could do was make an effort not to embarrass her sister. Years ago Emily had decided her face was an equation that added up to zero, which was not to say it was bad, only unremarkable. The eyes, large, gray, deeply intelligent she was convinced, were a plus; the mouth, too wide, too thin, too unyielding she'd been told, was a minus; the high forehead, a plus; the nose, straight but too long, a minus; the hair, reasonably thick and carved to a widow's peak, a plus; its color, a shade of brown that was best described as mouse, a minus. She stood and straightened her pleated skirt. It was momentarily but accidentally in style. She'd been wearing the same kind of skirt since college. She also owned a basic black dress and a strand of good pearls. But the neat, zero-level façade was not without advantages. Emily was convinced it contained and camouflaged an embarrassing tendency to emotional sloppiness.

"Just one drink, though. I want to get home before Peter." Emily saw the look on her sister's face and decided to beat her to the punch line. "I don't approve of latchkey children—even if they are thirty-nine-year-old college professors."

In front of the elevator bank Ned Sinclair, "T. Edward Sinclair" on the firm's letterhead, stood waiting. "Only the service one is still running." His smile was conspiratorial, as if they all were on this desert island together. Emily performed the introductions and watched her sister run the tally. Ned's fingernails were not only immaculate but manicured. His shoes—always the giveaway, their mother, Dottie, insisted—were cordovan and shined. The gold Rolex on his wrist told more than the time. The Brandt women were living proof of Dreiser's law of females and clothing. They made a profound connection between an individual's attire and his probity. When Ned managed to acknowledge the introduction without opening his mouth, he gained a few more points. Moving from Dreiser to Fitzgerald, Ned's accent, if not his voice, was full of money.

From behind closed lips he asked Hallie if she was an attorney, too. She explained she was the executive director of AWE. Emily always envied her sister's title. It sounded so impressive, as if Hallie were the goddess of reason or the muse of art.

"Alliance of Women Executives," Emily explained, because Hallie didn't seem to realize that AWE was not a household word, especially in the households of single men like Ned Sinclair. Ned had more going for him than his impeccable attire and implied credentials. He was the only adult heterosexual male Emily knew who paid neither alimony nor child support. No, that wasn't true. Come to think of it, though she rarely did, her former husband, Jake, was another.

"A professional group?" Ned asked.

"We provide a network, among other things."

"As in old boys'?" Ned said.

"Exactly!" Hallie answered, and they smiled at each other as if they'd both stumbled on the secret of DNA at precisely the same moment.

"How long have you known *him?*" Hallie asked after they said good-bye to Ned in front of the building and started walking up Madison Avenue.

"Don't talk in italics. You sound like 'That Cosmo Girl.' "

"Helen Gurley Brown's no fool. She turned a washed-up magazine into a multimillion-dollar empire. But what about Ned Sinclair?"

"He's had his picture in *People* magazine."

Hallie's smooth head lifted like a golden retriever picking up the scent. "There's nothing wrong with that."

"Maybe not, but there's something wrong with a man who tells you about it on the Bloomie's escalator."

"He's nice-looking," Hallie insisted. "He has a sweet, boyish charm."

"The first time I met Ned Sinclair he told me he was in the Social Register and into group sex—that was in the seventies, of course—and asked if I was too."

"In the Social Register or into group sex."

"I think either would have done. Hallie, I may not be married to Peter—we may be living in sin, as you and Laura so whimsically put it—but I do believe in fidelity."

"Does Peter?"

"As fervently as a child believes in Santa Claus."

"It's easy to see you don't have kids," Hallie said, and led the way into the hotel courtyard, glittering with hundreds of tiny lights and more promise than it could ever fulfill. Inside the venerable town house library given new life as a bar, Hallie outmaneuvered two other groups for the last sofa, ordered drinks, and got down to work.

"AWE has gone as far as it's going to as a networking organization. I'm desperate for new target markets. That's what this meeting tomorrow morning is about. A group that's into baby counseling."

"For executive toddlers?"

"Cute, Em, very cute. To help women decide if and when they're ready for childbearing. The future lies with the service industries, and baby counseling is the service of the future."

"Sometimes I wonder how I got into this family. You talk like an advertising slogan and Laura takes her philosophy from needlepoint pillows. Lately she's waffling between 'If you love something, set it free' and 'You can't be too rich or too thin.' What I don't understand—" Emily began, then stopped because she heard the anger in her voice.

"Is how she could have neglected to cover her ass," Hallie finished for her.

"I'm not the wordsmith you are, but yes. She has no career, no training, and no money of her own."

"I thought that was why she had you. To get her the last.

Which brings me back to AWE. Think about it, what does the young B-school graduate want?"

"I thought she had it all."

Hallie's smile was triumphant. "That's exactly the point. She doesn't have it all, but she wants it all. She wants children." Hallie dropped her eyes and sipped her drink, as if she'd suddenly remembered that Emily didn't. "And she wants help in deciding how and when to have them. Five years ago, when I got pregnant, I had to lie and tell everyone at work it was an accident."

"Why on earth did you do that?"

Again Hallie dropped her eyes and sipped her drink, but this time the embarrassment was not for Emily. "You know. I didn't want them to think I wasn't serious about my career."

"You'd rather have them think you couldn't master the mechanics of a diaphragm?"

"The point is," Hallie said, all business again, "I sensed that my biological clock was running down, but in those days a biological clock wasn't a household fixture. I had no network to resource with, no role models to follow. I had to make the decision for myself."

"But now you have *Time* magazine and market research to do it for you."

"You can laugh all you want, but this is a ground swell, and I plan to get in on the bottom floor."

"You're mixing your metaphors," Emily said, "but you're probably going to make a million dollars doing it. All right, tell me about this baby counseling group and what kind of deal you have in mind, and I'll see if I can reserve judgment long enough to be of some help."

"How's Daniel?" Emily asked her sister after they'd given the cabdriver their respective addresses.

Hallie pictured her husband as he'd be when she arrived home. Daniel's big shoulders would be slumped forward over the computer terminal, his eyes as red from hours of staring at the screen as an alcoholic's from a bout with the bottle. It was a portrait by Hopper, all sharp lines and desolate isolation. If his work were going well, he'd be at one with the machine. If he spied ruin lurking on the horizon, he'd be inconsolable. Either way he'd be beyond Hallie's reach. "Terrific," she said. "His company's stock is up to twenty-two. He's working like a dog, of course, but I can't complain. He put the entire AWE operation—everything from mailing lists to accounts—on floppy discs for me."

"That's the kind of talk that makes me understand the Luddites."

"Now you sound like Peter."

"I am like Peter," Emily said, and wondered at the things women told each other, and themselves, in the name of loyalty.

When Hallie let herself into the apartment, Daniel did not disappoint her. The only sound of life, other than the blissful yelps and tap dancing paws of Byte, the cockerpoo they'd bought for their daughter, Kate, was the whisper of computer keys from somewhere down the hall. She headed for the sound. Daniel sat as she'd pictured him. When he looked up from the screen, his face was as smooth and blank and well designed as the machine that still held his attention, if not his gaze.

She asked about his day. She mentioned her own. The conversation was as spare and to the point as one of Daniel's more elegant programs. Hallie continued down the hall to Kate's room. Sprawled across the youth bed, surrounded by Paddingtons and Snoopys and Stieffs, her daughter slept the sleep of the just, the affluent, the protected. Hallie stood looking at her for a moment, then closed the door and went back to the study. Daniel had not moved. She crossed the room and put her hands on his shoulders. He gave no indication of feeling her presence.

"Have you had anything to eat?" she asked.

"Naomi heated up the pot roast before she left." As he leaned forward to type in a command, he managed to shrug off her hands. She started out of the room. "It was good," he said. She presumed he meant the pot roast.

In the kitchen she noticed a peculiar but unfortunately not strange aroma. Byte walked to his accident and sat beside it in shame. Hallie cleaned it up quickly, trying not to gag, then went back down the hall to the study.

"Did you walk Byte?"

"Naomi walked him before she left," Daniel answered without taking his eyes from the screen.

"Then he's definitely sick. I thought you were going to take him to the vet. You promised to last Saturday when I took Kate to that birthday party."

"I forgot." Daniel typed in another command.

"Next time I'll program it into the computer."

He looked up from the screen, and Hallie wished he hadn't. After a certain point in some marriages naked emotion, like naked flesh, doesn't warrant display. "I know you find it hard to believe, Hallie, but I have other things on my mind. Five of my people have burned out in the last month." He pronounced the most dire words in the industry in the tone most mortals reserve for cancer, heart disease, and AIDS.

"We all have things on our mind, Daniel."

"My apologies. I forgot for a minute that I was talking to the executive director of AWE." His eyes moved back to the screen. "Listen, Hallie, I think it's wonderful that you're aiding and abetting the women of America. I think it's terrific that you're bringing home a little bacon—well, maybe an occasional egg—but you don't seem to realize the burden it puts on me. The attrition rate in this business doesn't give me time to drag Byte to the vet or listen to Naomi's complaints or pick up dinner on the way home."

"No one asked you to pick up dinner—" she began, then stopped. They'd been through it too many times before. Maybe that was why Daniel was no longer listening.

Two hours later Hallie stopped in the door to the study again and said good night. Daniel actually looked up from the screen and managed a smile. She went on down the hall and into the bedroom. Just as she was about to close the door to the bathroom, she heard his voice. The words escaped him in a long sigh. "Baby, you're terrific."

Hallie didn't bother to go back down the hall to the study. He hadn't been talking to her.

Daniel's voice awakened her. He was talking in his sleep, and now the words came out in anguish rather than pleasure. They were mumbled, but Hallie knew them by heart. The dream haunted Daniel's sleep the way nightmares of battle were said to trouble men home from war. "The system's down," he moaned. "The system's down."

She thought of Yossarian in *Catch-22*. She remembered Dana Andrews in *The Best Years of Our Lives*. Yossarian had been alone, but Dana had had Teresa Wright. She put one hand on Daniel's brow, the other on his shoulder and shook him gently. "It's all right," she said. "It's all right, Daniel."

He turned to her and opened his eyes. Whatever war he'd seen, it was hell. "The system was down, and three major clients were waiting for the product."

"It was only a dream," she crooned. "The system's not down." She went on holding him and gradually felt his body relax against hers. Well, not relax entirely. As she'd said, the system wasn't down. She moved her body. She moved her hand. She listened to his breathing. It was even. He was fast asleep.

Hallie disengaged herself and turned on her side with her back to Daniel. She tried to recall the last time they'd made love. It was more than two weeks ago, the night his company had sold the new payroll software to an international investment firm. And the time before that had been weeks earlier, when he'd returned from the convention in Las Vegas. She thought of the man Emily had introduced in her office. Ned

Sinclair. She thought of all the Ned Sinclairs in the world and wondered where she'd gone wrong. Then she remembered the trip to Las Vegas again. One of the salesmen had brought his wife a case of herpes. Daniel had returned home with nothing but a clear conscience and a few mementos. She thought of her sister Laura and a woman at AWE who'd just separated from her husband. She pictured the hordes of women she saw all over the city, their faces incomplete, their nerves ragged, like pieces of photographs torn in two. She turned on her other side toward Daniel and put a hand on his shoulder. He didn't respond, but he didn't shrug it off.

By the time Emily got home Peter was sprawled on the bed, his long body largely undressed, his longish fair hair entirely disheveled. The horn-rimmed glasses, always a little absurd on a half-naked man, were lopsided, as if in deference to the asymmetrical features. They were sharp, perhaps handsome at times, but they were not even. There was an oversize volume with flaking pages open on his lap and the indication of several other books beneath the quilt where he'd thrown it to her side of the bed. Either he'd brought home a lot of work or a dead body.

"What was Hallie's emergency this time?" he asked. "Another conversion? In the last decade your lovely sister has been into *est*, Zen, and the Episcopal Church—in that order—but as far as I can see the essential philosophy remains the same. Self-help Tinker Bell. The louder she claps, the more everyone else will believe."

"She's getting into baby counseling. The future lies with the service industries, and baby counseling is the service of the future."

He looked up at her, his long face creased by a smile that would have convinced a less receptive audience that the car had only three thousand miles on it or a vote for him was a vote for clean government or he really was crazy about her no matter what he said or did in moments of anger. "I have to hand it to Hallie. This city is full of celebrity-fuckers, but she goes them one better." Emily stood at the end of the bed, shifting from her left foot to her right, waiting for the other shoe to drop. "She's the only trend-fucker I've ever met."

Emily laughed, guilty at her betrayal of her sister, relieved at her acquittal. She hated her own moral weakness, but she hated coming home to Peter's sulks more and to his total silences most of all.

"Don't tell me. Let me guess. She talked about her biological clock."

"Not hers in particular. How was your reception?"

Something about the way Peter narrowed his eyes as he lit another cigarette made her think there might be a third shoe somewhere in the offing.

"There was a lot of talk about visiting lecturers from business and the arts—if you'll excuse the expression. Your ex-husband is going to give a daylong seminar on magazine publishing."

Emily wondered if the neighbors downstairs had heard the thud. Four years ago, right after she and Peter had begun living together, they'd run into Jake at a party. Peter had said nothing about the incident that evening, nothing at all, it turned out, for the following four days.

"Do you want me to freshen that?" She indicated the glass on his night table.

"There's nothing to 'freshen,' but I'd like another drink—as long as you're up.

"I signed you up for the seminar," Peter said when she came back with the fresh drink for him and one for herself.

"Thanks all the same, but I know all I want to about the subject."

He brought the dimples into play along with the political smile. She was reprieved. He hadn't found her guilty for the coincidence. "In that case I'll take your name off the list."

"You really are a bastard."

"So my ex-wife has told me."

"Estranged, lover, not ex." She walked to her side of the bed and pulled back the covers. In place of the pile of books she'd expected lay a long, awkwardly wrapped package that could have come only from a florist. She looked from it to Peter. He was wearing a different smile now, the strained, lopsided one that she'd had to sleep with him to discover.

"Thank you," she said.

"I know I was short on the phone, but it was just that I didn't want to go to that damn reception alone. No, it was more than that. I like being with you, and I miss you when I'm not."

She turned from the asymmetrical smile that made him look less handsome but more appealing and tore open the paper. Inside were long-stemmed red roses, four, six, nine. She stopped counting. She felt the bulk in her arms. She knew Peter. There were a dozen. She refused to consider the going rate of a dozen long-stemmed roses. She refrained from glancing at the top of his dresser, where a pile of unpaid bills lay in cavalier disarray. She dismissed the thought of the loan they'd had to take out in her name because though he had the children with overbites, she had the better credit rating. Peter regarded everyone from the local bookstore to American Express the way a Regency rake regarded his tradesmen—everyone, that is, except his estranged wife, who could set the clocks in the suburban house Peter had abandoned along with her and two children by the arrival of his checks.

"They're beautiful. Thank you. But you shouldn't have. I mean, they must have cost a fortune."

The smile slid into balanced formality. The eyes, under lashes that would have been unfair even on a girl, turned guarded. Peter didn't like to talk about money.

"Thank you," she said again, and went into the kitchen to put the roses in water. Peter never said he was sorry. Over the phone he suggested it, around the apartment he mimed it, in bed he expressed it eloquently, but he never said it. Of course, he hadn't exactly said it now, but Emily wasn't about to quibble.

She returned with the vase, put it on the windowsill across the room, and asked if he wanted a sandwich. He shook his head. She glanced at the half-full glass on his night table. "Another drink?" He said no. "Anything?"

Peter closed his book, put it on the night table, and turned the reading light to low. "I thought you'd never ask."

During the six years Emily had known Peter and the four she'd lived with him, she'd discovered a man of impressive strengths, prodigious weaknesses, and many idiosyncrasies. He was highly intelligent, if not as well informed as he occasionally pretended. He was pathologically possessive, but only because he cared so deeply and passionately for Emily. He found most living mortals, many dead heroes, and ninety-nine percent of contemporary culture wanting. He was a mass of moral and aesthetic prejudices, absurd insecurities, and charming quirks. There was only one area in which Peter harbored no irrational convictions: He was inhumanly sane about sex. He was also, fortunately for Emily, astonishingly proficient at it. No, *proficient* was the wrong word because that implied study, thought, or at least effort. Peter was a natural. It was evident in his long-legged walk, his confident stance, the secret promise of his smile, at least around women. Emily knew nothing about athletes, natural or otherwise, but over the years she'd come to learn a great deal about Peter. Women responded to him like major-league scouts in the market for talent. And from the very beginning Emily had been no exception, though for some reason Peter had singled her out from the crowd.

She lay in bed after one of Peter's more eloquent apologies listening to the sound of his sleeping. He really ought to leave his body to medicine, and she wasn't thinking only of his sporting expertise. Surely there was something miraculous about a man who could snore on his stomach and side as well as his back. The sound was unmistakable but not unpleasant. There was no doubt about it, Peter was extraordinary. Across the room the roses made a dark shadow against the street-lit window. On top of the dresser the mass of bills and dunning letters was less clearly defined.

She turned onto her side with her back to his dresser. It took some effort on her part. Peter's arm, a dead weight in sleep, pinned her to the bed that securely.

II

Emily spent the following morning in a particularly acrimonious examination before trial, and by the time she arrived at her office the usual stack of telephone messages had accumulated. Laura and Hallie said she was a cynic, but Laura and Hallie were wrong. A cynic's heart would not leap with expectation at the sight of those hurriedly scrawled notes, not after more than ten years it wouldn't. Somewhere in that pile of untidy pink slips, Emily was eternally certain, was the client she'd been waiting for all her life, the one who would put another ounce of justice on the legal scales and Emily in the casebooks.

Though her social conscience had withered over the years, and her ambition shrunk, her hope managed to limp on. There had been a time, in college, in law school, even during her first years of practice, that the three had flourished hand in hand. As an undergraduate she'd marched in demonstrations and marked time until the day she'd be able to throw her trained mind as well as her body into the struggle. In law school the words *pro bono* had whispered a promise: She would have professional success *and* a clear conscience. She'd gone into the world girded for battle in undergraduate skirts and worn sweaters, the feminine counterpart of the blue work shirt that in those long-ago predesigner days signified unity with the masses. But the masses she'd met, in the form of pushers, pimps, and prostitutes, had sported fur coats and hand-tooled boots that offended Emily's aesthetic as well as moral sense, and the contemporaries she'd hoped to defend for burning draft cards and disrupting political conventions had renounced both practices in favor of raising children and their own consciousnesses. Meanwhile, back at the ACLU, while her seniors were establishing women's rights to abortion, and schoolchildren's to free speech, she was answering incessantly ringing phones and writing endless letters. "Eternal vigilance is the price of liberty" ran the ACLU's motto, and they weren't kidding about the eternal. So gradually, almost imperceptibly, Emily had backed into her current practice, as she'd backed into so many things in her life. And simultaneously she'd managed to back out of her marriage as well. But that was another story, equal to, perhaps, but separate from her career.

As she walked to her office, she leafed through the messages. If there was a landmark case among them, it was in disguise. She recognized most of the names and could predict the reason for their calls. One woman would want to know if she could put her former husband in jail for missing his child support payment. Emily wished she could say yes. The husband, who had managed, legally if not actually, to rid himself of a small fortune before the separation, was chronically late with his payments. But the answer, unfortunately, was no. A second caller probably had another blind date and wanted to be absolutely certain that she could have dinner, not to mention sex, with a man who was not her husband without losing custody of her children. This time Emily wished she could say no. The woman was a babe in the sexual woods, and a year of one-night stands was wreaking havoc on her psyche, but the divorce was final and the answer yes. Other clients wanted justice, retribution, a pound of flesh, but all Emily had to offer were custody agreements, financial settlements, and legal equivocations. At the bottom of the pile of messages was one from her former husband, Jake Ferris. The box requesting a return call was checked.

There was no reason for Jake to call. Their divorce, involving neither children nor financial payments, had been neater
than their marriage. And there was no reason for Emily not to
return his call, none, that is, except Peter's antipathy to Jake
and Emily's lack of it after nine years.

Emily dialed his office number. It had a vague, evocative
familiarity, like the title of a book read many years ago. When
the secretary asked her name, Emily was glad she'd kept her
maiden one. Jake got on the line immediately. "I thought I told
you never to call me here."

As soon as he spoke, Emily knew he'd been not only waiting
for her return call but preparing for it. The bad one-liner told
her so. She was glad it had, because the voice still gave away
nothing. If Peter picked up accents like protective coloration,
Jake's voice was one of the enduring truths of life, at least of
Emily's life. The voice was like music in a minor key, low, insistent, haunting. There was a time when that voice had made
her itch with desire. There was another time, only a few years
later, when it had rubbed her nerves raw.

"I tried not to—call you there, I mean—but I couldn't help
myself." She asked him how he was and, in case he'd taken her
comment seriously, how the second Mrs. Ferris was as well.

"Funny you should mention that." The voice was suddenly
off-key. Emily heard the discordant note and knew she'd forgotten the first rule of cross-examination: Never ask a question
unless you're sure of the answer.

"I want you to represent me," Jake went on, still hitting the
wrong notes.

"Represent you in what?" she asked, and this time she was
sure of the answer.

"Naïveté was never your long suit, babe. What do you think
I want you to represent me in? A corporate take-over? My divorce."

His voice went flat at the last word. No matter how hard he
tried to pretend, Jake didn't think this was a laughing matter.

*   *   *

"Of course, I can't take the case," Emily said to Laura when she reported the conversation.

"Why not? It isn't unethical."

"Just inadvisable."

Laura thought of Ezra. She was separated from him, and if they ever got through the morass of legal arrangements, she'd be divorced from him, but she'd never be immune to him. "Because of Jake?"

"Partly."

"And because of Peter?"

"It's not that Peter's jealous, only that he once mentioned that if I were ever unfaithful, he'd shoot me and the corespondent. No mention was made of any self-inflicted wounds."

"You're right. Refer Jake to someone else."

"You're only turning it down because of Peter and his irrational jealousy," Hallie argued.

"Are you sure it's irrational?" Emily asked. "After all, I was married to Jake at one time."

"Do you still want to be married to him?"

"Of course not."

"Then what's the problem? Look," Hallie went on before Emily could answer, "you can make all the compromises you want in your personal life, but your career is a different story. Do you think a man would turn down a perfectly acceptable case because it might make his wife jealous? Do you think Peter would refuse an appointment because you didn't like his colleagues? Do I have to remind you of that promising grad student he took on a year or two ago? She was the only Civil War scholar who'd won her credentials in a *Playboy* spread. 'Girls of the Southern Conference.' "

"I hated her."

"With good reason. But I'm talking profession, not passion. I don't think you ought to start turning down perfectly good cases in deference to Peter. And if you do, don't ever rail against Laura again."

* * *

Emily took the case. The minute Jake appeared in the door to her office she knew she shouldn't have. She gazed at Jake, thought of Peter, and realized that she ran true to type. She always had been a sucker for a man who looked as if he needed a haircut, a good square meal, and a lesson in the intricacies, to say nothing of the importance, of the stock market. When she'd met Jake Ferris during her junior year in college, his mop of shaggy dark hair had called to her like a beacon in the sea of shorn Ivy League heads, his frame had been a walking testimony to days sustained on coffee and cigarettes, and he'd already come close to flunking the introductory course in economics. He'd liked to read to her from "Prufrock" and "Howl" and had a passion for Hemingway, though the single time in his youth he'd gone out to shoot duck he'd come home a bird watcher. It had taken her the better part of a year to find out that he hadn't really been named for Jake Barnes, a peculiar conceit on his part in view of those steamy and, until a week before Jake's graduation, unsatisfactory tussles in dark corners of Princeton, Bryn Mawr, and points between. Emily's former mother-in-law, a sweet-tempered but almost illiterate woman, had finished a single book in her life, a biography of the late Aly Khan.

Jake stood in the doorway looking back at her. She wished he wouldn't. Peter had the lashes, but Jake had the eyes. They were large and dark and like a camera shutter left open. The eyes had been the first thing she'd fallen in love with and the last thing she'd regretted renouncing. The eyes hadn't given an inch to the years, but time had made inroads on the rest of the face. When she'd first met Jake, the wide, pronounced cheekbones had reminded her of an empty hanger waiting for life to drape some character over them. Life had obliged, or maybe only the second Mrs. Ferris and the second separation.

He stood there for much too long, or so it seemed to Emily. Eventually he smiled, and the lower corner of his mouth pulled down in a small, surprisingly familiar movement. She'd remembered the arrogance of the smile but not the tender vulnerability of the tic that turned it inside out. The tic, she recalled, appeared when he was concentrating deeply, or nervous, or thinking of sex.

"Emily," he said finally.

"Jake," she answered, but then she had an excuse. She was a lawyer; he was the writer, even if, as he was always the first to point out, only for *Newsweek.*

She stood and extended her hand the way she always did with a new client, then dropped it to her side. "Oh, God," she said.

He took her hand, kissed her on the cheek, and moved to one of the clients' chairs as if he were crossing a court to make a shot. He was an inch or two shorter than Peter, and more wiry. Peter's movements were languid. Jake's were deliberate and even smoother. He made everything look easy, though he was not an easygoing man.

"Okay, babe," he began, "you're the only thing that stands between me and financial ruin." The voice was musical, the smile broad, but the tic at the side of his mouth gave him away. This was hurting.

"Are you sure you want a divorce?" Emily asked the question, once considered ethically imperative and now thought impertinent. Jake said he was sure. "Why?" she asked. "On what grounds?" she corrected herself.

He smiled, and this time there was no tic. "No fault to the second question." He took his hands out of his jacket pockets, and Emily noticed they were clenched into fists. "Does the answer to the first make any difference? Legally, I mean."

"You always did have a nice sense of honor," she said.

"You didn't always think so," he answered.

She reached for a legal pad and got down to work.

"How about a drink?" Jake asked an hour later. He managed to make the suggestion sound so natural that Emily decided it would be impolitic to remind him that he'd once sworn he'd never again have a drink with her in public, or, for that matter, private. In all fairness to him, that was after she'd cried in the Oak Bar of the Plaza and screamed in the local liquor store and stormed out of a neighborhood Greek restaurant.

There was no reason for her to have a drink with Jake, and no reason not to, especially since Peter was at one of those graduate student gatherings that always got him high on young wine and nubile adoration. Emily said she had time for one drink.

Jake suggested they go around the corner to the Rainbow Room. "Touristy but convenient."

"And I was hoping for Elaine's. Word has it you have your own table." Years ago, when he was starting on the magazine, he used to say he didn't trust a restaurant that advertised in the *Paris Review* rather than *Cue*.

"Who's been reporting on my restaurant habits?" Something about the way he kept his eyes focused on the lighted numbers over the elevator door as he spoke made Emily suspect she might have hit on one of the reasons for divorce after all. Had the second Mrs. Ferris married for the literary high life?

Emily said something evasive and inane about the size of the world, though she'd actually heard of his defection to the establishment from a couple they'd maintained in joint custody. During Emily's regular, if infrequent, lunches with the wife, reports of Jake enhanced the meal like a reliable wine— light, dry, and a whiff nostalgic.

On the street in front of Emily's office building the pale autumn sun turned the tops of the steel and glass towers a fleshy pink but gave no warmth. Emily pulled her scarf tighter around her neck, then looked both ways. Jake laughed. "Afraid we're going to run into someone?"

"Aren't you?"

"I'm a separated man." He paused just long enough to

worry her. "And a client. Come on, Emily." He started walking. "I suggested a drink, not a tryst."

It was strange walking beside Jake again. Peter marched like a soldier on parade, shoulders back, head up, eyes blind to the unwashed multitude swirling below him. Jake moved like a hunter, or an Indian, or merely a journalist, his shoulders hunched a little forward as if to protect some vital core, the photographic eyes registering each small beauty and every jarring obscenity of the city streets. At the crossings his hand moved to Emily's elbow. She chalked the gesture up to reflex.

Since the lounge was only half filled, they managed to get a table beside a window. Around and below them the lights of the city told their terrible lies about romance and success and happiness.

Jake asked what she wanted to drink. She said she still drank Johnnie Walker Red. She waited for the pack of cigarettes to appear, then realized he hadn't smoked in her office. She was pleased for him but felt a twinge of regret for herself. Emily liked people whose habits were sloppier than her own.

While she cast around for conversational gambits, she remembered the handful of times they'd talked since the divorce had become final and she'd stopped screaming and he'd stopped analyzing and editing her words in that maddeningly thoughtful way of his. The first time he'd called, almost a year after the divorce, he'd pretended he wanted to know if she had his old college edition of Auden. Emily had thought the Auden was a pretense, but she hadn't been interested. The marriage, to say nothing of the divorce, was still fresh in her mind. Six months later, after a long, cold winter, she'd called Jake and managed to break into an icy sweat while doing it. Her pretense had been even flimsier. She told him she'd searched her entire apartment and hadn't been able to find his collected Auden. He said he'd bought another. A little while after that she'd heard he was seeing someone seriously. Sweet as pie, the joint custody friend had reported at lunch, though of course, she couldn't measure up to Emily. Emily was surprised to find the news souring, as if the wine had turned, but its effects had been short-lived. They'd passed entirely by the time Jake called several weeks later. Emily would have seen him then, but she was leaving the following morning on vacation. It was just as well because she'd had a marvelous holiday in Spain and by the time she returned Jake was planning to marry. Emily had had no more news of Jake for almost two years. Then the joint custody friend had announced the arrival of a child.

Emily asked to see a picture of his daughter. She was beautiful, as Emily had known she would be. She told Jake as much. She believed in honesty and had a sneaking respect for self-flagellation as well.

He put the photograph away, leaned back in his chair, and turned his eyes on her as if he were focusing a lens. Was he recording the aging process? She lifted her chin a little. Weighing her genes against the second Mrs. Ferris's? The child in the photograph had strawberry blond hair. Gloating? She remembered an argument they'd had about children. It had occurred late at night—arguments frequently did—in the bedroom that Jake had used as a study and that Emily, during the previous few weeks that had been devoted to Jake's first cover story, had taken to calling the psychiatric ward. In that short time he had managed to go into a manic upswing about his genius, plunge into an almost suicidal depression over his lack of talent, turn paranoid about his chance of being fired as a result of this fiasco, and remain faithful to this obsession with the story throughout. Emily, for her part, had tiptoed around the apartment, washing coffee cups, emptying ashtrays, and feeling her jaw muscles getting tighter by the hour. When the fight had finally come, it had for some reason—maybe the subject of the cover story; she couldn't remember—been about children. Emily had screamed that any man who couldn't remember his wife's name under professional fire—he had called her by an old girlfriend's once and his former roommate's twice—

couldn't take on the additional responsibility of a child. "Unless," she'd shouted across the bed littered with books and papers, "we called it Jake Junior, regardless of sex. You can always remember that."

She'd forgotten the argument for years, and she wished she hadn't remembered it now, but if Jake was thinking of it, too, nothing in those eyes that went on measuring her in silence gave him away.

"I read your book," she said at last because unlike Jake, she believed banal conversation preferable to no conversation, at least in situations like this.

"Were you one of the five who bought it, or did you take it out of the library?"

"I took it out of the library." Actually she'd read it in the member's room of the Society Library because she hadn't dared take it home, where Peter would find it, but she wasn't about to admit that. "I liked it, though."

"You and five other people," he repeated.

"You got a good review in the Sunday *Times*."

"By a guy I went to school with and still see for lunch once a month—who wants his next book reviewed in *Newsweek*."

She'd known that, at least the part about going to school together, but admired Jake for admitting it.

"So you've become a hot matrimonial attorney." He managed to drain his drink and her sudden resurgence of admiration simultaneously.

"Don't be patronizing. Your name on the magazine masthead doesn't exactly make you Edward R. Murrow."

His laughter was soft, like a mineral vein running through the rocky arrogance. "I. F. Stone if you don't mind. Murrow was television. And I wasn't being patronizing. The report I got really was that you were a hot matrimonial attorney. Why else do you think I called you?"

Emily decided to treat the question as rhetorical. "Lukewarm. The more women I handle divorces for, the more women want me to handle their divorces."

"You mean I'm your only male client?" He sounded titillated, as if by some fortunate accident he'd stumbled into a seraglio.

"There are a few other enlightened men."

"What about the volunteer work? Still killing yourself for the greater glory of the ACLU?"

"Not exactly," she said, though "not at all" was closer to the truth.

"Pity."

"I never thought I'd hear you say that." Her voice surprised her. She'd been sure she had no bitterness left.

From the look on his face it surprised him, too. "I always admired the volunteer work."

"You could have fooled me."

"I admired the work," he said carefully. "I just thought you took the fact that you were doing it too seriously. All those First Amendment groupies sitting around talking about having the Bill of Rights as a client."

"As opposed to all those intense young magazine writers moaning about how some editor had butchered their deathless prose." His expression stopped her. The camera's eye had recorded a collision. "How in hell did we get back to this?"

"Our mutual regard for the past. And only those who forget it are doomed to repeat it. As I'm sure your resident historian has told you." At the reference to Peter the tic made a fleeting appearance.

He suggested another drink, but she said she really ought to get home. "You mean, he keeps a tight rein on you?"

"I mean, I have work to do tonight." She wondered too late, if he remembered that after a few ounces of scotch, she couldn't tell a contract from a deposition.

He must have been remembering more than that about her because when the check came, he managed to outmaneuver her so swiftly and smoothly that she didn't have a chance. He looked across the table and smiled. This time there was no vulnerable tic to soften the effect. "Look, Emily, I haven't forgotten the litany. I know there's no equality without economic equality. I know there's no independence without economic independence. I know all that, but I'm not sure the waiter does, so just this once could you put your calculator away and compromise your principles? I swear that's the only compromise I have in mind."

The apartment was empty, though when Emily turned on the lights, the signs of life were not only evident but inescapable. On the kitchen counter a package of English muffins stood open beside Peter's half-empty coffee mug. In the bedroom sheets and quilt lay in a tangle. In the bathroom damp towels were strewn across the floor. She supposed that was an improvement. A few weeks ago she'd thrown a tantrum about wet towels on the bed, and to be fair to Peter, she hadn't found a wet towel on the bed since. Still, it was no fun coming home each night to Peter's idea of gracious living. But you didn't live with a man for his housekeeping habits, any more than you read Thucydides for his punctuation, as Peter liked to point out.

Emily got out of her clothes, into her robe, and was halfway through straightening the apartment before she thought of it. There was no reason she shouldn't smell of scotch at nine o'clock at night, and even if she did, Peter, still reeking from California chablis and the sweet smell of success, wasn't likely to notice. But she wanted to make sure he didn't notice. She was a terrible liar. She went into the bathroom and brushed her teeth. And all the time she was brushing she kept thinking that for a woman her age, in her position, the gesture was slightly insane and more than a little degrading.

III

It rained all that autumn, or so it seemed to Laura. Every morning she awakened to apartment windows as filthy and streaked as the sky beyond. Each day the *Times* arrived limp and soggy, except for the want ads, which, tucked deep within the bowels of the paper, remained dry and unproductive. In the hall closet her Burberry hung continually damp, its lining giving off the thick, fuzzy smell of wet wool. On the street her open umbrella collided with everyone else's. On steaming buses it stabbed unknown people in inadvisable places. After twice starting out of restaurants with someone else's, she no longer left hers in receptacles provided for the purpose but tried to set it apart from its mates, just as she tried to disassociate herself from her counterparts. That rainy fall she saw them everywhere, the lone, lonely women, waiting for something to happen, or simply waiting, like Eskimos on ice floes, for death by natural causes.

Laura wasn't going to wait. She couldn't afford to wait. She had no career except that of a wife and mother, and the retirement benefits weren't what they were cracked up to be, but she did have experience. As a volunteer she'd led tours through every corner of the museum and learned the workings of the hospital inside and out. She'd given those institutions weeks, perhaps months of her life. Now she was going to ask for something in return. She was ready. Terrified, which was nothing new these days, but ready. Or almost so. What did you wear to go begging? Emily told her not to think of it as begging, but Emily had a degree in law. Hallie told her to go for broke in her Adolfo suit. "I just finished a column on professional dressing for the AWE newsletter," she explained. "A woman should dress not for where she is but for where she plans to be."

"The Adolfo is where I was."

"And where you'll be again. This time on your own."

As Laura hung up the phone, she remembered that Hallie was the only one of the three of them who'd been a cheerleader.

She wore the suit to the museum, nonetheless, and when she passed the other volunteers at the information desk, she was glad she had. When she entered the office of the curator with whom she'd made the appointment, she wasn't so sure. The woman looked up from her desk and gazed at Laura as if she were contemplating an old master. When she spoke, all Laura's doubt disappeared.

"I love my job, Laura, but, oh, your suit. Sometimes I think when I came to that proverbial fork in the road, I took the wrong path. I should have married wisely and well. What can I do for you?"

Precious little it turned out. Museums were a glamour industry. They paid abysmally and hired selectively. Training programs were for the underaged; jobs, for the overqualified. The curator sent Laura to the personnel office, where all she managed to land was a spot on her skirt and a chance to earn $3.85 an hour peddling reproductions in the museum shop. She said she'd consider it. On the museum steps among the lunchers holding their sandwiches and Sabrett hot dogs and the young lovers holding each other, she began to cry when she realized she might have to take the job.

The following morning, a Friday, she sent her suit to the cleaners, and put on an old skirt and sweater. They weren't expensive; they weren't chic; they weren't even, Laura realized as she was about to leave the apartment, flattering. They were, however, reassuringly similar to the uniform the head of the women's hot line at the hospital lived in, except that Laura's skirt and sweater were wool.

The woman looked surprised when Laura entered her office, though they had an appointment. "Are you all right?" she asked. "I mean, you look different ... tired ... maybe it's just your outfit. You look as if you were going to give a poetry reading." Laura hoped the woman did better on the hot line.

She began to explain her position, and the woman's mouth gradually tightened as if it were a purse and she were drawing in the strings. She must be better on the hot line. Otherwise, she couldn't have lasted this long.

"I wish I could help you—" the woman began in a voice that sounded remarkably like a recorded message. Laura swore that no matter what happened in her life, she would never dial a hot line.

By the time she reached home the rain had turned to a fine mist, too light for her umbrella, still heavy enough for her spirit. She stood on the corner opposite her apartment house watching the taxis swarm up Park Avenue. Friday afternoon, and the city was in a hurry, rushing to the country, the airports, cocktail parties, dinner. The tires on the wet pavement reminded her of bacon sizzling. Bacon sizzling reminded her of Ezra. The son of Orthodox Jewish parents, Ezra had discovered the twin sins of forbidden food and forbidden sex simultaneously. In those days before their marriage they used to spend weekends in Ezra's apartment, left discreetly to themselves by his roommates. They'd started with bacon and eggs and the missionary position, moved on to shrimp cocktail and oral foreplay, escalated to Chinese pork and Oriental practices. Ezra had given up bacon as soon as the cholesterol scare had hit. Laura supposed she ought to be grateful he'd stayed with her a bit longer.

She had to stop thinking of Ezra. She had to stop seeing him in every man she passed. Only this was no mirage. The man standing beside the spanking new BMW pulled up in front of the canopy of her building, the tall, only slightly stooped symphony in cashmere and Harris tweed, was none other than Dr. Ezra Glass. Even if she hadn't recognized her estranged husband, she would have known the license plate. It read "FREUD." When Ezra had arranged Isabel's duffel to his satisfaction, he closed the trunk, opened the rear door for Isabel, and climbed into the driver's seat. Beside him was a woman who was too old to be Isabel's guest but too young to be Ezra's, at least if there was any justice in the world. Laura knew all about her or at least more than she ought to for her own peace of mind. She could accept the fact that the woman was twenty-seven. She could even accept the fact that she was twenty-seven and beautiful. But she could not accept the fact that she was twenty-seven, beautiful, and had an M.B.A. from Harvard. Or maybe it was Stanford. Isabel had relayed the information haltingly, as if halfway through she'd suddenly realized she shouldn't, and Laura hadn't pursued with questions. Ezra adjusted the side mirror. The woman turned halfway around in her seat and said something to Isabel. Isabel smiled. Laura stood watching as the car pulled away. What's wrong with this picture? I'll tell you what's wrong. Someone's sitting in my seat.

Upstairs the apartment was empty. Only the mail waited for Laura. She riffled through it and came to a stop at an envelope from the building's managing agent. It was the middle of the month. She shouldn't be getting mail from the managing agent in the middle of the month. She hoped they weren't going to turn off the water for another four days. She prayed they weren't going to raise the maintenance again. She tore open the envelope. "Second notice" was stamped across the bill. "Please disregard this amount if already paid" was printed in smaller type. She hoped the second message applied, but remembered Isabel's tuition and the new BMW and knew it didn't.

* * *

As Thanksgiving approached and the holiday season shifted into high gear, women acquaintances began accosting Laura. Divorced, separated, widowed, still married, they ambushed her on street corners, sidled up to her in supermarket lines, took her aside at the museum and the hospital, where she continued to work with the same diligence, if not the same sense of dedication, and spoke in a single voice. The holidays, they warned, are the hardest time. These women, it seemed to Laura, set aside a time for grieving as religiously as those of their mothers' generation, the bachelor girls of questionable repute, had designated a time for hair washing and lingerie mending. But Laura knew they were wrong. Loneliness, she'd discovered, lay not in any particular moment but in every possible one. Living alone was like walking through a minefield. You never knew when you were going to trigger an explosion. She might start out for a Sunday afternoon walk only to be wounded by the sight of a young couple locked together with embarrassing abandon or, even more cruel, a middle-aged pair whose air of contentment clung to them as stylishly as their good tweeds, or a nuclear family bristling with the raw health and optimism of a television commercial. Laura would tell herself that the youthful affair had a life expectancy of two weeks, the middle-aged husband might be, in her mother Dottie's words, stepping out on his wife, and those name-brand offspring were unlikely to reach adolescence in a two-parent household, if statistics and her sister Emily could be believed. The argument was convincing rather than consoling. Laura still felt maimed by comparison. So, well-meaning women to the contrary, the holidays were not the hardest time. In fact, as she stood in the kitchen on the Wednesday evening before Thanksgiving, she was feeling pretty good. The pie dough was chilling in the fridge, the apples were whirring in the Cuisinart, and all was right with the world—until Isabel drifted in. She held out an envelope. "When I stopped at the drugstore, they gave me this." Laura dried her hands and tore open the envelope. Its second notice was stamped in red.

"Daddy said to tell you he's coming up in about an hour. He wants to pick up more of his books."

"Is he taking them one at a time?" The words had slipped out. She blamed then on the druggist's bill.

Isabel took a slice of apple from the bowl as Laura removed it from the machine. "Maybe he just likes to see you," she said, and started down the hall to her room. Laura fought the urge to call after her that she hadn't been the one to break up their happy household.

When Ezra arrived, he looked neither pleased nor displeased by her presence. In fact, there was some doubt in Laura's mind whether he noticed her at all. Laura handed him the druggist's bill. He glanced at it with the same lack of interest.

"These things have to be paid, Ezra."

"Of course, they have to be paid, but I've been busy."

"Then why don't you let me start handling them again? You can give me a check at the beginning of the month, and I'll take care of all the bills. I'd rather do it that way."

"But I wouldn't. I know your tastes, Laura, and I can't afford them any more. I'm supporting two households now."

"Whose fault is that?"

There was no doubt in her mind that he saw her now. He recognized her, turned away from her, and started down the hall.

"Did you take care of the maintenance?" she called after him.

"Didn't I say I would?"

She returned to the kitchen, opened the refrigerator, and took out the pie dough. She'd left it in too long. It was rock hard. She put it on the counter to soften. When she squeezed lemon juice into the bowl of apples, she lost two pits among the slices.

She heard Isabel wander down the hall to the study. A few minutes later she was back in the kitchen. "We're not going to Grandma and Grandpa Glass's tomorrow after all." She put her hands in the pockets of her jeans and shifted from one foot to the other.

Laura wasn't surprised. Ezra and holidays were an unstable combination. Add his parents, and the mixture became explosive. She remembered one Christmas that had begun with Ezra in smoking jacket and urbane humor and ended with him shrouded in guilt poring over a volume of Elie Wiesel. Even Mother's Day, known to most sentient adults as St. Hallmark's Day, had driven him to distraction. Thanksgiving was a little less dangerous—even Ezra couldn't work up much primal angst about the Indians—but it was still fraught with uncertainty. The plan to spend it with his parents had been only a ruse to win Isabel for the day. Laura's mouth closed in a firm, full line. When Ezra had first left, she'd sworn to abstain from denigrating him, at least in front of Isabel. She'd fallen off the wagon once this evening, but she had no intention of going on a binge.

"We're going to a restaurant," Isabel said.

Four-star, Laura thought, but kept her mouth shut.

"Isn't that depressing?" Isabel asked. Laura started rolling out the pie dough, which had begun to soften. "I think it's depressing. Like people without an apartment or a family or anything. Like bridge and tunnel people coming in for a big time."

Laura opened her mouth, then closed it, then opened it again. "You can still have dinner with us. Dottie and Herb will be upset that you're not here." Laura amended the thought: Dottie and Herb will be upset period. When her mother and stepfather had called to announce the flight they'd arrive on, they'd reminded her that though she'd always be their daughter, they'd come to think of Ezra as a son, and wouldn't it be nice if they all could celebrate the holiday together?

Isabel poked around in the bowl of apples till she found a slice that met her standards. "What about Daddy?"

Laura lifted the crust carefully into the pie plate. If you handled it too much, it became tough. "What about him?"

Isabel moved to her mother's side. "Couldn't we ask him to

have dinner here?" she whispered. "I mean, it's a holiday. And there'll be lots of people and all. Grandma and Grandpa are crazy about him. It would only be dinner."

Laura managed to tear the second crust as she slid it into the second pie plate. "I think he'd feel awkward," she said as she massaged the split together.

Isabel took another piece of apple and savored it as if it were victory. "You know Daddy never feels awkward."

Laura took the bowl of apples from her daughter and divided it equally between the two empty pie shells. "I'll ask him."

"Now?"

"Let me finish the pies first." Laura' fingers, which had put hundreds of crusts in place over the years and fluted hundreds of edges, suddenly belonged to the hands of a derelict suffering from delirium tremens. She finished glazing the top crusts with egg white and washed her hands but left on the professional cook's apron. It made her feel competent. Ezra used to love the way she looked in that apron. In front of the hall mirror she stopped to smooth her hair. She was doing this for Isabel and out of kindness and in the interest of getting those bills paid. She had no designs on Ezra. She glanced in the mirror again and decided she didn't need lipstick.

Ezra was sitting in the old wing chair she'd moved into the study with a few other pieces of stray, disreputable furniture from dark corners of the apartment and the storage bin in the basement, objects that had seen better days or had been mistakes from the beginning. Though the room was no longer empty, neither was it a candidate for *Architectural Digest.* It had a gloomy air of unrealized expectations and failed hopes. Ezra sat in the midst of it with a stack of outdated journals on his lap. When he looked up, he didn't appear annoyed at the interruption, only mildly impatient.

"Isabel said you're not going to your parents' tomorrow."

"My mother isn't up to making dinner. And they were

never much for Thanksgiving—if you remember." He smiled and smoothed the three tufts of hair on the crown of his head.

"Isabel wants me to ask you to have dinner with us. Herb and Dottie suggested it, too."

His smile was analytic now, boring through the ruses and obfuscations to the real meaning of her words. Isabel. Herb and Dottie. Really, Laura, after all these years of life in the analytic fast lane, you ought to know better. Isabel isn't inviting me. Herb and Dottie aren't. You are.

She smiled and shrugged. He had a point. They knew each other too well. She laughed. "You're welcome to come."

By the time Laura realized she was the only one laughing, it was too late. "I appreciate your generosity, Laura." His tone was smooth as cough medicine, the syrupy kind. "But I've made other plans." Though there was no reason to go on, Ezra did. "Actually, to be accurate, I have another guest. I guess I forgot to mention her to Isabel." A silly grin cracked the professional mask, and he pronounced the word *her* as if it were one of Krafft-Ebing's more titillating entries.

Laura went back into the kitchen and waited until Isabel, her overnight duffel slung under her arm, had come in to say good-bye and the elevator door as well as the front door of the apartment had closed. Then she began slamming the empty bowls and utensils into the sink. It was lucky there were pies in the oven rather than cakes. Now there was a career for her. The Heloise's Hints of marital disintegration. Boxer shorts: to iron or not to iron when you know they're being put on—or taken off—for another woman. Lipstick removal from collars, ties, and points south. Meals that can be kept on the back burner from seven till eleven. Wives who can be put on hold for even longer. She turned the water on full force, then realized her mistake. It was hydrotherapy in reverse. Water came splashing out of her tear ducts to meet the water rushing into the sink. She thought of the words *second notice* that arrived on entirely too many of her bills these days and the way Ezra had looked when he'd given her his own particular second notice earlier this evening. She turned off the water. If only she could stop the tears as easily. If only she could summon an icy fury rather than this petulant frustration. But she was still too full of Ezra. His influence lay over the apartment like a thin layer of dust, gritty, inescapable, and likely to be stirred up by the least movement.

"Are you sick?" Hallie asked.

Sitting at the computer with his daughter on his lap, Daniel didn't look up. "No."

"Fired?"

"Very funny. Get 'em!" he cheered as Kate pushed a key, and the screen exploded to an accompaniment of violent sound effects.

"What are you doing home so early?"

"It's the Wednesday before Thanksgiving. We closed early."

"That's never made any difference to you before."

"Keep it up, and I'll go back to the office."

Hallie walked into the study, stood behind them, and put her hands on Daniel's shoulders. "Sorry. The surprise of it all sent me into shock."

He actually looked up at her. "I thought we could go out to dinner."

"You know, I really like you when you're in your human mode."

They went to a neighborhood restaurant that Hallie had had the foresight to cultivate before the reviewers discovered its briny shellfish, ebullient pasta, and bright basil-flecked tomato sauces and promoted it to the big leagues. Her vision had paid off. They would have to wait at the bar, but at least they were permitted to wait. They'd finished a second round of drinks, and Daniel and his stomach both had begun to grumble, when

Hallie saw Ned Sinclair at the far end of the room spreading a little noblesse oblige over the bartender. He caught sight of her immediately, pointed his index finger like a revolver, and fired the first shot. "Hallie Fields, the executive director of AWE, Inc."

Hallie introduced the two men. Ned took a bead on their glasses, ordered another round from the bartender by name, and launched into a story about the cab ride uptown with a celebrated client and a typical, if apocryphal, New York taxi driver. Hallie began to counter with an anecdote in kind, but Daniel headed her off. "So you're an attorney." You had to say one thing for Daniel, he knew how to stop a conversation in its tracks.

Ned admitted he was. When Hallie began to explain that he was a partner in Emily's firm, Daniel ambushed her again. He had some serious questions about the legal ramifications of the electronic revolution that couldn't wait.

Half an hour later the maître d' came to summon them to their table. Since Daniel was in the men's room, Hallie took matters into her own hands and did the only gracious thing. She invited Ned to join them. The boyish face collapsed in despair. He might have just discovered that he hadn't made the varsity team. "I'd love to," he said. "Really," he added, establishing his sincerity once and for all, "but this damn last-minute packing. I've got to catch a plane at the crack of dawn."

"Going home for the weekend?"

"Would that I were. Strictly business. Have to hop over to Paris. Hell of a way to spend a holiday weekend."

Over Ned's shoulder Hallie saw Daniel picking his way through the maze of tables. "You should have taken the Concorde," she said quickly, as if racing against Daniel's return. "It doesn't leave until one."

The look on Ned's face, as Daniel joined them, was one of pure respect.

* * *

Emily hung up the phone and went into the bedroom where Peter was sitting up in bed reading exams to the accompaniment of a televised hockey game. "Your mother sends her love. She said she didn't want to bother you if you were working."

Peter looked up with the smile of a coach who finally has the team playing according to his strategy. For the first three years Emily and Peter had lived together, his mother had refused to recognize Emily's existence. Then, after his father's death, his mother had had intimations of mortality or at least second thoughts. Now she called often and, since answering the phone was against Peter's religion, regaled Emily with the latest bulletins from Whitmore, Owings, and Kerr. It was just like his mother, Emily told Peter, to put together a team of medical specialists who sounded like an architectural firm.

"She said she's going to your aunt's tomorrow but she'll see us Saturday."

"I don't expect to be alive by Saturday. Not after a day with your family."

"It's only a few hours," she pleaded.

"It may be a few hours with your family to you; it's a lifetime to me."

"Be fair, Peter. For three years I kept a profile so low your mother thought you lived here alone. Now she and I are practically joined at the hip. She calls almost every day—at the office half the time—to give me recipes for pot roast or tell me there's a sale on silver polish at Altman's. And every time we see her you disappear into the last century or at least the next room to watch some game on television while I stay and carry the conversational ball."

"In other words, you were dissatisfied when she wouldn't accept you, and now you're dissatisfied that she has."

It served her right for getting mixed up with a man who'd been exposed to the Jesuits in his formative years. "I didn't mean to complain about your mother. I just wish you'd understand that your spending time with my family is no different from my seeing her."

"Except that I admit my mother's a pain in the ass, bless her sainted soul."

"In other words, if I admit my family's faults, you'll go graciously."

"If you see what they're like, I can't understand why you want to spend the day with them, or"—his eyes remained focused on some nasty bit of violence being played out on the television screen—"half your life on the phone with your sisters."

She told herself to give it up—Peter had agreed to go; he didn't have to be eager to go—but the master of ceremonies in her had to keep everyone happy. "At least you'll eat well. Laura's dinners are positively Edwardian."

"I've heard the Perrier flows like champagne."

Emily paused for breath. He'd heard that from her. She'd made the crack after one of Laura's more fashionable dinner parties.

"You can talk to Herb," she said. "He always makes a point of reading at least one historical biography before he sees you."

"Let's just say he manages to read another ten pages of that Lincoln biography you gave him five years ago."

"You say Hallie's intelligent. Misguided but intelligent."

"Brilliant. I'll be spending Thanksgiving with the best and the brightest."

"There's Daniel." She was getting desperate and knew it. "You can discuss computers and the role of demography in revisionist history."

"Daniel doesn't discuss. He gives input."

She gave up. "Look, if you don't want to go, you don't have to. I'll tell them you went to your aunt's with your mother. I'll tell them your wife decided not to take your kids away after all. I'll tell them you died and went to heaven."

"I said I'd go, Emily. Just stop trying to make me enjoy it."

IV

Emily awakened early on Thanksgiving morning. Beside her Peter, whose biorhythms kept time to an academic beat, shifted position in his sleep. She lay staring at the ceiling and calculating the odds on familial disaster striking within the next eighteen hours. She tried not to remember the previous Christmas. She and Peter had struck a bargain. If she wouldn't keep a mental tally of his drinks—he insisted he needed every ounce to get through a day with her family—he'd be ineffably charming. By the time Peter turned his charm on Ezra it was 86.8 proof. He inquired about the use of graduated fee schedules in the practice of psychiatry. A thoughtful discussion ensued. Social consciences were mentioned. Economic realities were considered. Ezra grew a little touchy, but Peter had the last words. They came out somewhat slurred. "You're a fucking robber baron!"

The statement was out of character, as Emily pointed out when Peter sobered up and apologized to her, if not to Ezra. She would have expected him to call her brother-in-law a fucking carpetbagger. Peter had countered that his knowledge was broad as well as deep, and—reaching across the bed for her—his interests eclectic.

He shifted position in his sleep again, and his hand hit Emily accidentally. When it recognized the terrain, it turned intentional. He might not be awake, but he was definitely alert.

"You can sleep," she whispered.

His only answer was the slight but unmistakable movement of his hand.

"I really ought to get up."

This time his leg entered the discussion.

"I promised Laura I'd cut up the crudités," Emily said, but her heart wasn't in it.

Peter let his fingers do the talking.

Emily had one last tussle with her conscience. "If I don't get up, I won't get the vegetables cut up, and there won't be enough hors d'oeuvres, and we'll all have too much to drink on empty stomachs, and Dottie will take Laura aside and tell her how to lure Ezra back, and Laura will lock herself in the bathroom, and Hallie and Daniel will start sniping and end up threatening divorce, and Herb will corner you and ask why we aren't married after all these years, and you'll call him the fucking grand inquisitor, and he'll disown me, and the whole damn day, not to mention the whole family, will go down the drain. I mean, if a war could be lost for want of a nail, think of the holiday havoc a hard-on can wreak."

Peter laughed, but he didn't stop what he was doing, and in all fairness, Emily hadn't wanted him to.

By the time Laura awakened on Thanksgiving morning the bedroom was bathed in sunlight. Her eyes blinked against the glare, but her spirit welcomed it. Ever since Ezra had left, she'd taken to raising the shades last thing at night. Ezra had insisted on midnight blackness for sleep—the slightest glimmer of light from the street had the same effect on him the pea was reputed to have had on the princess—and a soothing, or so he thought, gray gloominess for awakening. Laura liked opening her eyes to the day outside. On rainy mornings she luxuriated in the sense of isolated security. On fair ones, like this morning, she loved the way the sun flooded in, washing the provincial chintzes to a brilliant clarity, bleaching the white backgrounds to a blinding purity. On a morning like this it was impossible not to expect the best from the day ahead. Across the street the church bell pealed the hour. The sound reverberated up and down Park Avenue and out over the Upper East Side exactly as if it were a New England village. Laura got out of bed and walked to the window. The scene was as peaceful as that New England village. Across the street a man in a bulky turtleneck and tweed jacket waited patiently while a dachshund pawed through the brown leaves at the base of a tree stripped naked by the previous month's wind and rain. Another man, walking as straight as the crease in his immaculate trousers, held the hand of a small girl in black Mary Janes and a fawn-colored coat with a velvet collar. At the corner a young couple in shorts and sweat shirts jogged in place while waiting for the light to change. Laura liked family holidays, even if her family was not intact. Let Ezra take his guest to a restaurant, though she wished he weren't taking Isabel as well. She would make a proper Thanksgiving.

In the bathroom she raised the shade over the frosted glass window. No sun flooded in from the north, but the light was unforgiving. It washed and bleached her reflection in the mirror over the sink. She tried to look at herself objectively. Somewhere she'd read that Chanel said by the time you were forty you had the face you deserved. Somewhere else she'd read that Jeanne Moreau said she loved the lines in her face because they reminded her of the men who'd put them there. She thought of Ezra again, pulled down the window shade, and turned on the shower.

Under the stiff spray of water she started with *Madama Butterfly*, decided it was inappropriate—or too appropriate—and switched to Noel Coward. She ran through her repertoire fortissimo. There was something to be said for having the apartment to herself. Not as much as the media and certain friends had suggested, but something.

She dressed slowly, taking special care with her makeup, then made the bed, smoothing the spread into perfect folds. In the kitchen the two apple pies she'd baked after Ezra had left with Isabel in tow stood on the counter, their aluminum foil covers shining like crowns in the sunlight streaming in from the window. She made coffee in the small pot she'd bought after Ezra had moved out, took the turkey from the refrigerator, and turned on the oven. As she unwrapped the bird, she admired the butcher's trussing and the small neat packages, like party favors, of innards and basting lard. When Laura and Emily, fresh off a confrontation with Ezra's attorney, had discussed the holiday, Emily had suggested a supermarket turkey, but Laura had stood firm. A Thanksgiving turkey with a pop-up thermometer in its breast was un-American. A turkey with a pop-up thermometer, preferably a frozen turkey with a pop-up thermometer, was, Emily argued, quintessentially American. Laura yielded the point but not the turkey. She unwrapped the package of innards and started the stuffing.

By the time Emily stepped off the elevator at Laura's floor the aroma of roasting turkey hung in the hallway like bunting. When Laura opened the door, the fragrance reached a crescendo, like the clash of cymbals in martial music. Laura stood on the threshold of her apartment, one arm holding the door wide, the other reaching out to draw her sister in. As she looked past Emily to the empty hall, a frown replaced the smile of welcome. The first problem of the day: Peter wasn't going to show.   .

"He'll be over later," Emily explained. "I came early to help." She took the shopping bag full of crudités into the kitchen. Naomi, dressed in an ivory silk blouse Emily remembered seeing on Laura several years ago, was taking each Lenox dinner plate out of its plastic slipcover. Her strong hands moved with reverence. Naomi, as Laura occasionally pointed out, was as close to an old family retainer as anyone was likely to find these days. Dottie had discovered her, Laura had shared her, and after Kate was born, Hallie had inherited her. Only Emily was odd woman out. By the time she'd overcome her scruples sufficiently to pay someone else to scrub her floors, wash her dishes, and clean up her mess, Naomi had claimed a full schedule. Actually Emily suspected Naomi had had the time but not the inclination to care for an apartment she deemed a love nest.

"Hi, Mrs. Brandt," Naomi said.

For some years now Emily and Naomi had been waging a political battle over forms of address. Whenever either of her sisters' telephones was answered by Naomi, Emily identified herself as Emily, but Naomi continued to address her as Mrs. Brandt. For Naomi the coveted form of address was like virginity in reverse. Once you'd won it, you could never lose it. Regardless of the last name—maiden, married, or some hyphenated hybrid—if a woman had seen action in the marital wars, she was entitled to permanent rank. For a while Emily had taken to calling Naomi Mrs. Charles, but Emily's convictions were no match for Naomi's political and social assumptions.

Emily followed Laura into the dining room. Between them Laura and Naomi had set an exquisite stage. Emily owned the same Lenox, Waterford, and Tiffany sterling—Dottie did not believe in playing favorites—but unlike Laura, Emily rarely used them.

In the living room a variety of hors d'oeuvres was arranged with an attention to color and detail that would have done Louis Comfort Tiffany proud. "You throw a great Thanksgiving," Emily said. "Everything is perfect, as usual."

"Except everything isn't quite as usual, though God knows I tried." Laura's eyes slid away from her sister's. "I invited Ezra."

Emily looked at her the way a childless woman looks at children. There was affection in her face, and compassion, but neither understanding nor affinity. "Did he accept?"

"He said he thought it would be awkward."

"That's the first time Ezra has made sense since this whole mess started."

"He said he thought it would be awkward because he had his own guest for the day. In addition to Isabel, that is. He left no doubt as to her gender, not to mention sex."

"I take it back. He wasn't making sense, merely points." Emily's voice was soft with wonder as well as sympathy. Her profession had accustomed her to jealousy, greed, and vengeance, but gratuitous cruelty still shocked her.

"I'm glad he said no," Laura said.

"It's really much better this way. Those holiday reconciliations never work. They confuse the kids and are hell on the adults."

"This way it will be just the family."

Then the family arrived. Dottie and Herb didn't so much enter a room as overtake it, like a train they were afraid of missing. Dottie was in the lead by a step or two, but she still managed to hold Herb's arm as if it were an imperial scepter, sweeping him along in her wake like royal robes. Herb was a second husband, a stepfather, a stand-in for a first love and natural father who'd died before he had a chance to do much in life besides start a family and provide for their future, but he was a man and gave Dottie legitimacy.

They bustled around the foyer, looking for resting places for their expensively wrapped packages. Dottie was a trim woman with neat features. Herb was a large, neat man. They matched in the surprising way of physically dissimilar people who have lived together for a long time. Dottie stood on the toes of her smoothly polished Helene Arpels shoes to kiss her daughters. Herb bent to embrace each of them in turn. He didn't so much imitate his wife's gestures as underline them. He too had a sense of his role in the scheme of things. Besides, he loved his family. The fact that it had come to him instantly and almost effortlessly, like some well-packaged soup or soft-drink mix, did not detract from its value in his eyes.

As soon as Laura had hung up their coats, they began picking up the packages they'd just set down. It was a process less of presentation than of explanation. While Dottie insisted that the cake had to be refrigerated and Herb gave them the pedigree of the new nuts he'd discovered, their eyes searched for signs of Ezra and Peter.

"Ezra isn't coming," Laura said.

Dottie turned back to her daughter with a look of genuine surprise. "I didn't ask if Ezra was coming. Herb," she called for confirmation, "did I mention Ezra's name?"

"It's all right," Laura said. "I wasn't accusing you. I just wanted to get it out of the way. I asked Ezra, but he had other plans. He's going out for dinner. Unfortunately he's taking Isabel with him, but she'll be back later.

"Very strange," Dottie said, "a man who'd rather eat restaurant food than good home cooking. Especially on a family holiday."

"Very sad," Herb added, "a man who doesn't know how to celebrate a family holiday with his family."

Laura was relieved. If they weren't ready to condemn, at least they were willing to criticize. For the first time since she'd announced Ezra's departure over a long-distance wire thick with static and her own half-swallowed grief, she didn't hear that accusing question in their voices. *What did you do wrong?* She took the packages they were still pressing on her and kissed them both.

Herb took another gift-wrapped bottle from one of the shopping bags and handed it to Emily. "This one's for you, you and Peter."

"Where is Peter?" Dottie asked, as if she'd just thought of the question, though everyone knew it was not a new idea, merely one whose time had come.

"He should be here any minute," Emily said. "I let him sleep late."

Dottie beamed approval. Letting a man sleep in on weekends and holidays was a wifely gesture. Emily had let Peter sleep in this morning. Therefore, Emily was wifely, despite all current evidence to the contrary.

And then, as if on cue, Peter appeared. He apologized for being late but admitted he'd made a stop on the way over. He held a bouquet of flowers out to Laura. Emily could have kissed him. Instead, she took his arm. Like every man she'd ever known, he tightened tendon and muscle. But he was not like any man she'd ever known. He was wearing the challis tie she'd bought him the previous week, though she suspected he didn't really like it. She squeezed his arm. Tendon and muscle tightened again.

"I've been reading a biography of Lincoln," Herb said.

"What do you think of it?" This was a new accent for Peter. It came from somewhere in America's heartland and was suffused with sincerity. Emily took his hand.

Hallie and Daniel arrived with Kate swinging excitedly between them, and the family surged into the living room. They crowded onto the two long sofas that faced each other across the low Chinese coffee table. There were other chairs around the perimeter of the room, but no one wanted to be left out. Dottie, who could make church steeples of her slender fingers and babies in a hammock out of her handstitched handkerchief, lured Kate to her side. Daniel passed bloody marys. Laura urged everyone to try Emily's crudités. The conversation rose and fell like recitative, interrupted now and then by individual arias. Even Peter seemed to be enjoying himself. He was standing in front of the fireplace talking to Herb. Emily felt a surge of possessive pride at the intelligent profile and the unruly fringe of hair that grazed his shirt collar tenderly. "What you have to remember," she heard him say, "is that Lincoln freed the slaves south of the Mason-Dixon line."

The Emancipation Proclamation didn't affect those north of it, Emily predicted.

"He wasn't about to mess with those north of it," Peter said, "not in the middle of a war."

"Is that true?" Dottie asked. Emily was surprised. History was not her mother's long suit. "Is it true what Laura told me over the phone? Is Jake Ferris getting another divorce?"

Across the room Peter's expression didn't change, but Emily knew from the way his chin edged forward that he'd heard. It was not the sort of sentence he was likely to miss. She mumbled a "yes" that managed to deny all responsibility for or any connection with her former husband's actions, but Peter was not taken in. Emily recognized the tilt of head that said he was listening as well as talking. "It was a political act," he said to Herb, "not a moral one."

"I'm not surprised he's getting another divorce," Dottie went on. She didn't sound smug, only relieved. The flaw lay not in her daughter but in the man she'd chosen, at least the man she'd chosen first. "But I am surprised he wants Emily to represent him. What kind of a man uses his first wife as an attorney in his second divorce?"

"So Lincoln wasn't quite the saint that he pretended to be or that we make him out to be." Peter shot Emily a vicious smile and moved to the bar. As he reached for the ice bucket, the profile that had inspired lust only a moment ago now reminded her of a bird of prey. When he turned back to the room, he was wearing his public smile. It took in everyone except Emily. She recognized the cruelty to the curl of mouth. It was as treacherous as the icy veneer of his voice. "I don't know about anyone else," he said, "but I'm for a little football before lunch." As he started off down the hall, Daniel fell into line behind him, and Herb, who felt more comfortable discussing marriage and masculine responsibility to the tune of an all-American sporting event, followed.

Half an hour later, when Peter returned to refill his drink, Emily followed him back down the hall. "Peter," she said, but he kept walking. "Please," she added, but he seemed not to hear. When she put her hand on his arm, he stopped and turned back to her. She wished he hadn't. His face was frozen. A film, like early-morning frost on a window, masked his eyes.

"Please don't be angry."

"What makes you think I'm angry?" His voice, as cold as

his face, was tinged with a British accent now. Had he been watching rugby rather than football?

"Peter, please don't do this."

He stood there staring at her as if she were a colonial—simple, childish, morally illiterate. "I'm not doing anything." The accent was growing more clipped.

"Peter, please."

He straightened his shoulders as if under the weight of the white man's burden. "Don't be an ass, Emily!" The words came out as if they were an order, straight from high command. Peter executed a smart military turn and marched away from her down the hall.

On her way to answer the front doorbell Laura tried not to look at Emily and Peter. She didn't have to hear the words to interpret the universal language they were speaking. She could see it on their faces, sense it in the way Emily's body curled toward Peter's and his arched away from hers, hear it in their hushed voices as clearly as she heard the noisy laughter of the rest of the family. The sound and the sight and the memory made her momentarily queasy. At least she was free of that particular fear. The nausea passed. Then she opened the door.

Ezra stood with one arm around his daughter's shoulders, the other outstretched with an oversize bouquet. Flowers, it seemed, were the order of the day. The men carried them as if to a grave.

"We came after all. The prodigals returned." Ezra moved forward into the apartment.

Laura took a step back. "I thought you had other plans," she said, but behind her Herb and Dottie, converging from opposite ends of the apartment, remembered the parable even if she didn't.

"What other plans!" Dottie dismissed the very idea. "Someone get Ezra a bloody mary."

"Maybe he'd like a real drink," Herb countered. "I brought a bottle of Glenlivet. You can't beat Glenlivet."

"Come over here, Isabel, and let me look at you." As Dottie reached out for her granddaughter, she managed to touch Laura's shoulder. A casual observer might have thought she'd done it accidentally, but Laura was not a casual observer. She knew Dottie had nudged her, and she knew what the gesture meant. Take his coat. Get him a drink. Welcome him. Forgive him. And all the while pretend there's nothing to forgive.

Laura put down the bouquet of flowers and took Ezra's coat. "What happened to your plans?" she asked again, but Ezra only smiled, smoothed his tufts of hair, and glided off to the living room with one arm around Dottie's shoulder and the other reaching out to welcome Herb's glass of Glenlivet.

Ezra always had liked surprises. There was the time he'd taken the house in East Hampton for the summer and hadn't told her about it until they arrived for a supposed weekend with friends, and the two tickets to London tucked into her Christmas stocking along with the small, silly jokes, and the week at the Golden Door he'd sprung on her last winter. And Dottie and Herb always had appreciated Ezra and his generosity. Only last winter they'd said, Wasn't it just like Ezra to make sure Laura had a week of rest at a spa even though he couldn't get away? She watched them moving, arm in arm, into the living room and remembered the first time she'd taken Ezra home. Dottie had introduced him to an aunt and uncle who'd been summoned for the occasion as Dr. Glass, though the title was premature at the time. Herb, who had still had trouble offering Laura a glass of sherry, had poured Ezra a hefty scotch before dinner and offered him a Cuban cigar after. And all through the evening she'd basked in the the pride and approval that had glowed as steadily as the twin candelabra on Dottie's dinner table.

Laura opened her mouth and for a fraction of a second wondered what would come out. An order to Ezra to leave the apartment for which he refused to pay the maintenance. An agonized cry to her parents to stop this injustice. A simple no.

"Dinner's ready," she said.

Without being told, Naomi had laid two more places. Propelled by years of habit and depths of instinct, Ezra moved to the head of the table. Drawn by the other sides of those same coins of habit and instinct, Naomi carried the turkey, so perfect it might have been made of bronze, straight to his place.

Late-afternoon sunshine streamed through the windows. An expectant silence hung from the high ceiling of the prewar building. Only the organ music was missing, but strains of it soared in Laura's head. Ezra glanced around the table, bestowing his attention on each member of the family as if it were a blessing. When he reached Laura, he inclined his head as if in prayer—or penance.

And from her end of the table Laura, returning his gaze, joined in his worship. Her husband, her daughter, her family, her home. Her sisters had told her it wasn't enough, and sometime in the last two decades society had done an about-face and seconded the opinion, but the organ music kept playing in her head. She gave thanks and added a silent prayer from childhood: Please, God, let me have this, and I'll never ask for anything again.

Deliberately, solemnly, Ezra picked up the carving knife and fork from the table as if they were his connubial responsibilities. He turned from his congregation to the work at hand. Raising the knife high above the turkey, he plunged the fork deep into the breast. The table erupted in conversation so jubilant it might have been congratulations.

After the apple pies that had been conceived in hope, baked in fury, and consumed in joy, the men drifted back to the last quarter of a football game, leaving empty coffee cups and full ashtrays behind like the bastard children of a former army of occupation. The women—Emily and Hallie on one of the two sofas, Laura and Dottie on the other—remained to compose the ballad that would commemorate the day. Kate was glued to the television in Laura's room; Isabel, to the phone in her own.

"You see," Dottie said. "I knew Ezra would come back." Her voice was so liberally laced with pleasure that none of them answered.

"I know what you're all thinking," Dottie went on. "One dinner does not a reconciliation make. But the point is one dinner makes whatever you want it to."

Still no one answered.

"Of course, it takes work. Everything worth having in this world takes work."

The adage from childhood met with another silence.

Dottie looked at the three women, her daughters. "I'm not blind, you know. I see what's been going on. And don't for a moment think I condone any of it. Just because I'm nice to Ezra doesn't mean I approve of what he's done—or will ever forget what he's put Laura through. But that doesn't mean I won't give him a second chance. That doesn't mean I'm going to cut off my nose to spite my face."

Another favorite adage. Laura was beginning to feel like an oversize adult careening crazily through a child's playroom. "You can't meet every crisis in life with a cliché," she said. "And you can't give a man a second chance if he doesn't want one."

"Does a man who doesn't want a second chance come home for a holiday dinner and bring his wife flowers?" Dottie turned to Emily and Hallie. "You were both here. Is that a man who doesn't want a second chance?"

"It's hard to say," Hallie answered.

"I wouldn't read too much into this afternoon," Emily added.

"For God's sake," Laura interrupted, "Ezra wants out. He doesn't think marriage is a viable institution anymore."

Dottie's eyes moved from her daughter's face to her own

carefully manicured hands with the old but not outdated diamond engagement and wedding rings. "When a man talks like that, you don't listen. Ezra needs a wife. And a family. He can't fend for himself. Men can't."

Laura's face was red now, as if she'd been scalded by the argument that had finally boiled over. "That's what you taught us. And I believed you. I was sure that as soon as Ezra realized that his shirts didn't know their own way to the laundry and piccata was not the natural state of veal, he'd be back. I was sure that because I'd done all those things for him for all those years, he needed me to go on doing them for him. I was wrong. Ezra drops his shirts off at the laundry every Saturday morning on his way to play tennis and, according to Isabel, makes a mean osso buco. Ezra doesn't need a wife, Mother. He's got a maid who comes in three times a week."

Dottie was twisting the rings on her left hand with abrupt, desperate movements. "I meant more than that. I never taught you—"

Laura stood so suddenly she hit the end table. The china and crystal made a polite rattle on the polished wood surface. "Haven't you heard anything I said? I never thought cooking and cleaning and domestic service were enough. I thought they were the last goddamn cards I had to play. After the appeals to seventeen years of marriage and Isabel and love or loyalty or whatever you want to call it had failed. But they didn't work, any more than the color in my hair or the constant interest in his work or the perfect little dinner parties with the perfect conversation he used to be so proud of. So don't tell me what you taught me, Mother, because it didn't work. And whatever you do, don't you dare tell me I didn't try hard enough."

"I never said—" Dottie began, but Laura had already careened out of the room and down the hall. The lampshade on the table was still swaying. It was the only movement in the room.

"I never said she hadn't tried hard enough," Dottie insisted. Emily and Hallie were silent.

"I never even thought it."

Emily watched her mother twisting the twin rings around and around on her finger, exposing the strip of pale flesh, like an unhealed wound, on the tan hand. She felt the pull of separate pities and divided loyalties, but she knew the truth of certain facts. "You did think it." She stood. "And you implied it. Every time you talked about hard work and working things out. The implication was always that Laura was too lazy or headstrong or just plain incompetent to make her marriage work. The implication was always that it was Laura's fault, that she was the one who had to keep the marriage going. All Ezra had to do was be there. And even now, when he refuses to be there, you go on blaming her."

Dottie opened her mouth to defend herself, but Emily was already halfway down the hall on the way to her sister's room. As she passed the den, she noticed Peter slumped in a chair with a mean look on his face.

By the time she reached the master bedroom Laura had closed herself in the bathroom. Emily called her sister's name.

"Leave me alone." Laura's misery seeped around the cracks in the door like a noxious fume.

"Dottie didn't mean anything."

"Don't you believe it. She meant it's all my fault. She meant I was a failure."

"I thought that was my role."

"Not anymore."

"Come on out, Laura. Please."

The sound of crying is probably the single noise intensified rather than muffled by a closed door.

"She knows you did everything you could. That's why she says such stupid things. Out of frustration. Because she knows you did everything you could, everything she believes in, and it didn't work."

"She thinks I'm a failure."

"She thinks she's a failure." Laura blew her nose noisily,

and Emily went on. "My divorce was one thing—from the day I came home and said I wanted to go to law school she knew I'd screw up where it really counted—but she believed in you. You were her justification, her pride, her achievement. You were proof that she was right. And now she isn't right anymore, and she doesn't know what to do."

"You think I do?"

Emily heard heavy footsteps in the hall. She listened as if to Morse code, trying to decipher the message. Was Peter following her to continue the argument, tell her he was leaving, apologize? The footsteps, which didn't even belong to Peter, disappeared into the bathroom across the hall.

"I think you're doing a damn good job of handling things. Or you were until you locked yourself in the bathroom. Please come out." Emily waited for an answer. "In two minutes Herb's going to be in here. And Ezra." There was no sound from the other side of the door. "Be reasonable, Laura. You don't want Isabel dragged into it."

As Emily waited, she studied her reflection in the mirror on the back of the bathroom door. Her mascara was smudged, and her face sallow and wrinkled like the page of a legal pad that had been written on, crumpled, and tossed away. When she'd passed the den, Peter's expression had been ugly, but his face still handsome. "Laura," she pleaded, "you have to come out."

There was another silence, and when Laura spoke, she sounded embarrassed and a little grudging. "I will."

"When?"

"In a minute. I just want to fix my face."

Emily went back down the hall. In the foyer Hallie and Daniel, standing toe to toe, were locked in anger as intimate as an embrace. Daniel's voice hissed as if it were the steam of passion. "It's almost ten, Kate's asleep, I still have a couple of hours of work, and you aren't ready to leave."

"I said I can't leave. When things get emotional, Daniel, not all of us run for our machines."

Emily kept walking. The living room was empty. She went on to the kitchen. Naomi had left some time ago, and now Dottie stood at the sink, loading the dishwasher with cups, saucers, and pie plates. Her hands, so nervous a few minutes ago, performed the domestic ballet smoothly.

"Are you all right?" Emily asked.

"*I'm* fine." Like a ballerina displaying her technique, Dottie's hands picked up speed. "Where's Laura?"

"She'll be back in a minute. She's putting her face together."

"I shouldn't have said anything."

Emily was silent.

"It's all my fault."

"Come on, Mother, it can't *all* be your fault."

Dottie bent lower to the dishwasher. The ballerina had become a small, crumpled woman. "No, I've failed. First with you and now with Laura. It's my fault you never had children."

Emily had been wondering how long it would take to get around to that.

"If I had been a better mother, you would have wanted children of your own. It's because you were in the middle. I neglected you."

"That's pop psychology." Emily remembered the closets full of clothes her mother had selected, the dates she'd dissected with girlish enthusiasm, the letters she'd read without permission until Emily learned to hide them. "You never neglected me."

Dottie closed the dishwasher. "Then why don't you want children? You used to love playing with dolls. You were better to your dolls than either of your sisters. You took such good care of them."

"Do we really have to go through this tonight?"

"I just don't understand why you think getting people divorces is a better thing to do with your life than raising children."

"I don't. But I don't think replicating yourself is mankind's highest achievement either."

"If everyone thought the way you do, the race would die out."

"I think about that sometimes. I'm not being facetious. I do. The only answer I've come up with is that most people don't think the way I do, fortunately."

"What I want to know is, what happened to the old values?" It was another question Emily occasionally pondered. "What happened to loyalty? What happened to standing by someone through bad times as well as good?"

The kitchen was hot, and the dishwasher noisy. The heavy smells of grease and coffee grinds rose like fumes from a swamp. Emily thought of Peter and the hard time ahead of her tonight. "I believe in all that."

"In other words, if Jake had lost his job or gotten sick, you would have stayed with him, but since you just didn't like him anymore, it was all right to walk out."

"It's not that simple."

Dottie dried her hands. "It's not that hard."

Laura returned from the bathroom with fresh blusher that looked as if it had seeped down from her reddened eyes; Hallie and Daniel declared a truce, packed up their daughter, and left; and Emily managed to lure an icily correct Peter from the den. He helped Emily on with her coat. Herb watched with approval. Only Emily could sense the malice of Peter's actions. It emanated from him thick and acrid as the odor of perspiration after sex, except that Emily was drawn to Peter's sweat while this sore, smoldering anger sickened her.

Herb took her face in his hands and kissed her good-bye on one cheek, then looked at her, and kissed her again on the other. No one had told him of the explosion among the women, but he sensed something. He sensed it, but he was going to stay away from it.

He turned to Peter and extended his hand. "Now remember what I said. If I were you, I'd call my broker first thing in the morning."

"Actually," Peter said, and Emily recognized the thick, resonant cadences of brandy, "I don't have a broker."

Herb was intrigued. "Buy and sell through your bank."

"Actually," Peter repeated, "I don't buy and sell."

"No stocks, eh? Just CDs and money markets? What do you think of these tax-free municipals?"

"Not a thing," Peter said. "Not a goddamn thing. I subscribe to the Errol Flynn school of finance. 'Any man who still has ten grand left when he dies is a failure.'"

"And so," Emily said on their way down in the elevator, "the day turned out just as I predicted."

Her only answer was Peter's back as he preceded her out of the elevator. Louis, the doorman, wished her a happy holiday.

After her family had left, Laura walked around the living room, plumping pillows, moving an ashtray here, picking up a crumb there. Her efforts were superficial and cosmetic, more necessary for her well-being than the room's. Thanks to Naomi and her mother and sisters, it showed few signs of the day's turmoil. She wished she were as resilient, but Ezra and Dottie had left marks, deeper than any scratch in the furniture, more stubborn than any stain on the upholstery. They'd left hope.

She walked down the hall to Ezra's former study. He was sitting in the threadbare wing chair.

"It was nice having you for dinner," she said.

He smoothed the stray tufts of hair on the crown of his head. "Thank you for inviting me."

"Or as Daisy Buchanan said to Nick Carraway, 'I always like to see you at my table.'"

Ezra's smile was knowing. He loved literary references. "It's always nice to be at your table, Laura."

"Always?"

The smile faded. The pale eyes looked suddenly bleached. "You have to keep pushing, don't you? You can't leave well enough alone." He stood, exposing the threadbare upholstery of the chair, the worn spot in her hope.

"Well enough for whom, Ezra?"

"Well enough for Isabel, of course. I thought we could be friends for her sake."

"You didn't show up today for Isabel's sake. You came because you were stood up and had nothing better to do. So you figured, why not drop in on old Laura and the family? After all, it's cheaper than a restaurant. Especially since you've decided to stop paying the bills."

He passed a hand over his eyes, and they emerged all professional distance and dignity once again. "It's late. I'd better be going." He started down the hall. The session was over.

She trotted after him. It seemed to her she was always running after him these days. "Did you get the second notice from the insurance company?"

"I got it."

"When I went in to order the turkey, the market said last month's bill was still outstanding."

He turned to face her, his Burberry half on, half off, like the man in the old Jimmy Durante song who couldn't decide whether to stay or go, but Laura knew Ezra had made up his mind a long time ago. "You know, Laura," he began, and his voice had a new distance to it, as if he'd already left, "every time I see you these days, every time I speak to you on the phone, you begin nagging about money." His eyes traveled over the entrance hall and came to rest on a Frank Stella lithograph they'd bought years ago. "And it seems to me you have precious little to complain about. I see patients twelve hours a day to keep you in Frank Stella prints and designer clothes and Isabel in private school. I camp out in a one-bedroom rental while you live in a Park Avenue co-op."

"You have your coat, Ezra. Don't forget your crown of thorns."

Ezra's frown was etched with smugness. He'd been listing facts. She was stooping to insults. He pulled on the other arm of his Burberry. "I always thought of you as a fair woman. I hope you're not going to change now. After all, we agreed to an amicable divorce."

She opened her mouth, and his name came out in a shriek, but he was too fast for her. He thanked her for dinner and was out the door before she could do anything but repeat his name in a second accusation. Her fists flailed at the closed door, then stopped when she heard the record come to an end in Isabel's room. Her daughter's voice floated on in the silence of the apartment.

Laura went down the hall to her own bedroom. A small china box in the shape of a heart stood on her dresser. *Je t'aime à folie* was written across the top of it. Violets climbed and curled around the fine gold script as if it were a trellis. Ezra had given her the box one Valentine's Day. She went back to the kitchen, found the hammer, and returned to her room. Isabel was still singing, and Laura closed the door, spread newspaper on the parquet floor—neatness counts—and put the china box on top of it. The hammer made a thick, dull sound, much louder than the shattering of the china, which resembled the faint tinkling of a small and distant bell. Neither was as loud as the sound of Isabel's record, which had started up again. Laura rolled up the newspaper and put it in her wastebasket. The box hadn't been expensive, though it had come from Tiffany, and until tonight she'd thought it valuable.

Hallie opened the front door—Daniel was carrying Kate— and was welcomed by a joyful Byte. Bliss turned to euphoria at the first whiff of turkey scraps. By the time Hallie had put Kate to bed Daniel had managed to race the dog around the block once and was back at his computer.

"You're not going to work now," she said, though she knew perfectly well that in this case appearances did not lie.

"I had an idea this afternoon," he answered above the whisper of the keys. "A real brainstorm. I'll just be a minute."

"So the man said when he went out for a pack of cigarettes twenty-five years ago."

"Christ, Hallie, you don't think I'm doing this for my health, do you? I'm fighting for my goddamn life in this business."

Hallie looked at her husband. There was no doubt the struggle was hazardous to his health. She wondered when the handsome fair-haired—literally as well as figuratively—boy she'd married had become this middle-aged man with a softening jaw and shoulders that sagged under the weight of the race for technological superiority. But she couldn't help thinking that like other addictions, this one gave Daniel his necessary high. The little devil in his lap took in his every word and spit it back on demand. He tickled her keys when he felt like it, and she responded on cue. Nice terminals did not take the initiative. And most important of all, he could turn her off whenever he damn pleased. All it took was a flip of the switch.

Hallie went down the hall to the bathroom, removed her makeup, brushed her teeth, and stood looking at her reflection in the mirror over the sink, but it was no good. You could never tell what you really looked like. She remembered a party she'd gone to alone—Daniel had been working—the previous week. The party had been strictly A-list with half a dozen women who looked like models, dressed like socialites, and pulled down at least a hundred thousand a year in blue-chip professions. During the entire evening only two men had shown any interest in Hallie. The first was wearing pinstripe all right, but it was the kind of pinstripe that looked as if it came with a machine gun under one arm. The second, who was turned out perfectly presentably, asked Hallie her sign. "No standing," she answered, and moved on. Say what you wanted about Daniel, he'd been swaddled in natural fibers and taught that certain subjects were unmentionable in polite conversation.

She took her diaphragm case from the medicine cabinet and opened it, half expecting to find a prehistoric artifact, shrunken, cracked, damaged beyond repair, but it lay there in its compact, a cared-for, inanimate object. Only her imagination turned the film of powder into a layer of dust. She thought of Laura with her dwindling self-worth and growing stack of bills. She thought of Emily, self-supporting, independent, but imprisoned by Peter's possessiveness and jealousy. She thought of Daniel and his hands. He had the most beautiful hands she'd ever seen on a man. They were thin with long, arching fingers and perfect moon nails. The first time she'd seen him, he'd been rolling a joint. She'd watched in fascination. Later that night, on someone's water bed, she'd watched them on herself. She took the device from its case. Such a foolish-looking object. Such a pathetic trampoline of hope. She decided to give it one more bounce.

Without putting on a robe or even a nightgown, she walked back down the hall to the study and stood in the doorway, one hand on the frame, the other on her naked hip. "I don't suppose I can interest you in a few strokes, Lord Bottomly—of golf, of course."

He looked up from the screen. When he saw her, his face creased in a smile she'd almost forgotten. "What's a nice girl like you doing in a place like this?"

She crossed the study, stood behind his chair, and put her arms around him. "Is that an automatic rifle in your pocket, or are you just glad to see me?"

This time he laughed.

"You'd better come to bed. I'm getting cold and running out of salacious one-liners."

"One minute. Five at the most."

She kissed the top of his head. His hair was still thick. It smelled clean and vaguely spicy. "You get four minutes and fifty-nine seconds. I don't want you to think I'm easy."

Half an hour later she closed her book, turned out the reading light, and turned onto her side. The spring had gone out of her hope. She felt dusty and unused.

Peter opened the door to the apartment, followed Emily in, and poured himself a tumbler of vodka without a word. Emily couldn't imagine why she was surprised. They'd left Laura's in silence, walked home in silence, ridden up in the elevator in silence. He'd said good night to her family and good evening to the doorman. Those were four more words than she was likely to get for the next four days.

He took one of his volumes on the Confederate generals from the bookcase and settled down for an evening with men of courage and cause, if not vision. Peter was among his peers. And like them, he had his principles, pure, hard, unswerving.

She took a coaster from the bar and slipped it under his drink. He didn't thank her. He didn't even notice her.

"Don't mind me, Massa Peter." She shuffled her feet a few times. And sure enough, he didn't.

She poured herself a drink to rival his, although unlike Peter, she added the amenities of ice, went into the bedroom, and closed the door behind her. She looked at the pile of books and magazines on the night table. The *New Republic* reminded her of her own failings; *Vogue*, of everyone else's success. A chronicle of the last decade of the women's movement read more like a century; a novel about a blocked writer had managed to block her interest. She checked the late movie listings, usually her favorite escape, but decided she didn't have the stomach for them tonight. Although she knew men and women didn't meet, fall in love, and live happily ever after, Louis Mayer, Darryl Zanuck, and Adolph Zukor hadn't seemed to be privy to the same information.

By the time she finished her drink she felt better. In fact, she felt so good she went into the living room and poured herself another. Peter's glass, which had been half empty by the time she'd closed the door, was full again, too. She wondered if he'd allowed one of the house slaves to refill it. He couldn't have done the job himself.

She settled back in bed with her fresh drink and her own histories, less tangible but equally vivid. She remembered the time she'd been feverish with a summer cold and he'd made her walk the battlefield at Gettysburg in a sticky ninety-eight-degree heat. "Now you know what it really felt like," he'd exulted, as encouraging as old Georgie Pickett himself. When she'd snapped that Georgie's boys hadn't lived to cherish the memory, he'd told her she had no romance in her soul. She supposed he was right. A true romantic wouldn't give a second thought to the fact that the whole grim but overpriced weekend was going to end up on her credit card since Peter's cards were temporarily out of order. American Express, MasterCard, and Visa had no respect for the prerogatives and perquisites of a gentleman. She recalled the time she'd taken him to a party full of corporate lawyers and he'd first given his lecture on the causal relationship between the proliferation of corporate litigation and the decline of the American economy. That had been an early draft of the speech—not nearly so polished as the version he delivered these days—but it had had a certain power to offend that had dwindled with time, or so it seemed to Emily. She summoned up the weeklong depression that had followed her weekend at a convention of matrimonial lawyers, the nightlong sulks in the days when she still went out for an occasional evening drink with a colleague, and the four-day silence after they'd run into Jake at that party.

She thought of the time he'd actually left her for two and a half days. She hadn't been happy. *Light-headed* was the term. Of course, she'd known all along that he'd be back, but she kept trying to feel what she thought she'd feel if he left for good. One night she came in from a movie—she didn't mind going to movies alone—and turned on the radio for company. Mildred Bailey was singing "Thanks for the Memory." Emily turned up the volume. The song should have been sad or at least poignant, but Mildred Bailey didn't sing it that way. Emily reveled in the swingy jubilance. She wondered why she'd never heard the record before. Then she remembered Peter. He went into a sulk whenever she put on a Billie Holiday record. He would have hated Mildred Bailey if he'd ever heard her. Emily danced around the apartment. The following morning she awakened to Peter's hand, impatient and insistent, on the doorbell. In his rage he'd left his keys as well as her.

She tried not to remember the time she'd come home from the office earlier than planned and found him reading a box of letters from Jake that she'd stowed in the top of her closet. Betrayed, invaded, raped of her privacy, she'd ranted about old-fashioned morality and common decency, but Peter had managed to place the guilt where it belonged. She had loved before him. Worse still, she had made love before him. Some of the letters had come from Jake's Henry Miller period. And it was no good arguing that it was all over, because then why the hell did she keep his letters in the top of her closet? For the same reason, Peter's tone implied, that adolescent boys hide girlie magazines under their pillows.

Emily didn't have to study this history. She'd been committing it to memory for years. She could trace the chronology, marshal the details, answer any question—except one. Why did she put up with it? She didn't have Laura's excuses. There were no children. She was self-supporting. The way things were going these days she'd have fewer debts without Peter. She had her work. She used to have her life. And she wasn't afraid of divorce. Like most transgressions, it was a sin only the first time. She didn't need Peter. So it must be love. Either that or self-destruction. She flipped through the pages of her mental history again. Self-destruction won. It was time to get out.

She finished her drink, turned off the light, and turned onto her side. Her future, alone, independent, free, stretched before her. Want to discuss the four freedoms, Peter? Freedom from apologies for her family, her friends, the way of the world; freedom from excuses for herself; freedom from guilt; freedom from—and here was the clincher—fear of displeasing Peter. She appropriated his pillow and drew up her knees in a fetal position. Her cold feet were literal rather than figurative. It was time to overcome her prejudices. She'd always been wary of sleeping beneath anything electrically charged, but when she thought of Peter, Ezra, even her former husband, Jake, she decided electric blankets were probably the safest thing going.

Emily awakened at five with aching temples and cold feet. This time they were figurative as well as literal. Only the double bed was none the worse for wear. She was a neat sleeper. Peter's side of the bed remained pristine. She padded to the bathroom, downed two aspirins, put on a pair of tennis socks, and got back under the quilt, but it was no good. She wasn't going back to sleep. Her feet grew only a little less chilled.

So this was it, the beginning of her new life. She thought of Laura. She thought of Laura's pillow philosophy. Today is the first day of the rest of your life. You're not getting older, you're just getting better. The only one that applied was, I have a feeling we're not in Kansas anymore, Toto. She turned over and buried her face in the pillow. It smelled faintly of soap and aftershave lotion. She crossed her arms over the back of her head. She wasn't afraid of lingering aromas and leftover impressions, but she was afraid of Peter. In an hour or two or four, depending on how much he'd had to drink and how late he'd stayed up, he'd open his eyes, realize he'd gone to sleep on the living-room sofa, and make his own particular sense of the previous day, if you could call Peter's behavior sensible. Then, like a courier, he'd appear in the bedroom door with the news. Icy silence as he marched past to the bathroom? Eloquent rage as he stood at the foot of the bed cataloging her moral faults and more mundane defects? Diplomatic overtures for peace negotiations as he slipped silently into bed? Emily knew all the maneuvers but not which he might put into play on any particular occasion. Like a good general, Peter had mastered the element of surprise. But this morning she was immune to every tactic. Her position was impregnable. She recalled still another forced march of her past, a dreary hike in a slate gray drizzle over the hills of Manassas. There stands Emily Brandt, like a stone wall. She heard the sound of a match striking in the living room. Peter was awake, smoking, thinking, plotting. She heard the doorknob turn and saw Peter's silhouette in the doorway, outlined by the light from the living room. Talk about your goddamn stone walls. Lean as he was, his shoulders almost filled the space; his presence did fill the room. She steeled herself against the attack.

He took one step into the room, then a second. The stealthy approach. With a third he reached his side of the bed, lifted the quilt, and got in beside her. She went on pretending sleep. You're too late, Peter; the war's over; the enemy lies dead on the battlefield.

"Em," he said.

She gave no sign of life.

"Em," he repeated, and his arm circled her in a brilliant outflanking move. "I'm sorry."

Talk about surprise tactics. Those two magic words of surrender would have been enough, but Peter was determined to bring out the big guns this morning. A short involuntary—she was sure it was involuntary—sob followed.

She turned toward him, and they got down to the slow, meticulous process of hammering out the peace treaty. And at odd moments for the rest of the weekend Emily stopped and wondered at the disastrous mistake she'd almost made.

V

Most people Emily knew ground to a professional halt during the holidays. One of the advantages of spending your entire life in school, Peter said, was the annual Christmas break. Other people took less official, though no less substantial, vacations, but Emily might as well have worked in a department store. Parents battled for children like gifts on a bargain table, squabbled over finances like a couple of collection agencies, and called to complain as if they'd got Emily's number mixed up with customer service. Last Christmas one of her clients, still in possession of her husband's credit cards, though not of her husband, had managed to drop fourteen thousand dollars in fifteen minutes in Bergdorf's fur department. Another, enraged by Emily's report of her husband's recalcitrance on some minor point—it was always, Emily knew, the minor points—had picked up scissors, which for some reason had been left on Emily's desk, and proceeded to cut her married name out of the lining of her mink coat. The husband of a third client, a woman who was an ardent vegetarian devoted to a variety of save-the-animal causes, had sent their daughter back Christmas night in a coat sewn from baby bunnies. The fur had certainly flown last Christmas, and from the look of things on the Monday morning following Thanksgiving, this holiday season wasn't going to be any better.

Emily picked up the phone to begin returning calls, then put it back in its cradle when Ned Sinclair stopped in the doorway, coffee cup in hand, beatific smile on face. He said he hoped she'd had a good holiday weekend, taking care to accent the second syllable of weekend, as if to indicate he'd spent his at an English country house, Blenheim at the very least. She glanced over his shoulder to the hall in search of British clients, but unlike Peter, Ned was not an inadvertent mimic. He knew exactly what he was doing.

He turned to go, then thought better of it, and lingered in her door a moment longer. "How about letting me buy you a drink tonight? We haven't had one in ages."

Ned was wrong. They'd never had one. And she couldn't figure out why he wanted to now.

"I'd love to, Ned. Really." She shouldn't have added the "really." It was overkill. "But I'm tied up tonight."

"Another time," he managed to answer without opening his mouth and headed back to his own office, a halfhearted sheep in exquisitely tailored wolf's clothing.

The phone rang before he was out of sight. "I trust you had a pleasant holiday," Jake said. "I learned how to make stuffing—for a rock cornish hen."

Emily laughed. "Poor baby. I'd weep for you, if I didn't know that your mother makes a sensational oyster dressing."

"It's nice to know you're reminiscing," he answered in a voice that implied he'd been doing nothing else the entire weekend. "I've got those profit-sharing papers," he went on before she could contradict him. "How about making the drop over a drink tonight?"

Emily speculated on this sudden need of half the men she knew to ply her with alcohol, remembered the weekend, which had turned out far better than she'd expected Thursday night, and steeled herself against Jake's voice. She told him to put the papers in the mail.

"They'll take longer that way."

"There's no rush."

He laughed. The sound, like his voice, was seductive. She told him to send the papers by messenger.

* * *

The holiday season, people warned Laura, was no time to look for a job, but Laura kept at it. It was that, she told Emily, or daytime soaps. "Which can't hold a candle to my own miniseries. I haven't gotten a dunning letter for more than a week, but I have the feeling Ezra has another surprise in store. And I don't think it's going to be as much fun as that weekend he arranged for our tenth anniversary."

Laura was right. Ezra's lawyer called Emily on the Tuesday following Thanksgiving. When Emily returned his call a few minutes later, a whispery voice geared more to a dial-a-porn service than a law office told her Mr. Kron was gone for the day. He must have called on his way out the door. Emily did not reach him until Friday. Gary Kron was a master of the missed connection, the ominous delay, and the escalating fear. When it came to tactics, Peter had nothing on Kron.

"Emily, sweetheart," he began when they finally spoke, "what's this you're trying to put over on my client?" He paused to allow her to anticipate the worst. She obliged. "I thought we were talking equitable distribution." He pronounced two of the most sacred words in divorce litany, second only to *no fault*, with reverence, but like all revealed truths, they were open to interpretation. "I don't call a beach shack equal to a Park Avenue duplex."

Emily counted to ten silently as Herb had taught her to during the summers she'd worked in his office. If the pause didn't make Kron nervous, as intended, at least it gave her time to beat the raging animal in her voice into its cage. "The apartment is not a duplex, Gary, the house at the beach is anything but a shack, and we've already agreed on all this."

"Come on, sweetheart, you know nothing is settled until the papers are signed."

"All right, Gary, exactly what are you after?"

"We just want to even up the pots a little. The house is worth maybe a couple of hundred thou. With the apartment we're talking three-quarters of a mil." Whenever Gary Kron talked money, he shortened the denomination, as if to indicate he was on intimate terms with it. "We figure she could buy him out."

"With what?" The wild beast in Emily's voice came raging out of its cage. "Ezra's a successful analyst. Laura's a woman who's spent the last seventeen years keeping his house, raising his child, and furthering his career."

"I thought she was going to get a job."

"She is, Gary, she is. At the moment she's waffling between an offer to run General Motors and feelers from the search committee to find a new president for Harvard."

"Can't she even type?" Gary made no effort to tame his own voice. The disgust ran free.

"She can bake a mean cherry pie. Apple, too. What is this about, Gary? Laura isn't going to find a job that pays enough to buy Ezra out of that apartment, and you know it."

"Concessions, Emily, sweetheart. It's about concessions. God knows you've got room for them. Like this business of putting a financial value on Ezra's degree."

"Don't forget Laura supported him while he finished med school."

"Laura isn't about to let anyone forget that." Kron's voice was friendly, even intimate. Just two good old boys getting a kick out of one more bitch's avarice.

"All right, Gary."

"All right, what?" The joke was over. Kron was suspicious.

"All right, we'll let a judge decide whether Laura's entitled to the apartment in which she has spent most of her adult life making a home for the husband and dependent child."

"You know, sweetheart, I was thinking of you and this court business just last night. I was telling my youngest kid the story of the boy who cried wolf."

"Gary, sweetheart," she said, and cringed at the sound of her own voice, "if you think we won't go to court over a seven-room co-op on Park Avenue, you've been reading too many fairy tales."

* * *

And then Laura surprised everyone. The job wouldn't enable her to buy Ezra out of the apartment, but it might allow her to pay the maintenance—if she and Isabel gave up eating. At least it would cover an occasional movie.

"Tell everyone you're looking for work," Hallie had advised. "And that includes Naomi and all your doormen. You never know where a job's lurking." Behind the sleek, antiseptic equipment in her periodontist's office, as it turned out. Since Dr. Seth Goodnuf had left his first wife and made his office manager his second, he and his associates needed a girl to run the office. When Laura, for the first time in her life, said she was a woman, but she'd take the job anyway, the probe slipped. The pain was slight, but Goodnuf had made his point. There'd be no bra burning over his sterilizer.

Emily and Hallie took her to lunch to celebrate. "Talk about the downward path to wisdom," Laura said. "I never thought I'd be happy about working in a periodontist's office."

"Whoever told you work was going to be a meaningful experience?" Emily asked.

"Several thousand feminists, by rough count."

"They lied."

Isabel bought her a bunch of freesias. "Today an office, tomorrow the world."

"I'll be cutting gums before you know it."

"That's disgusting."

"That's the world, sweetie. But at least I'm employed. Also employable. I was beginning to wonder."

Dottie and Herb were distressed. They couldn't imagine why she was so eager to rush out and get a job, especially a job that was clearly beneath her. "It isn't as if Ezra can't take care of you."

Won't is more like it, Laura thought, but didn't say. She was asking for congratulations, not trouble.

Ezra was outraged. "A dentist's office! With your education, Laura!"

"My education equipped me to discuss literature, appreciate art, and be a helpmeet. I'm grateful for all that—or at least the first two—but they're not worth much on the open market."

"I'm sure you can do better. You could teach.

"Teachers like me without special training are a glut on the market."

"You haven't tried."

"I have tried, Ezra. And with all due respect, your knowledge of the American labor market is surpassed only by your sensitivity and generosity."

"You're trying to humiliate me!"

"I thought you'd be pleased." For a moment the wounded pride in her voice discouraged her more than Ezra's reaction. "You keep complaining about supporting two households, about how hard you work and how well I live."

"You're doing this intentionally," he shouted. "To make it look as if you're being screwed!"

"I believe the baby tycoon has that honor." Her voice, she noted with a new pleasure, was several decibels below his.

That was Wednesday. On Thursday Isabel dined, as Ezra liked to phrase it, with her father. "Daddy's really upset about your job," she reported.

Laura said nothing.

"He said you're purposely trying to embarrass him."

"I'm purposely trying to put my life together and bring in a little money."

"But a periodontist's office!" Laura found it disconcerting to watch Isabel open her mouth and hear Ezra's voice come out. "Jenny's mother works in an advertising agency. She's always pointing out her commercials on television. Claire's mother went back to school to get a Ph.D. in psychology. They're doing something fulfilling."

"All I'm trying to fulfill are my financial obligations to the butcher, the baker, and the building's managing agent."

"Daddy said he takes care of all that."

"Daddy lies. He takes care of all that occasionally. And complains mightily. At last report he was on his way to the poorhouse—in his new BMW."

"You don't have to be bitchy," Isabel mumbled.

"My so-called bitchiness," Laura answered carefully, "is the only thing that stands between me and Payne Whitney. Would you like it better if I walked around with my heart on my sleeve? Would you be happier if I came to you moaning every time Daddy—"

"I don't care what you do," Isabel muttered, and started for her room. "Just don't tell me about it. You and Daddy both. I don't want to hear."

Laura told herself it was a minor argument, and Lord knows they'd had those before. She reminded herself that life with a thirteen-year-old daughter was as volatile and passionate as any romance celebrated by the Cavalier poets. She told herself all that, but she wished there were somone else to tell her as well. She thought of calling Emily, but what Emily knew about raising children could be put on the head of a pin and still leave room for several thousand angels. Hallie wouldn't be much more help. She defined the generation gap as the three feet that separated her height from Kate's. And she certainly wasn't going to call Dottie. Ezra was the logical choice. No, not logical but customary. Since the day Isabel was born, Laura and Ezra had explored the terrain of parenthood hand in hand. But Ezra had left and taken the maps with him. In dealing with Isabel, as in everything else these days, she was alone.

Emily wrapped the ham and cheese sandwich in Saran and stood staring at it, torn between the prospect of an ice-cold sandwich or Peter's death by botulism. She opted for the former, put the sandwich in the refrigerator, and went back to the bedroom where Peter was suiting up for the game. At least he was suiting up mentally. Physically he remained unclothed and slothful under the disordered sheets and quilt.

"I left you a sandwich in the fridge," she explained. "You know where the beer is. There's milk, too, and some coffee left over from breakfast. Just put the flame on high, then turn it down as low as it will go."

"I know how to work the stove, Emily."

He could have fooled her.

"I could even have made my own sandwich."

She sat on the bed beside him. Beneath the quilt the Sunday *Times* crackled under her weight. "You could have, but last time you did you dropped a jar of mustard. And the time before that you broke a plate."

"Don't stop now, precious. Aren't you going to bring up that time three years ago when I put the boiling pot on the counter and left a charred circle on the Formica?"

She had been building up to that. Instead, she ran a hand over the sparse patch of hair that made a light shadow between his breastbones. It was fine and soft to the touch. "My theory is that you do it intentionally so I won't let you in the kitchen."

He covered her hand with his own. "Sure you don't want to hang around till half time?"

She stood. "Thanks, but I don't like sex by the clock."

"For you, precious, I'd skip the third quarter."

He would. And had. During the first football season they'd lived together, he'd missed a great many third quarters. That was before he'd grown accustomed to her, and she'd discovered the cleated clay feet of this god of the intellect.

"I'm just going for a walk and a quick pit stop at the museum. I'll be home before you know it. Certainly before the second game starts."

"Give my regards to culture," he called as he turned on the television and settled down to a marathon of admirable skill or astonishing violence. It was all in the eye of the beholder.

At the doors to the Metropolitan Museum modern technology separated the real world from that of the spirit with a blast of hot air. It grazed Emily's icy face like a cheek-kissing acquaintance. She spent an hour wandering among the Impressionists, shamefaced and guilty for her limitations. Peter said she was narrow, and in this case she supposed Peter was right. She walked corridors of Oriental artifacts with unseeing eyes, entered the Egyptian wing only to get to another, and had never set foot in the hall of weapons and armor until she'd met him. Like the horses girded for battle in those rooms, she wore blinders. She sat for a few minutes in the garden of the American wing, contemplating the equally bleak views of the wintry park and her own shortcomings. Then she decided if she was going in for self-flagellation, she might as well have the right setting and headed for the medieval hall.

The mournful Gregorian chants, threadbare tapestries, and musty aroma conjured up hair shirts, vows of poverty, chastity, and obedience, and cities worth a mass, but the assembled multitude had other matters on their minds. Tourists with faces burnished by the cold and eyes glazed with exhaustion yanked at children's mufflers, mittens, and appendages as if they were launching another Inquisition. Several young couples in down vests stood clutching each other and swaying in an ecstasy that might have been religious but that Emily suspected was either erotic or narcotic. A scattering of local natives, men in their off-hours boys' clothing and young matrons, sleek-haired, smooth-faced, mink-clad animals, stooped to point out the fine points of the terra-cotta angels and cherubs to their raw-cheeked, runny-nosed versions. And among them stood Jake with one of his own. Her cheeks were red but smooth, her nose clean as a whistle, her hair a silky strawberry blond that was probably cut from her mother's cloth. If there was a god behind all this religious pantomime, he was one hell of a prankster.

Jake too had been stooping to point things out, but when he spotted her, he straightened and smiled. It was that damn intimate smile that implied he'd been waiting for her all along. He picked his daughter up in his arms and circled the outskirts of the crowd to get to Emily. The photograph he'd shown her that night they'd had a drink had done justice to the girl but not to the relationship. The hair might belong to the second Mrs. Ferris, but the dark eyes, round as question marks, and sharp chin were Jake's. Her nose started out straight and fine as his, then changed its mind and direction upward. She was, not to put too fine a point on it, adorable.

Jake introduced his first wife to his only child. Nina hid her face in her father's neck. Emily managed to mumble something without stooping to baby talk. Children made her feel more awkward than hanging judges, and this particular child made her feel more awkward than most. The relationship between a first wife and the child of a second marriage was a little like that between an aging artist manqué and her early promise.

Jake explained that they were on their way for something to eat. "Nina can't decide between Burger King and McDonald's." Emily told Nina she was a pushover for Burger King and felt as if she'd just gotten off an epigram worthy of Oscar Wilde. The child looked unimpressed; Jake, merely amused. She wondered if he remembered her insecurity with children. She was always sure they could see right through her.

He put Nina down, and she clung to his thigh as she had to his neck. While they stood talking, his hand moved to the child's head and lay over the silky hair like a strong shell protecting the soft, translucent organism within. It was a side of Jake Emily had never seen.

Outside the museum in the hard winter twilight, icy blasts of air swept up the stairs, stinging her face and bringing tears to her eyes. She headed east toward Madison, where the wind moderated itself out of deference to the solid buildings with their windows full of worldy goods. Gold glowed in the dusk, antiques whispered their pedigree, and an enormous tin of caviar spilled its glistening innards onto the pristine white tile of a shopwindow. Here was a different holiday, a Christmas unmistakable, inescapable, unambiguous. This Christmas tore at your pursestrings rather than your heartstrings. It didn't hint at the spiritual blessings you might win but came right out and rubbed your nose in the material rewards you had to have. This was a Christmas Emily could confront, combat, live with. She walked home conjuring up extravagant presents she and Peter might give and receive. Peter would like that.

Still in bed, though with the remains of his lunch strewn around him, Peter sprawled, blissfully oblivious of the season which, whenever Emily allowed it to intrude upon his life, he took as a personal insult to his sensibilities and intelligence.

"You missed half time." His enunciation was impeccable, his accent democratic, his cadences combative. He sounded as if he were auditioning as a sportscaster.

"I take it from that euphoric tone that the Giants won."

"The tone was supposed to be lustful."

"That means they played well and won." She took off her coat and boots, straightened the fallout around Peter, and settled beside him on the bed with the remains of the *Times* and a drink for each of them. He reached over and put an appreciative hand on her thigh. "Stick around. There's another half time coming up."

"Watch yourself," she said. "Christmas always makes me maudlin. I think my biological clock may have started ticking."

His hand on her thigh remained steady, as if he weren't about to fumble the ball with half time just around the corner. "You don't need a child, Emily. You have me."

Three days before Christmas Ezra's lawyer called Emily with more holiday cheer. "Emily, sweetheart, we're going to make you an offer you can't refuse."

"Does that mean you take us out in the New Jersey marshlands and shoot us immediately, or do you break our arms and legs first?"

"My client will relinquish his claims to the apartment if Laura will cut this crap about his M.D."

"This crap, as you so eloquently refer to it, Gary, reflects three years of teaching in a slum school, which paid better than a private school, during which time I might add, Lau—my client was threatened with a knife."

Gary hummed "Hearts and Flowers." Emily countered with current figures on the value of Ezra's degree and practice. "The longer this drags on, Gary, the more his practice is likely to be worth. Ezra's a young man just coming into his prime. And of course, if we take this to court, we'll have to ask for top dollar. Not to mention my fees."

"You're her sister!" Kron shouted.

Emily told him she was touched by his familial feeling. Kron said he'd talk to his client. Emily decided it was time to call hers.

"I was just thinking of you," Laura said. "Of course, the fact that I'm standing here alone confronting a naked Christmas tree and eight boxes of ornaments has something to do with that. You wouldn't care to drop by tonight, would you? If, that is, Peter will unlock your leg irons. My intentions are strictly opportunistic."

"Thank you, but I have a naked tree of my own at home."

"To say nothing of a naked man, but I'd rather not go into that. Do you realize, if I'd conceived last time I had sex, I'd be delivering next week."

"I love you when you're feisty."

"Is that what it's called? All I know is the Gristede's delivery boy, half of Isabel's friends, and Mr. Wallace in the dry cleaning store are beginning to look good. Mr. Wallace has a pacemaker."

"Speaking of hearts, or rather those without them, I just spoke to Ezra's lawyer." Emily presented a substantial, if sanitized, version of the conversation.

The story hadn't been cleaned up enough for Laura. When she spoke, her voice sounded like the thin wire she walked in this new life. "What do I do now?"

"Nothing. Just sit tight. I think Ezra's running scared. He's grasping at straws."

"A seven-room co-op on Park Avenue is not a straw, Emily."

"I usually hate to go to court—the last judge I drew was fresh off his own divorce and heavily into male bonding—but in this case I think Ezra's got more to lose than we do. The courts love women like you who have stayed home to preserve the old values."

"They're the only ones who do."

Emily told Laura not to worry, and Laura promised she wouldn't, but when she got off the phone, she walked through the apartment, room by room, toting up its emotional value. Her life, with Ezra, with Isabel, alone, lingered like indentations in the upholstered furniture, fingerprints on the polished surfaces, pictures on the walls. She was standing in the door to Isabel's room, remembering the white enamel youth bed with Winnie-the-Pooh painted on the headboard and Eeyore at the foot and the matching toy chest that used to stand in one corner, when Isabel, who had long since forgotten all of them, came up behind her.

"I know, I know, just occasionally you'd like to see if there's still a rug under that mess."

"I wasn't even thinking that."

Isabel put an arm around her mother's shoulders. They were eye to eye, but in another year or two Isabel would have the edge. "What were you thinking?"

Laura put an arm around her daughter's ribs. Their fragility never failed to surprise her. "About your old bed with Winnie-the-Pooh and Eeyore on it."

Laura was wrong. Isabel hadn't forgotten. She put her head to one side in mock childishness, but she was more serious than she pretended. "And Christopher Robin. You forgot Christopher Robin. When I was afraid to be alone in the dark, you used to tell me I wasn't alone. Pooh and Eeyore and Christopher Robin were with me." Isabel straightened and shook her mop of wiry hair. "Weren't we fey?"

"Fey?"

"Whimsical."

"It means doomed."

Isabel shrugged. "From where we stand now, I guess you could say that, too."

Where we stand now is on the edge of eviction. It wasn't a piece of information Laura wanted to pass on. She swallowed the words but didn't like their taste.

"The doorman gave me this to give you." Isabel handed her an envelope. "He said it was delivered by hand this afternoon."

Even the name of the building's managing agent in the upper-left-hand corner looked threatening. Laura took the envelope back to the living room and put it on the coffee table. She went into the kitchen and poured herself a glass of wine. When she came back the envelope lay like a white flag among the ornaments. There was the lamb she'd bought when Isabel was a baby and the dove she and Isabel had bought together a few seasons later and another lamb, this time curled between the paws of a lion, that she'd bought only last Christmas. The story of her marriage to Ezra. The lamb lying down with the lion or peace at any price.

The phone rang and Isabel managed to get to it on the first ring. "Daddy," Laura heard her daughter sing into the phone. As in "My Heart Belongs to," she thought. Laura went into the kitchen, returned with a fresh glass of wine, and picked up the envelope. When she tore it open, her movement was so violently clumsy that she managed to rip the notice inside. She held the number indicating the December maintenance in her left hand, the larger figure indicating October, November, and December, in her right. Should she bother to Scotch tape the pieces together before sending them to Ezra? There didn't seem to be much point since despite her pleas and Emily's escalating threats, he was determined to ignore them.

Laura picked up a china angel and put it down again. It was one of the more valuable ornaments, and her hands were trembling too badly to handle it. She sat on the sofa, put her head in her hands, and wondered where she'd go. She thought of Isabel and her in a one-room studio, a garden apartment in Queens, the guest room at Herb and Dottie's. Her living accommodations, like her life, were shrinking.

"That was Daddy." Isabel flung herself across the opposite sofa. She was grinning with the closemouthed smile that meant she'd just swallowed something delicious. "Guess where I'm spending Christmas."

The only question was north or south, cold or warm, skiing or swimming. "Katmandu."

"Close but no banana. St. Martin. Daddy just called. He said he decided last week but didn't want to tell me until he was sure he could get reservations. It isn't easy this time of year."

"So I've heard." Laura looked at the undressed tree. "How long are you going for?"

"Ten days."

Laura calculated the cost of ten days for two people, perhaps three, in St. Martin at the height of the season. Of course, when you didn't pay bills, there was more left over for the necessities of life.

"Who said Daddy's not generous?"

Laura pressed her lips together. Not I. I might think it. I might have nightmares about it. But wild horses couldn't drag the information from me.

"I'm going to get absolutely black."

"Be careful. That sun is death to your skin."

"Come on, Mom. Give me a break. I'll start worrying about crow's-feet the minute I turn eighteen. I promise."

In place of an answer, Laura stood, picked up her empty wineglass, and headed for the kitchen. When she returned with another refill, Isabel hadn't moved, but the expression on her face had changed. Though she didn't believe it now, someday she too would have to worry about frown lines.

"I'm sorry, I didn't mean to be bitchy."

Laura put down her glass, picked up an ornament, and began trimming the tree. "I was just worried about your getting too much sun. It isn't good for you at any age."

Isabel took the china angel from the table and hung it carefully on one of the upper branches. "If you don't want me to leave you ... I mean, to go away"—she surveyed the ornaments and chose the fuzzy lamb from her infancy—"if you'll be too lonely, I'll tell Daddy I can't go."

Laura picked up another angel. This one was unbreakable. Ezra was raising the ante, but she'd be damned if she'd match him. Isabel was too valuable to gamble. "And be the only girl in the first form who comes back for the hols without a tan! I can take anything, sweetie, except being hauled up on charges as an unfit mother."

Laura waited until the following morning to call Emily. Emily didn't waste that much time. Kron's secretary reported that he was "in conference." Emily replied in a voice she associated with grammar school teachers and Con Ed customer service representatives that she'd wait while he was called out.

Kron sounded short of breath. He'd obviously been dragged kicking and screaming from the conference room. "I've just got a minute, sweetheart. What's your problem?"

"Actually it's your problem, Gary. If I don't have a certified check from Ezra for three months' maintenance on my desk by four o'clock today, we're going to court for a temporary support order. I am not crying wolf, but in case you've been spending more time on fairy tales than casebooks lately, I'll remind you what that means. There will be no more negotiations, just court orders. And if Ezra doesn't pay those, the court can stop visitation rights. There'll be no more holidays in St.

Martin and no more weekly dinners and, as far as Ezra's concerned, no more Isabel."

The check arrived at three-thirty. Emily had to wait until after five to telephone Laura. Dr. Goodnuf did not brook personal calls in his office. Not when human life hung in the balance and each pair of gums hung on a twenty-minute schedule.

"You're a genius," Laura said. "Or a magician. How did you do it?"

"I threatened court—and meant it. And I reminded him that if Ezra didn't pay the court-ordered support once we'd got it, he'd lose visitation rights."

"Oh."

"What's wrong?"

"I wish you hadn't used Isabel as a pawn."

"I didn't use her as a pawn, but I needed some leverage."

"You don't understand, Emily. You don't have kids."

Emily wasn't going to argue the point. "That's right, I don't. And now you don't have a maintenance bill that's three months in arrears."

Hallie had bathed Kate, read to her for fifteen minutes from *A Child's Christmas in Wales*—she firmly believed that children should have to grow into their books but never into their clothes—and tucked her in bed. She'd even walked Byte, but Daniel still hadn't turned up. He'd promised he'd leave his office by six. He'd sworn he'd be home in time to get the tree. After all, he was the WASP in the family. She could barely distinguish between a balsam and a Douglas fir.

Naomi came out of her room to remind Hallie that she had to leave by eight. She too had a family. Hallie wasn't so sure about the "too." She dialed Daniel's number. A strange voice told her he couldn't come to the phone now. He was with the mainframe—the computer age equivalent of a *cinq à sept.*

She put on her coat, told Naomi she'd be back in an hour, and cursed Daniel once more for good measure. How in hell was she going to get the tree home?"

Outside the apartment, on sidewalks temporarily narrowed by walls of trees for sale, holiday crowds rushed about their business. Women fluffy as foxes and raccoons, exotic as tanuki, domestic as minks hurried by on polished boots or spindly heels. Every one of them, Hallie was certain, had a perfect marriage, a vibrant sex life, and a holiday schedule of A-list parties. Men, carrying briefcases worn to an expensive patina and shopping bags of silver and gold foil and bright-colored paper, cut through the crowds with entrepreneurial initiative. Every one of them, Hallie was sure, had a six-figure income; a working knowledge of contemporary painting, literature, and film; and a healthy respect for the art of conversation. It was so damn unfair.

She kept walking down Madison, past the spindly trees in front of the A&P and the merely respectable ones in front of Gristede's to the glorious specimens in front of the Greek florist. All her life she'd been comparing her Christmas trees to the ones she saw in ads and commercials and finding them wanting. She paced the line of trees once, a second time, a third, and finally came to a stop in front of one of them. It wasn't the tallest, but it came close, and it was definitely the fullest. A small paper tag hung from one of its branches like an ornament. She lifted it. A hundred and five dollars. She gave the man her American Express card. When he offered to deliver the tree and set it up for another ten dollars, she decided to go for broke. The only people who dragged trees home themselves were the laughing couples in cigarette ads, and she neither smoked nor, for the moment, qualified as half of a couple.

Only after she started walking down Madison again did she realize that the tree was probably too tall for the apartment. Lucky Laura with her prewar ceilings. It was the first time in months that Hallie had thought of her sister as fortunate. She must have smiled at the irony because the man coming the other way smiled back. She started to look away—only out-of-towners and prospective rapists smiled at strangers on Madison Avenue—then recognized Ned Sinclair. He was carrying two small Tiffany shopping bags and a third from Gucci. With a single smooth take-over he engineered a corporate merger of the bags and took Hallie's hand with his free one. "I've just broken the back of Christmas," he announced through clenched teeth.

"And I've barely gotten a running start."

He looked past her to the awning of the Carlyle. "I don't suppose you have time for a quick drink?"

Hallie thought of Naomi, then remembered Daniel, and said she had time for just one.

They sat at a miniature table in the requisite dark corner. Ned's knees grazed hers.

Hallie led with Woody Allen. Ned said he'd just heard the plot of his next movie. She followed with Sam Shepard. Ned confided he'd just been asked to invest in his next play. She segued into a Pulitzer prizewinning novel. Ned's face fell. He admitted its brilliance as well as his own inability to do it justice. "I read it in London. It's a little hard," he apologized, "to get into a drunken bum who's down-and-out in Albany when you're staying at the Connaught." Hallie knew from the way Ned ducked his head with a boyish grin that he could not have been more embarrassed by the confession.

He suggested a second drink. Her conscience flexed its muscles. Naomi was too valuable to offend.

"You know," Ned said as he helped her on with her coat, "you're something of a schizophrenic." She turned to face him. He wasn't as tall as Daniel, and his face was almost level with hers. The smile wasn't boyish, she decided. It was positively impish. "With your husband you're one person. On your own you're an entirely different woman." He stopped smiling, but he didn't stop staring at her. "You come alive."

For the first time in her life Hallie understood the meaning of the word *frisson.*

When she returned home, Naomi was noticeably lacking in holiday spirit. Hallie gave her an extra twenty dollars to pay for the cab and expiate her own guilt. After checking on Kate, she sat down to wait for Daniel and the tree. A few minutes later she looked in on Kate again, then went back to the living room. She moved a chair to make space for the tree and tried to look at the room with objective eyes. The two freestanding columns, a real postmodern bargain, were too big for the postwar proportions of the apartment. They needed a loft to set them off. On the coffee table a single white rose lay on a marble slab. It was living minimalism, and Hallie had to change the rose every few days. She moved it a fraction of an inch. It had looked terrific in the gallery but was grim in the apartment, like a nurse mugged in a hospital corridor, Emily said.

Hallie turned on the radio. A Christmas carol gave way to a mournful-sounding voice singing "Stay with me through the holidays." She switched off the radio.

She called the florist. The tree was on its way. She thought of calling Daniel and decided against it. She settled down with the third section of the *Times,* the one she saved for last.

Her eyes alighted on an article about how the rich and famous were planning to celebrate Christmas. A best-selling author was taking his muse, mistress, and children by several previous marriages to Mégève to ski. The wife of a real estate developer responsible for more urban blight than the Luftwaffe, RAF, and American Air Force combined was fleeing with a dozen of her most intimate friends to the solitude of her Mediterranean Island. A well-known actress was holding a séance for all her former incarnations.

The journalistic fare turned more serious. Twenty noted artists met to discuss government aid to the arts. They were in favor of it. A man whose psyche had been scarred by his girlfriend's abortion was organizing a group of his peers into

Father's Against Deprivation, acronym FAD. If men could be present during delivery, why not during abortion? A headline about workingwomen and sex caught Hallie's attention. A rising number of women who had returned to the work force were complaining of inadequate sex lives. Since husbands could no longer control these wives by withholding money, a noted California psychologist explained, they were now manipulating them by withholding sex. And all this time Hallie had thought she was alone. For once she found no consolation in the fact that she was on the cutting edge of a trend.

She went down the hall and opened the door to Kate's room again. It was no help. She went into her own bedroom, picked up the phone, and dialed Daniel's number. This time he answered, but his voice was distracted. He was still with his mistress.

"I decided what I want for Christmas," she said.

"Mmm," Daniel answered.

"A divorce."

Her only reply was the whisper of computer keys while Daniel finished whatever he'd been up to. Neither snow nor rain nor the dissolution of his marriage would keep him from accomplishing his appointed course. "This is no time for jokes," he said finally. "I know I said I'd try to get away early, but all hell broke loose around here. The system went down three times today."

"Which is three more times than I have in the last month," she shouted, and hung up the phone. Then she began to cry.

When Emily got off the phone, she stood for a while thinking about Hallie and Laura and Dottie's reaction. She wasn't going to take a third divorce in the family well. Three strikes, and she was out as a mother. Emily supposed that some sleight of hand or mind would allow Dottie to snatch an ounce of victory from the jaws of defeat. After all, Emily's failure was in the past. She was settled now, more settled than she'd ever been in marriage. She thought of Jake and his daughter, then glanced at the pile of presents she'd spread out on the coffee table to wrap for Peter's sons. She supposed she could even lay claim to a family of sorts. She didn't see Peter's boys often, but she got along with them well enough when she did. She was settled all right.

That was five days before Christmas. On Christmas morning Hallie and Daniel were still together. In the middle of the argument that had raged when Daniel had finally arrived home that night, Kate, awakened by the shouts, had wandered into the room to ask if it was Christmas morning yet. As Hallie and Daniel looked at each other, recognition became familiarity and finally affection. They began to laugh. The sound started quietly, like a secret underground spring suddenly bubbling up, then grew shrill. In the past few hours they'd both stood on the edge of a terrifying future. Now they pulled back with a wild relief.

When Christmas morning actually did arrive and Kate came out to open her presents, Hallie and Daniel were still together and planning a week in Barbados to celebrate the fact. But Emily was alone. Peter had moved out. Or rather, as he phrased it, she'd thrown him out. It all depended on your point of view.

VI

I have already been here, Emily thought four days before Christmas. With Jake and with Peter.

"I have already been here," she said aloud, afraid the words might echo back at her from the half-empty closet. Running true to form in domestic matters, Peter had executed a dramatic but far from thorough departure. He'd taken his three favorite jackets, a suit, several ties, and one pair of loafers and another of cordovans. In the dresser behind her—the drawers left open as if by a ransacking burglar—the underwear and shirt drawers were empty, but several sweaters he hadn't worn in years, some sets of cuff links he'd never worn, two ties from his mother still in last year's Christmas box, and a rook and two pawns from an old chess set lay like the artifacts of an architectural dig. Without going into the bathroom, she knew that his toilet kit would be gone. In the living room there was a hole in the bookcase where the four volumes of *Battles and Leaders of the Civil War* had stood until this morning, and marks on the wall where three cavalry sabers had hung. It wasn't that Peter traveled light, merely that he knew his priorities.

Emily went into the kitchen, poured herself a scotch that would have done Peter proud, and came back to sit on the end of the bed, headboard and frame a relic of her marriage to Jake, box spring and mattress selected, if not purchased, with

Peter. She sipped her drink and stared at the pillaged closet and ravaged dresser. On its top Peter's set of keys lay in a morass of unpaid bills and dunning letters. She'd worked this site before all right. She remembered the last time he'd decamped with his personal effects and cherished valuables and without his keys. She didn't count the time he'd stormed out of the apartment saying that he was going for a walk and that Emily was to have his things packed when he returned. They'd laughed about that line when he'd come back. She wasn't laughing this time. And she wasn't taking him back. She hummed "Thanks for the Memory." Mildred Bailey had the style, but she managed to carry the tune.

She put her drink on the night table, stretched out across the bed as if she were laying claim to it, and tried to figure out how she'd come so far so fast. Twenty-four hours ago she'd been worrying about Hallie and wallowing in her own unexpected stability. Twenty-four hours ago she and Peter had been bound together by love, predilection, and the previous United States census. They were a unit, a couple, a household. Emily looked at the clock on the night table. It was a little before eight. Twenty-four hours ago, strictly speaking, they hadn't been together at all. Peter had gone off to the departmental Christmas party. He'd sworn he'd be home by eight, and when Emily returned to an empty apartment a little before nine, she'd decided to get started on the Christmas wrapping.

She hadn't been angry. Emily sat up, sipped her drink, and thought about it. No, she hadn't been angry. She punched Peter's pillows and her own into a comfortable mound and lay back against them. She'd known Peter wouldn't be able to drag himself away from all that intellectual skulduggery and heady adulation early, and she enjoyed wrapping Christmas presents. Unlike washing dishes or making beds, the work, once done, stayed done, at least until next year. She put Christmas on the radio, Peter's favorite robe on herself, and a little scotch and soda on ice.

Even with time out for Hallie's phone call, which had gone on for a bit, she'd managed to wrap all the gifts for her family and make a dent in Peter's to his mother and kids by the time he got home.

Above the carols on the radio, the noise of his arrival was unmistakable. He was either having trouble with his key or using a blunt instrument on the lock. She opened the door for him. He breezed past her like a gust of wind from the winter night, cold and bracing.

"What a bunch of horse's asses." The fat vowels and precise consonants were Peter's impersonation of a sober man.

"Noel, noel to you, too."

He dropped his coat on the sofa, his long body into it. "Shapiro gave one of his asinine monologues on the French Revolution and the salt tax. Complete with all that horseshit about re-vi-sion-ist de-mo-gra-phy." He let out a bark of disdainful laughter. Across the coffee table, where she'd spread out the presents to wrap, she caught a whiff of distilled arrogance. "Shapiro couldn't argue his way out of a paper bag. I wiped the floor with him." With a sudden lurch he heaved himself out of the sofa and toward the bar, where he proceeded to drop an ice cube and pour several ounces of scotch on the floor before discovering the opening in the glass. He showed no sign of mopping up either, presumably because Shapiro was not handy.

He found his way back to the sofa. "If there's one thing I can't stand it's goddamn nit-picking academicians. Fucking fact collectors. Pissant 'picklock biographers.' "

Emily recalled an academic party Peter had taken her to a few weeks after they'd met. He'd given a brilliant, or at least dazzling, lecture on the central fallacy of Proust, complete with rolling *r*'s and nasal *an*'s. Emily had been swept off her feet by this American Civil War scholar who knew his Proust like a pro and spoke French like a native. Only months later had she discovered that, with the exception of the first fifty pages of *Swann's Way*, his knowledge of Proust was entirely secondhand,

and his command of French, beyond a few catchwords, nonexistent. She decided this was no time to dredge up that particular incident or Shapiro's superior knowledge of the French Revolution. "Wouldn't you rather have some coffee or at least something to eat?"

He took a long swallow of his drink. "The beautiful part of it was this little graduate student Shapiro was putting the make on. The whole damn lecture was for her benefit. Flexing his intellectual (sic)"—he made the word sound like a hiccup—"muscles. She started out panting. Like she's listening to Newton tell about this fucking apple that fell on him. You know that bright-eyed, tense-titted look."

Not as well as you do, Professor.

"By the end she was laughing at him."

But not at you, Professor. "Did you tell her about Proust, too?"

"Proust?" He took another swallow of his drink. "We were talking about the Revolution. Proust's Third Republic."

"Thanks for the chronology."

"So this kid—she was no dope—"

"Just bright-eyed and tense-titted."

Peter looked at her blankly. Alcohol, as she knew from experience, did little to improve the immediate memory. "Her body wasn't all that good. Chunky. A little like Teddy Roosevelt in drag."

Emily decided to let it go. "Who else was there?"

"That asshole Flaherty. Holding forth on his new book. A psychohistory of Ramses the Second. Talk about exercises in futility. I told him we don't even know what they spoke, let alone how they thought."

"You must have endeared yourself to your colleagues."

"Asses," he repeated.

Emily picked up a gardening book she'd bought for Peter to give to his mother. "It can't be easy being the sole representative of truth and right in the world."

"They're like ants, bees, drudges. Small minds. No vision."

He slid his shoes off and put his feet on the coffee table. They were the one thing the table, laden with wrapping paper, ribbon, tape, and scissors, had been missing.

"Look, Peter, if you don't want anything to eat, why don't you go to bed?"

He held up his empty glass and looked at her through the distortion. One more ant, bee, drudge. One more small mind lacking vision. "You know what your problem is? You're obsessed with bodily functions. If I don't want to eat, I have to sleep. Can I pee on the way?"

"I just thought—"

"You just thought that because I went to a party, I must be drunk. *Partio ergo drunko.*"

"I didn't say you were drunk."

"Didn't have to, precious. Your face says it all. Holier than thou. You look just like Shapiro."

Emily was suddenly aware of her mouth pressed firmly closed in a narrow line. She took a sip of her drink, though she knew that unlike two heads, two drunks were not better than one. "I'm just trying to get these damn presents wrapped. For *your* mother and children."

"Christ! Let a Jewish girl near Christmas, and she turns it into an orgy for martyrs." He heaved himself out of the sofa and toward the bar, where he refilled his glass. A single ice cube floated lonely as a cloud in the dark amber. "I'll wrap the fucking presents."

Emily's mouth closed in the thin, firm line again, then opened. "I am not a Jewish girl. I am a woman, born of the Jewish faith, grown to agnosticism, now in the full flower of her atheism. And what you'll do is threaten to wrap the presents until Christmas Eve, when you'll turn them over to me. I may be a martyr, lover, but you're no slouch in the persecution department."

He returned to the sofa and put his feet back on the table. Emily fought the urge to push them off. "You're a lousy

Christmas wrapper anyway," he said. "You always buy those chintzy stickers that fall off so the tape shows. You're not supposed to see the tape."

"Forgive me. I don't have your superior Jesuit training. Besides, we lapsed Jews like to see the tape. It reminds us of the martyrdom of wrapping."

He poked a recently wrapped present with his toe. "The ribbon's coming undone."

"Let's hear it for the quality assurance department." She retied the ribbon.

"Oops, forgot about you and criticism. My mistake. The ribbon was perfect. It was a fucking Platonic ideal of a tied ribbon."

The ugliness was beginning to clank and pound like the apartment's old radiators when they started to give off heat. "Please, Peter, I've had a lousy night, and I'd like to get these presents wrapped and go to bed."

"Not bed, precious, sleep. We all know how you feel about drunks, in bed or out."

She closed her mouth again. Her lips felt as numb as if she'd just emerged from the dentist's office.

"Okay, let's have it. Why did you have such a lousy night?" Peter sounded as if he might really want to know.

No sane woman, she warned herself, tried to reason with or even talk to a drunk. She moved the present she'd just wrapped from the table to the stack on the floor. Two of the stickers fell off, exposing the functional Scotch tape.

"All right. Don't tell me. Let me guess." He sipped his drink and stared off into space in an ugly parody of thoughtfulness. "Laura called. In tears. Ezra won't give her enough money. What she thinks is enough money. Hell, you lie down with robber barons, you don't get up with a philanthropist. To put a new twist on one of your mother's favorite clichés."

"It isn't Laura. It's Hallie. She and Daniel are getting a divorce."

Peter let out a hoot of pleasure appropriate to the discovery of gold, oil, or another valuable resource he'd been prospecting for all along. "Sibling rivalry rears its ugly head. What one of the Brandt sisters has, all the Brandt sisters must have." He knew she hated it when he called them the Brandt sisters, as if they were one of those brassy singing acts. He waved his hand in front of her face like a silent slap. "And don't tell me you're the only one who still has the name. The blood of the Brandts runs thick and glutinous. Too thick and glutinous for some poor schmuck like Daniel to stay afloat in."

"Christ, doesn't anyone in this world hurt except you?"

"Not everyone has your fathomless"—the scotch-soaked voice flooded the word—"depths of compassion. Mother Teresa of the legal world. Two hours to listen to Laura's problems. Three for Hallie. How long do you spend on Jake Ferris?"

"We've been through this."

"I'm talking about time out of the sack."

She flung the reel of ribbon across the table. "We don't get out of the sack!" she screamed. "I'm doing the negotiating for this one between the sheets. All four of us. Jake, his wife, her lawyer, and me. Strange positions! Perverse practices! Is that what you wanted to hear?"

But Peter had heard enough. He managed to propel himself off the sofa and toward the bedroom. Despite his condition, his balance was not so precarious that he missed the bottle of scotch on the way or failed to kick the door closed behind him.

She wrapped a few more presents, without the niceties of stickers, and crept into the bedroom to get a pillow and blanket. Peter's heavy breathing filled the dark, fetid silence. She hit her knee on the end of the bed and cursed. He groaned, mumbled, and went on breathing.

The sofa was too narrow for sleep, although Emily was a neat sleeper, and each time she turned the blanket twisted around her. They'd been through it before, Emily had told Peter, only they hadn't. In the years they'd lived together they'd never worked anything out. Peter didn't believe love was negotiable. Whatever held them together must be pure, natural, effortless, like one of nature's gems. Discussion might crack it; compromise would surely deepen the fissure until it shattered completely. And so they'd stayed away from both. When a flaw appeared, one of those little tricks that nature plays on even its most perfect creations, they'd polished the surface with nature's oldest amalgam, sex. And when it came to burnishing, Peter was a master craftsman, one might even say artist. He made the surface glow and shine and glitter so that it blinded the naked eye to those tiny black imperfections deep within.

She awakened a little after five to the queasy certainty that all was not well. Through the closed door she could hear Peter snoring. An hour later, when she tiptoed through the bedroom on her way to the bathroom, he was still snoring. By the time she came out of the bathroom he'd stopped. When she dropped a shoe from the pile of clothing she was carrying into the living room, he didn't move. She was sure he was awake. In sleep he would have made some protest at the noise.

As she finished dressing in the living room, she heard the sound of a match being struck in the bedroom. She wondered how many mornings of the last four years she'd sat in one room trying to interpret the sound of striking matches in another. Was he smoking in fury, biding his time, working up to a reconciliation? She sat on the disordered sofa and stared at the pile of presents, mostly oversize ones, that had still to be wrapped. The chemistry set for Peter to give his younger son had presented difficulties. Peter hadn't approved of the first one she'd bought, and she'd had to exchange it for this one.

Suddenly she felt like a detective who'd tracked the culprit to her own door. All she could blame on Peter was selfishness. She was guilty of stupidity, weakness, and willful self-destruction. She was guilty of buying and exchanging and wrapping presents so he wouldn't have to, and taking out the loan so he wouldn't be harassed by his estranged wife, and answering the phone so he wouldn't have to talk to his mother, and lying to her family so he wouldn't have to see them, and backing down and bearing up and giving in. She felt something brackish and sour rising in her chest, as if she'd drunk too many cups of coffee on an empty stomach, though she'd had none so far this morning.

On the other side of the closed door Peter struck another match. She grabbed her coat and fled the apartment. That was the only word for it. She was *fleeing* her own apartment.

When Peter hadn't called by lunchtime, the nausea subsided enough for Emily to have a cup of soup at her desk. Some atavistic instinct made her order pea soup, but it came from the coffee shop downstairs and was thickened with flour rather than with long, tender care.

Emily spent the afternoon preparing her case. She would not give in. He could apologize, cry, break out the goddamn *Kama Sutra.* She'd made up her mind. Now she had to make sure he didn't change his. This time she'd pack his things for him if he asked. She'd find him a sublet. She'd arrange for the movers. She knew how to do all that, but she didn't know how to convince a six-foot-three thirty-nine-year-old opinionated man to change his venue if he didn't want to.

She left her office before five. As she passed Ned Sinclair's door, he noticed her coat and asked if she was ill.

"Christmas," she explained.

He pointed his index finger at her as if it were a revolver. "Right."

The key in the lock was her first clue. The bolt hadn't been thrown. Someone had closed the door, maybe even slammed it, but not locked it. Inside, someone had left, but not necessarily for good. Emily had examined the half-empty closet and the half-full drawers, known again that she'd been there before, and sworn that this time she was going to stay.

She turned to the digital clock on the night table just in time to see 8:59 become 9:00. She'd been lying on the bed for so long that for a moment she thought she might have dozed off.

She got up and closed the door to Peter's closet and his dresser drawers. Then she went into the living room and plugged in the lights of the Christmas tree. They shone steadily for a few seconds before they got up the nerve to try any fancy blinking. She went around the room lighting the candles. Shadows flickered in the drafts from the windows.

The presents she'd been wrapping when Peter had come home last night were still piled on the coffee table and the floor around it. He hadn't bothered to take the gifts for his mother and kids when he'd left. Peter didn't care about material things. His shoes were there, too. She picked them up, carried them into the bedroom, and flung them into his closet. Then she went into the kitchen, took the four largest shopping bags from the cupboard, and began dividing the presents. Those for Peter's family went into the bags; those for her own, under the tree. She stood staring at the chemistry set and several oversize games that had yet to be wrapped, then caught herself. Love might not stop overnight, but service did. She had to go back for another bag, and when she'd finished, she put the five full bags beside the front door. Then she went into the bedroom and opened the second drawer of her dresser. Beneath the underwear and pantyhose lay a pair of cashmere-lined men's gloves, a silk muffler—both were too functional for Peter to regard as gifts—a small, frustrating puzzle that was this year's Christmas craze, two books, and a Colt navy revolver. It was the gun that had won the West, and Peter had been talking about buying one for years. Emily had made a dozen phone calls and talked to as many men, several soft-spoken antique dealers, three John Wayne impersonators, and one ghoulish gun nut before she'd tracked down this specimen.

She took the gifts from the drawer and spread them on the bed. She'd had her eye on the muffler all along, and the gloves, books, and puzzle could be returned. She supposed the dealer would buy back the revolver, though she knew he wouldn't buy it back for the $450 she'd paid him. The shadow of Peter flickered through the room, coloring and shading everything in it like the blinking tree lights. How like Emily to be worrying about spilled milk when she ought to be grieving over slain passion. Small mind, no vision. Behind her Peter's shadow snickered. The phone rang. She regretted her Luddite sympathies. An answering machine would head Peter off. A backbone would do the job as well.

Emily picked up the phone. Her voice sounded as if she were about to lose it. Peter's walked a tightrope between contrition and surliness. A push in either direction, and he'd fall.

He asked how she was. She recognized the ploy. He was playing for time, trying to gauge just how contrite he'd have to be.

Emily considered the question. Abject? Obviously a lie. Jubilant. No point in erring on the other side. "All right."

She heard a match strike. Peter inhaled. Even over the phone she could sense his disapproval. "All right" was the wrong answer.

"Where are you?" she asked, though she knew she oughtn't to, and he wouldn't tell her anyway.

"It doesn't matter."

He smoked noisily into the long silence. "Em," he said finally, "can't we stop all this?"

"I'm trying to." She heard him exhale in pleasure. This was more like it, more like her. "I'm trying like hell to put an end to the fights and the craziness and us."

She heard a gasp of breath again, but this time it had nothing to do with his cigarette. "Do you know what you're saying?"

"I'm saying I don't think we ought to go on living together. I just can't take it. I can't take the—" But Emily did not have to explain what she couldn't take. Peter had hung up.

She sat staring at the phone. It rang again immediately. "Listen, Emily," Peter said, "you don't mean that."

"I do."

She supposed she'd known it was coming. "You've found someone else."

"There's no one else, Peter."

"Your ex-husband."

"I'm not going through this."

"If it isn't Ferris, it's someone in your office."

"Just someone? Not the whole office?"

"It's got to be someone else. There's no other explanation."

This time she hung up the phone. It didn't ring again for twenty minutes. She could tell Peter had had a drink in the interim, though he wasn't drunk. "I want to stop this, Emily."

"Then stop calling."

"You know what I mean."

"You should have thought of that last night when you came home spoiling for a fight. Or last week when you went into a sulk because I got home late from Christmas shopping—Christmas shopping for your kids. Or Thanksgiving when you—" It was Peter's turn to slam down the phone. Emily hung up her own receiver gently. It was hard to believe they masqueraded in the world as adults.

She went into the kitchen and freshened her drink. If it wasn't going to be a productive night, she might as well make it a painless one. When the phone rang, she picked up the kitchen extension.

"Look, I'm sorry." But the words had lost their magical power. "I don't mean to keep hanging up on you."

"I don't care if you keep hanging up. I just wish you'd stop calling." The sour brackishness she'd thought she'd banished this morning surged in her chest. She was, as Peter had frequently pointed out, a coward.

"Do you mean that?"

"Yes."

"You really want to end things?"

She took a long swallow of her drink, but it didn't wash away the bitter taste. "I really want to end things, Peter."

"You don't mean that."

"I do."

"You really want me to leave?"

"You have left," she pointed out, but Peter would not be sidetracked.

"You want to end it?" he repeated.

"I've been telling you that all night."

"You mean it?"

"Yes, Peter."

"Are you sure?"

The sickening brackishness exploded inside her. "God damn it, Peter! I said it, and I mean it! It's over! I want out!"

"I just want to make sure."

"No," she shouted. "You don't want to make sure. You want to get your way. And you think if you keep badgering me, I'll give in." She took a deep breath. It was a mistake. She'd drawn all the ugly black rage back into herself. "Why not? I always have in the past. I played the goddamn dog to your goddamn Pavlov. You badgered, I gave in. But not this time! Not anymore!"

"I'm not badgering you. I just want to make sure you mean it."

"You are badgering me, and I do mean it."

"Are you sure?"

"Peter!" Her scream filled the empty apartment. "It's over!"

"It can't be."

"I'm hanging up now." She replaced the receiver gently because he was still talking.

The phone began ringing again almost immediately. She waited until it stopped, then went into the bedroom, took the receiver off the hook, and placed it beneath the pillows. God knows she and Peter had their faults, but she'd never thought an abject lack of dignity was one of them. She'd been wrong.

VII

"He'll be back," Laura said.

"I don't want him back."

"I didn't say you did, but that doesn't mean he won't keep trying."

"I don't think so. Peter's persistent, but he's also proud. I saw him with his wife. When things were over, they were really over. In a few days or a week, when he realizes I'm serious, he'll relegate me to the past, and I will be forever known in story and song as That Bitch."

There was a moment's silence, and when Laura spoke again, her voice was tentative. "How do you feel about Peter and another woman?"

Emily considered the question. She thought she felt nothing at all, but it was always risky to predict those things. "Fine—so long as she doesn't turn out to be Sandra Day O'Connor."

He'll be back," Hallie insisted. "I think it's sheer perversity. Laura would do anything to get Ezra back, so of course, he won't come back. I can't blast Daniel out of the apartment." Hallie was having second thoughts about the reconciliation. They were going through with the trip to Barbados, but she wasn't sure they'd be able to go through with the marriage.

"That's because you don't really want to."

"Let's say I'm ambivalent."

"Who isn't? You don't just get up one morning and decide it's all over."

"You did."

Emily remembered Thanksgiving night and half a dozen others in the past year. When had compromise, which she regarded as a virtue, at least if you were trying to live with another human being, become surrender? And when had the white flag begun to fray? The time she'd listened to Mildred Bailey? The evening she'd rushed home from Laura's to make dinner for Peter only to discover he wasn't speaking to her for going there in the first place? The night she'd brushed away the traces of a drink with Jake Ferris? "This didn't happen overnight," she said to Hallie. "It's been a long time coming."

"And I still think Peter's going to be a long time going. He knows where his bread is buttered."

Talk about scorched-earth policies. Hallie had managed to destroy four years of Emily's life with a single torch.

Hallie heard the silence on the other end of the phone. "I didn't mean to suggest he wasn't in love with you, but face it, Em, where else is he going to find another woman to call in twice a day, pay for his kids' braces, and never go anywhere except his mother's apartment and faculty parties?"

Emily wished she'd never told her sisters about the loans. She wasn't sure what had happened with Peter, but she knew that whatever it was, it couldn't be summed up in a single image of buttered bread. The idea made her sick. She was tired of the queasy feeling that came and went, the hands that trembled as she lit the unfamiliar cigarettes Peter had left behind, the endless talk that destroyed rather than illuminated. "Where is he going to find a woman to do that?" Emily repeated. "In every class he lectures, every seminar he gives, every bar he walks into, every dinner party he's invited to, the Metropolitan Museum, the Whitney, the Guggenheim, Bloomingdale's, Brooks Brothers, Paul Stuart, and the local supermarket, to name only a few. In other words, everywhere but the men's room."

"You have a point." Hallie took a deep breath. It sounded like a sigh. "And I am one woman on whom it isn't lost."

But it was Dottie who provided the real surprise. "How do you feel?" she asked after Emily had broken the news.

Emily assured her mother she was fine. "After all, I've been here before."

"It's not like playing the piano, Emily. Practice doesn't make perfect." There was a silence, as if Dottie were regretting her words. "I don't like your being alone. At least Laura has Isabel."

"We're not going into that now, are we? Anyway, Isabel's in St. Martin for the holiday." Her attempt at deflection boomeranged.

"Maybe you ought to stay with Laura. She could use the company."

Emily pictured Laura and herself tiptoeing around each other to make coffee every morning, circling each other every evening as they prepared dinners of steamed vegetables and spare salads, sidling up to each other every night as, anesthetized by nightcaps, they pinned Ezra and Peter to the dissecting boards and began cutting, carving, and probing. As girls they'd frequently shared bedrooms. As women they shared opinions, and probably not enough of those. "I'm fine alone. I like being alone."

Then came the surprise. "I never did like the way he treated you."

"I thought you wanted me to marry him."

"As long as you wanted him—wanted to live with him—I thought you ought to marry him, but to tell you the truth, Emily, I'm glad he's gone. Maybe I shouldn't say that, but I am. There are worse things in the world than living alone."

"I know that, but I didn't think you did."

"And after all, you have your career."

"Wait a minute, is this my mother on the other end of the phone? Dorothy Baum Brandt Kramer?"

Dottie laughed. "I keep telling you I'm a modern woman. And speaking of your career, how's Jake? Is his divorce final yet?"

So Dottie hadn't surprised her quite so much after all.

There was a certain dispiriting satisfaction to being proved right. At least Emily wasn't leaving a stranger. Peter lived up to her predictions. After three days of round-the-clock calls, he'd retired to an island off Puerto Rico to slather suntan lotion on his festering wounds and rum punches on his lacerated vanity. She wondered how you said "That Bitch" in Spanish.

Peter was gone, but his possessions lingered on. Emily had her work cut out for her. On New Year's Eve she stood staring at the stack of empty boxes she'd dragged home from the liquor store over the past few days. It was a hell of a way to usher in the new year. Outside her apartment the city was filled with drunks and people in love. Inside, her apartment was empty of both for the first time in years.

She opened the door of Peter's closet. He'd left the silk dressing gown she'd bought him two Christmases ago, the son of a bitch. As she began folding it, she noticed a cigarette burn on the cuff and several stains on the lapel. They should have made her feel better about giving him up, but they didn't.

She'd finished packing his clothes and was starting on his books when the phone rang. Dottie was early. Emily had been certain she'd call at a little after midnight to wish her Happy New Year. First Laura, then Emily. She had the sentiment right but the voice wrong. Or rather the voice was exactly right. Jake Ferris sounded as smooth and rich as all those exotic foods the rest of the city was enjoying on this festive night, or so the media assured her.

Emily looked at the digital clock next to the phone. It was 10:17. On New Year's Eve. Her imagination and experience ran the gamut of possibilities. The second Mrs. Ferris had picked this night to serve Jake with papers suing him for adultery, every penny he was worth, sole and exclusive custody of his daughter.

"I'm at a party," he said. "Not really a party, more like a dinner." He mentioned the name of the joint custody couple. In divorce law, one point was inviolable. Men won custody of the dinner invitations. "I just heard the news. About your separation. I'm sorry."

He didn't sound sorry. He wasn't gloating, but he wasn't grief-stricken either. "We thought you might like to join us."

"It's after ten."

"It's New Year's Eve."

It was not what you'd call repartee.

"Some other year."

He took her up on the suggestion. "Okay, how about brunch tomorrow?"

She looked around her at the open suitcases and half-filled cartons. There were several stacks of books on the floor that she couldn't make up her mind about. If Peter had read a book and urged it on her, did it qualify as his? If she'd given him one because she liked the author and wanted him to as well, was it hers? There were entirely too many books between them.

"I don't think so."

"Why not?"

The question was so like Jake she started to laugh. "The first law of contemporary survival," she explained. "Never trust a newly separated man."

"Even if you're a newly separated woman?"

"Especially if you're a newly separated woman." She wished Jake a happy new year and went back to dividing up the books.

On January 3 Emily called Peter at his office to tell him his worldly possessions were packed and waiting for him.

"I can't discuss it now," he said.

"There's nothing to discuss. Tell me when you're coming,

and I'll leave everything with the doorman. I'd like to get your stuff out of the apartment."

"I'll pick it up in my own good time."

"Be fair, Peter. It's no fun living with a room full of cartons."

"It's no fun being harassed the day I get back."

"I'm not harassing you. And I thought it would be a good time to call. I thought you'd be rested from your vacation."

"Some vacation. It was hell."

So, she thought, was war. She asked him to have his things out in two weeks. In less time than that they'd gone from intimacy to enmity. Emily had seen it happen to her clients, but never quite so quickly. Someone was running the film at the wrong speed.

The phone became a lifeline to a sickroom. Laura used it to take the patient's emotional temperature several times a day.

"Did you sleep last night?"

"Have you gotten out at all this weekend?"

"Are you *all right?*"

Hallie used it less frequently but delivered massive doses of medication.

"I have a book you absolutely must read. *Creative Divorce.*" Emily said she didn't like science fiction. "It shows how to make your emotional profit and loss statement come out in the black."

"Just when I thought it was safe to declare Chapter Eleven."

When it came to self-improvement, Hallie was indefatigable. "Have you thought of joining a health club? You never know whom you're going to meet at the Nautilus machine."

"I know whom I'm going to meet at the Nautilus machine. Someone who thinks *Thirty Days to a Firmer Fanny* is one of the great books of the Western world, believes that Jane Fonda is a choreographer, and has more tucks behind his ears than character in his face. Besides, I'm not ready to meet people. Separation has its stages, as *Creative Divorce* and every pop psychologist will tell you. You don't want me to jump the gun do you?"

Hallie was even able to look on the bright, or at least the advantageous, side. "I'm thinking of getting into divorce mediation," she announced one evening.

"Has Daniel agreed to it?"

"For AWE. It's a burgeoning industry."

"I thought that was baby counseling, the wave of the future."

"First one, then the other. We aim to be a full service organization. I thought perhaps you could recommend a reputable divorce mediator."

"For a divorce mediator try our niece, Isabel, who's taking an introductory course in psychology, Naomi, or any denizen of your local OTB office. For reputable, I'm still looking for an honest man."

Emily bought an answering machine. It was less than a square foot in size but big enough to hide behind.

Emily stopped fighting Hallie and met her halfway. She signed up for a dance class. There were, she knew from clients who had bought entirely new wardrobes, moved halfway across the country, or taken up with the sixteen-year-olds who delivered their kids' pizza, more drastic ways to start over. The class was not expensive, irrevocable, or contagious. Besides, with Peter gone, she figured she needed all the exercise she could get.

The first class was not a success. Within minutes she was out of breath, step, and her element. Without her glasses she couldn't see her image in the mirror, the instructor, or even the other women in the class. Everything was off-focus. The class, she decided, was a metaphor for her life. She told herself to stop conducting morbid interior monologues and put on her glasses. Everything fell into place.

She began accepting all the invitations Peter had sneered at. It was odd going out again. It was even more peculiar going out alone. She went to a dinner party of high-powered attorneys and investment bankers at which she was the only person who'd never been to China or, what was worse, "21." She went to a brunch given by a socially conscious lawyer and his newly acquired young wife. The other guests were dressed like extras from an old MGM movie about simple, goodhearted peasants who'd cornered the market on passion, virtue, and folk wisdom, and the decor and food made a statement about the plight of the Native American. She went to the thirty-second-floor penthouse of a garish new high-rise for a party to raise funds to save the wilderness. By that time she was fair game. A man approached.

"Are you married?" he asked.

Emily decided there was a physiological difference between the male and female optic nerves. Women's eyes were drawn to wedding bands by a law of nature. Men's were blind to them. She admitted she no longer was.

"Why?"

"Why what?"

"Why'd you break up?"

Emily mumbled something noncommittal, unincriminating, and apparently unconvincing.

"Bullshit."

In a room full of lawyers she'd managed to find the only poet.

"There's always one reason. One real reason. I'll tell you mine."

I'll show you mine if you show me yours. No dice, Emily thought, but the poet needed no encouragement.

"My wife screwed around. She was twenty-seven, but she was insecure about getting older, so she screwed around."

Emily debated the appropriate response. "I'm sorry" seemed hackneyed, "Too bad" a little frivolous, "Serves you right for robbing the cradle" unnecessarily cruel. "At least you're not bitter."

"Oh, I'm not bitter," he assured her. "The bitch got the apartment in town, the house in the country, and a bundle, but I'm not bitter."

She accepted an invitation to a weekend in the country. Peter had always refused to spend a night under another man's roof. It was an invasion of privacy, he insisted, though he meant his rather than his host's. He had no intention of sharing a bathroom, the first cup of coffee of the morning, or every waking moment with relative strangers. Peter had exaggerated, but not by much. There was no rush on the three baths, and Emily, unaccustomed to the strange house, was down early enough to have coffee alone. The rest of the day was something else. She was strapped to skis, lashed to the back of a tired, asthmatic horse, and forced into a nature walk that had all the charm and amenities of the Bataan Death March. On Sunday evening in the car going home several guests swapped horror stories of urban existence, grew misty-eyed over the moral superiority of the simple rural neighbors who had scowled at them from their pickup trucks and snowmobiles, and confessed to a deep and abiding desire to return to nature. Emily was silent. Occasionally she spotted a sign that indicated the mileage to New York. She thought of several clients whose hands she'd held over the past few years. One, abandoned by a novelist, had taken up with a rag trade mogul who claimed he read books rarely and fiction never. Another, divorcing a fervent Zionist, had run through a spate of lovers who could have passed the Third Reich's tests for racial purity. A third, who had met her former husband at a civil rights demonstration, fallen in love at a peace rally, and had her first orgasm in the back seat of a car as LBJ announced he would not run for a second term, had rushed headlong into a second marriage with a power in the National Rifle Association. Last year she'd sent Emily a Christmas card assuring her that people killed, guns didn't. This year she'd been ominously silent. Emily was sure there was an object lesson there somewhere. And she'd learned it this weekend. Peter wasn't as right as she'd once thought, but he wasn't entirely wrong either.

It was the year of the homeless, or so the media said. That winter the newspapers counted them, the magazines interviewed them, and the local television networks took them to their outraged investigative hearts. Emily saw, and sometimes tried not to see, them everywhere. In the midtown area near her office they came and went with anonymous faces and interchangeable maladies and rags. In the neighborhood they staked out a particular block and took on the discomforting familiarity of old friends down on their luck. She began crossing the street to avoid them. One Sunday afternoon on her way to the museum the light changed before she could escape. With the averted face, closed in guilt, of the hardened native, she walked past the outstretched hand of a woman about her age. When she got to the corner, she turned around. The woman was ransacking a trash basket. Emily started back toward her. The woman picked up an empty plastic soda bottle—five cents on the open market—and an old copy of the *New York Post* and started down Eighty-eighth Street. She was fleet and lithe on her torn moccasins. Emily had to run to catch up.

"Excuse me," Emily said, and the woman turned. Filthy rags framed her face like an ex-communicant's wimple. Her skin was streaked with dirt. Her hand as it closed around Emily's dollar bill was black, too. Her smile was mischievous as a child's or an imp's or a madwoman's.

"Go to a shelter," Emily said. "Get in out of the cold. Do you know where to find a shelter?" Emily found herself shouting the way stupid people do when they're trying to communicate with someone who doesn't understand the language.

The woman's smile shrank to a small black hole. Her cracked, filthy hands pushed the dollar back into Emily's glove.

"Don't tell me what to do," she said, and Emily realized she spoke the language well. "Don't play Lady Bountiful with me. Not for a lousy dollar."

Emily pushed the bill back in her hand. "I'm sorry."

The woman considered Emily for a moment. Then she tucked the dollar into the folds of dirty fabric, turned on her moccasins, and danced off down the street, her crazy-quilt rags billowing about her like untended sails in the wind.

VIII

February set in. People with disjointed marriages began to think about joint tax returns. The previous year had not been a good one for Dr. Ezra Glass. Thanks to several deadbeat neurotics, the income from his practice had dropped by almost a third. He had taken a vicious beating on several investments. But despite setbacks, dutiful son that he was, he'd managed to set up a trust for his parents a few weeks before he'd left his wife.

For the first time since they'd started negotiations, Kron took Emily's call immediately. "Emily, sweetheart," he greeted her, "enough of this dicking around. Are you ready to get into bed with us or not?"

Her stomach lurched. There was still something to be said for celibacy.

"I just got Ezra's financial statement for last year. Who transcribed the numbers, Rosemary Woods?"

Even Kron's laugh was slippery. "I'm going to miss you when we settle this divorce, sweetheart. You're one funny broad. My client had a bad year. What can you do when a couple of patients don't pay up?"

"What Ezra's always done. No pay up, no lie down."

"We're talking about a doctor, sweetheart, a dedicated psychoanalyst, a man who helps and heals."

"If I may cite Ezra citing Freud, the payment is part of the cure."

"Yeah, well, you know what I mean. Anyway, with this drop in his income, you can see how he can't carry that apartment. If she wants to live there, she'll have to find a way to pay for it."

"She wants to live there with the dependent child."

"Exactly. She gets the kid and the apartment. He gets the bills. That's not what I call equitable distribution."

"Of course, we'll fight it," Emily told Laura. "Full disclosure and all that. But something Kron said gave me an idea. I know how you feel about joint custody, but I was thinking it might not be such a bad idea. Just listen for a minute. I'm talking about legal joint custody, which is more cosmetic than anything else, especially at Isabel's age. She goes on living with you, but Ezra feels he's getting something for his money."

"I'm not signing over my daughter."

"You're not signing her over, Laura. All you're doing is giving up a meaningless title to win some real advantages and allow Ezra to save face. It's called negotiating."

"Not in my book. Isabel is my daughter. I raised her. I stayed home with her so she'd grow up with a mother's love rather than a hired woman's impatience, and I taught her how to read so she'd have a head start. I was there when she cried about the girls who wouldn't let her into their fourth-grade club and when she got her first period and on several hundred other occasions. Ezra attended one flute recital. He always had an opinion—advice about what I should do or a judgment about what I'd done—but I was the one who was there. I raised her, and I'm not about to turn her over to him now."

"You're not turning her over to him."

"You don't understand, Emily. You don't have kids."

It was the only argument to which Emily had no answer. Maybe that was why her mother and sisters used it so often.

That weekend Laura began looking at two-bedroom apartments. Emily told her she was premature, but Laura said she liked to be prepared. She was merely appalled. For half a million and eleven hundred a month she could get a perfectly nice two-bedroom. For a quarter of a million she could get a one-and-a-half with a breathtaking view of an air shaft.

At a little after three she gave up. The broker had given up on her even earlier. "Maybe you ought to try one of the outer boroughs," the broker suggested, and hurried off to the Arabs and Japanese, who had real dollars to spend.

Laura stood alone in the middle of a Saturday afternoon as the crowds around her with surer footholds climbed toward the peak of the weekend. No rope bound her to other climbers. She was at loose ends.

She walked aimlessly for a while, but the day was too cold for aimless walking. Couples and families passed her on the street. Their words curled into ribbons of frost connecting them to each other.

She found herself in front of Bloomingdale's. It opened its arms to her like mother church to an apostate. She went inside.

Devotion was in progress. Sacrifices were being made, faith restored, hope renewed. There was an escalator to heaven. She got off at housewares. Machines that churned out the sacraments of pasta and popcorn and peanut butter stood like icons on every surface. Copper and aluminum and enamel glowed like votive candles. Here truly was the promise of a better life. Laura took the plastic card from her wallet as reverently as if it were a relic. In twenty minutes she managed to buy three hundred dollars' worth of indulgences.

She took the escalator to linens. The offerings grew richer. Towels the color of emeralds and rubies and sapphires spilled over each other. Smooth sheets promised otherworldly pleasures; soft comforters, solace. These linens wouldn't merely change your life, they'd redeem it. Laura bought them all, for her bed and Isabel's, for her bath and Isabel's, for her salvation and Isabel's.

She took a taxi home. She hadn't taken a taxi in months. When the cab pulled up in front of her building, Louis, the doorman, looked vaguely relieved, as if God were in his place and all was right with the world.

That Monday Laura spent her entire lunch hour on the phone with Bloomingdale's customer disservice department. Half the purchases arrived nonetheless, and she had to spring for another taxi to return them all. She mentioned the incident to no one, not even Emily.

"Have you ever had pasta with caviar?" Isabel asked her mother when she returned from her weekly dinner with her father that Thursday.

"Nope." Laura was sitting up in bed reading, the tray with the remains of the tuna salad she'd had for dinner beside her.

"Absolutely yummy. The best of *nuova cucina*."

So Ezra had switched his allegiance from France to Italy. "How is your father?" Laura asked in what she firmly believed was an excellent imitation of Jeanette MacDonald.

"All right." Isabel's wide mouth described the gentle arc of a frown. "He says he's a little lonely."

Laura's stomach flopped over like the fish she'd landed that summer in the south of France. "I'm sorry."

Isabel walked away from the problem with a light adolescent step but returned in a few minutes wearing one of Ezra's old shirts and a pair of fuzzy rabbit slippers. The pink ears flopped as she walked. Laura felt a thrill of pride at her daughter's long, thoroughbred legs and a stab of tenderness at the childish slippers.

"Daddy said you want to move. He says you're going to sell the apartment."

"He—" Laura started, then stopped immediately. The sound had been less a word than a cry of rage. She forced her eyes back to the book on her lap, though the words had blurred. "I don't want to move, but we may have to. It's still only a possibility, though, and I don't think you have to start worrying about it."

Isabel sat on the end of the bed. "In other words, you're going to spring it on me. Like the divorce."

Now the whole room blurred. Laura felt as if her head were reeling from a slap. Only the memory of that Sunday almost a year ago was etched clearly in her mind. At 11:42—Laura had sat staring at the digital clock because its glowing face had been warmer than Ezra's—he'd told her marriage was no longer a viable institution. Somewhere around 6:00 they'd summoned Isabel to the dining-room table and told her the things that Ezra's training and all the books said were right and Laura knew were wrong because what was happening was wrong. "We didn't spring the divorce on you, Isabel." I had a few hours' running start, that's all, she railed silently.

"You said you hadn't been getting along for some time. How come nobody bothered to tell me for some time?"

Because it wasn't true, Isabel. It was the party line. You're not supposed to make one parent look bad. You're not supposed to tell children that Daddy's suddenly discovered something called the prime of life and Mommy's just found out she's past it. You're not supposed to tell children the truth. Let them find out for themselves. "We told you as soon as we were certain what we were going to do."

"Just like you're going to tell me as soon as *you* decide we're going to move. Well, what about me? I don't want to move. I don't want to go to some awful new school."

"No one said anything about a new school."

"Daddy did. He said you could decide to leave New York. He said you could move anywhere on some whim or something."

"Some whim! Look, Isabel, I don't want to move. It's your father—"

Isabel got off the bed. "I don't want to hear it. I don't want to know anything about it." She started for the door. "You say it's Daddy's fault and he says it's yours and you're both lying."

So she'd found them out.

Laura picked up the phone and dialed Ezra's number. Her

fingernails sounded like shots on the buttons. "Dr. Glass," the familiar voice answered. He sounded so sure of himself, so full of himself. Laura could hear the conversation to come as clearly as if it had already taken place and been recorded on the answering machine. She'd hurl accusations. He'd counter with questions. She'd call him names. He'd suffer the injustice in silence. She'd hang up, still angry, ashamed, and looking for a meaningless object to smash. She put down the receiver without a word.

Sorry, Ezra. Not this time. Not with Isabel caught in the middle. She got out of bed and followed her daughter to her room. Isabel was lying on her back on the bed, staring at the ceiling. Laura sat on the side of the bed. Isabel didn't move.

"Look, Isabel, I know you don't want to talk now. Just let me say this. I don't want to move, but we may have to move. If we do, I'll discuss it with you first. And I promise—" Laura faltered; she'd never made a promise or a threat to Isabel that she couldn't deliver "—I'll do everything in my power not to leave New York and not to make you change schools. I promise you that."

Isabel gave no sign of having heard her. She went on staring at the ceiling as the crease between her eyebrows grew deeper and longer, like an angry exclamation mark. Laura wished she'd cry. When she hadn't made the fourth-grade club, Laura had held her and rocked her as she cried. Now she didn't dare touch her.

Laura got up and went back to her own room. It seemed terribly empty and larger than she'd ever noticed, larger than necessary, Ezra would say, for one person.

The next afternoon Isabel called Laura at her office to ask if she could stay overnight at a friend's. There was nothing unusual about Isabel's spending a Friday night at a friend's, but Laura couldn't help feeling there was something different about this Friday night.

She hung up the phone and leaned her head against the

curved Plexiglas wall that separated the long desk where all the girls, as they were called, worked from the room where the patients waited. She'd never figured out whether the wall was supposed to keep them in or the patients out. All she knew was that it made her feel as if she were trapped in a cage.

Behind her two of the girls—Laura had come to bristle at the term, but they were young enough not to—were whispering. They were closer to Isabel's age than Laura's, yet they liked Laura. They laughed at her naïveté about the clubs they went to, the music they listened to, the rituals they lived by, but they heeded her, too. When they went on forays into the greater world, they even sought her advice. She told them that pink anklets and punk men's shoes did not qualify as timeless fashion investments, that a book of art reproductions or photographs was always an appropriate gift, that sponges were not as safe as diaphragms, and that they really ought to question their gynecologists about the relative risks and advantages. She coaxed and counseled them, alternately amused and impressed them, took the private messages they were not supposed to get, and even wrote for Nancy, the oldest of the group, an answer to a *New York* magazine personal ad from a self-proclaimed "Kristofferson look-alike" who had so many physical, intellectual, and emotional qualities Laura couldn't understand why he was having trouble finding a mate, even a slim mate over five feet six inches tall and under twenty-eight years of age. Laura had had reservations about answering the ad. She couldn't help thinking that advertising for love was asking for trouble. The girls had only laughed. But they hadn't shut her out. Her daughter had done that.

She didn't see Isabel until Sunday night. Ezra had managed to scare up two ballet tickets for Saturday evening, and since Isabel spent the night at his apartment, Sunday brunch at Tavern on the Green just naturally segued into an afternoon movie and dinner in Chinatown. Even in the old days, as a penniless medical student, Ezra had been good at courting.

When Isabel returned home a little after nine, she went straight to her room and the demands of an English essay. Laura conceded that she'd never had to nag Isabel to do her homework.

"It'll blow over," Emily told Laura on the phone later that night. "A natural side effect of divorce. I had one client whose teenage daughter didn't speak to her for an entire summer. And that isn't a euphemism. The kid didn't utter a single word for two months. Then she started a new school. In a week she was on the phone nonstop. By the end of the month she and her mother were best friends again."

"I hope you're right."

"Trust me. I may know nothing about kids, but I'm an expert on divorce." Emily glanced across the room at the stripped bookcases. But practice, as her mother had warned, did not make perfect.

"Have you thought of professional help?" Hallie suggested to Laura. "For Isabel, I mean. Or for both of you, for that matter. I believe in relying on professionals."

"Ezra's a professional. Still, you may have a point." Laura had lost confidence in Ezra and her faith in his tenets was dwindling, but she couldn't afford prejudices when it came to Isabel.

She approached the issue gingerly, but then these days anytime she approached Isabel it was gingerly. She'd made veal piccata and fettucine, Isabel's favorite dinner. She was setting the scene, as if for a romantic proposal. "Isabel," she began, "I know you're angry at your father and me. It's only natural. And I understand that you feel you can't talk to us about certain things." Laura stopped to taste the veal. It was a little too tart. She'd been heavy-handed with the lemon. "But maybe you'd like to talk to a third person. An outsider. A professional."

"You mean a psychiatrist?"

"Or psychologist or someone like that," Laura lied. Isabel

would enter the office of a shrink unblessed by the New York Psychoanalytic Institute over Ezra's literally dead body.

But Isabel knew her father's prejudices as well as Laura did. "You trying to get back at Daddy?"

"I'm trying to help you."

"I don't need any help," Isabel said, and finished her veal in sour silence.

Ezra's call came only a few nights later. "That was highly irresponsible of you, Laura," he said as soon as she picked up the phone. Apparently he had no time for the niceties of a formal greeting.

"What was irresponsible, Ezra?" You didn't live with an analyst for seventeen years without learning to ask a few questions of your own.

"Trying to force Isabel to see an analyst. Or, even worse, someone less."

"I wasn't trying to force her to do anything. She's upset, and I think she might like to talk to someone about it."

"I haven't noticed that she's upset."

"You don't live with her."

There was a silence. "I see a lot of her. And I have the advantage of professional training and experience."

"With all due respect to your professional training and experience, I think you may be missing something. I think she may put up a front with you."

"Are you questioning my judgment?"

"You're questioning mine."

There was another silence. "Yes. Yes, I am, Laura. I have been for some time now. And this is just another example of it. Isabel is fine when she's with me, which can only mean that it's her relationship with you that's troubled. How can I do anything but question your judgment and your adequacy as a mother?"

A nausea, sudden and overwhelming as morning sickness,

swept over her. Her stomach churned and roiled as it had with the first stirrings of Isabel, and Laura knew she was going to be sick. She remembered those headlong rushes from bed to bathroom, but now there was no safe place to run. And now she couldn't afford to be sick. She couldn't afford the momentary release of spitting up all the nauseating rage festering within her. During her pregnancy she'd renounced medications and alcohol in the interest of a healthy child. Certainly she could renounce the cold comfort of anger.

"If my relationship with Isabel were troubled, I doubt she'd come straight to me with every lie you tell her. Like the one about my wanting to move. And one more thing. If you keep this up, I'm going to begin telling her the truth. About more than the apartment."

"What are you talking about?"

"I'm talking about a certain baby tycoon."

"I'm not seeing her anymore."

"The point isn't whether you're seeing her now, Ezra. The point is when you started seeing her."

"You have no proof!" he shouted.

"I don't need proof. I'm not talking about suing you for adultery. I'm talking about telling Isabel the truth."

There was a silence while Ezra slipped back into his professional skin. "I don't understand what's happening to you, Laura. You used to be a reasonable woman. But suddenly you've become obsessed with money. And with vengeance. You're becoming a bitch." He hesitated, and she knew he was going to bring out the big gun. "A ball-cutting bitch."

There was a time when the epithet would have devastated her, but these days the big gun made no more than an ineffectual pop. "I'm not a Freudian, Ezra. I have no designs on your private parts. Just keep your hands off Isabel."

Laura's voice had been smooth, but her hands were trembling, and she dropped the receiver putting it back in the cradle. The nausea returned, not a violent, stomach-wrenching illness but a dull, sickening ache. It was less a pain than a dread, a repulsive fear of Ezra's judgment, displeasure, anger. Then it came to her. Ezra had already judged her and found her wanting. He was displeased with her. From the sound of his voice on the phone just now, he was angry as hell. There was nothing he could do to her that he hadn't already done.

She went back down the hall to Isabel's room. The door was closed. It seemed to Laura it was closed more and more often these days. Of course, that was the age, and the music. She was glad it was closed now. The building was prewar; the walls were thick, the doors heavy. Maybe Isabel hadn't heard. She knocked.

Isabel was stretched out on her stomach, her elbows propped up, a book resting on the pillow. She didn't look up from the pages when her mother entered. Laura asked what she was reading.

"A book."

A moment went by while Laura debated.

"I'm sorry." Isabel sat up. *"The Invisible Man."*

"Which one?"

"What?"

"There are two. One by H. G. Wells and one by Ralph Ellison. Though I think one of them doesn't have an article before it."

Isabel looked at the cover of the book. "You're right. Ellison. No article. I've got a smart mom," she said, and went back to the book.

Laura was certain she hadn't heard her on the phone.

IX

In the Barbados sun Hallie and Daniel took on the color and patina of a set of expensive matched luggage. They swam and played tennis, had conversations and sex. On their last afternoon they lay on the beach sipping rum punches and basking in the warmth of their renewed marriage.

When they returned home, Kate was overjoyed to see them. They hugged her and passed her back and forth between them like an *objet* to be admired. Their plane landed late Sunday afternoon. It was Tuesday night before they had their first quarrel. Of course, that might have had something to do with the fact that Daniel didn't get home from the office till after ten on Monday.

On Wednesday morning Ned Sinclair called Hallie's office. "I can't keep waiting until I run into you around town. Let me buy you dinner."

She thought of Daniel. She thought of Barbados. She thought of the argument they'd had the previous night and the way Daniel had curled up like a fist with his back to her on his side of the bed. Ned said something. The words were garbled. "I can't hear you," Hallie said. "It's a bad connection."

"Damn these car phones," Ned said. "You'd think a nation that can send men to the moon could design a phone that works in your normal, garden-variety limo."

Hallie said she'd love to have dinner with him.

The maître d' greeted Ned by name. The waiter took Hallie's drink order but brought Ned's vodka without asking, and a phone. Ned cursed politely, took the call, then told the waiter to take the phone away. "I trust you're sufficiently impressed," he said, and ducked his head in that boyish way.

Hallie laughed. "Bowled over."

"I was having lunch with another attorney at the Polo Lounge last week. And he really was trying to impress me. As soon as we sat down, he asked for a phone and started making calls. I had to explain to him that the point isn't to make calls, it's to get them."

She laughed again. He said he liked it when she laughed. He reminded her that that evening they'd spent with her husband she hadn't laughed at all. He didn't sound nasty, only a little sad. It was hard to believe that someone so nice—that was the only word for him—could be so successful.

"We'll have to do this again soon," he said as he put her in a cab later that night. Hallie was stung. He might as well have suggested she have her girl call his.

She didn't hear from Ned Sinclair for almost two weeks. Of course, she wasn't in her office for part of that time. One day she stayed home with Kate, who was running a fever of 104°. Two other days she was away at meetings. Still, there were no messages.

First she was disappointed. Then she told herself she was relieved. Finally she grew angry, at herself as much as at him. She was the executive director of AWE, not the sweetheart of Sigma Chi. She had just finished reminding herself of the fact when Ned called.

"I've wanted to see you all week, but I got tied up on the Coast. Just got back on the red-eye. I don't suppose you're free for dinner." She could tell from his voice that he was ducking his head as he asked. She decided she'd have dinner with him, but only dinner. She already had an absentee husband. The last thing she needed was an elusive lover. Besides, there was a hole in the thigh of her pantyhose. She'd noticed it while she was getting dressed that morning, but she hadn't had another pair in the right shade.

At three o'clock that afternoon her secretary said Mr. Sinclair was on the phone. Elusive and unreliable, Hallie amended the judgment.

"This is the damnedest thing," Ned said, "but I've got to fly to North Carolina tonight." Hallie was silent. Let him get out of it on his own. "They're sending the company plane for me. I don't suppose I could convince you to come along for the ride. You'll be back by midnight."

Hallie said she'd love to go along for the ride. She called Daniel and told an extremely sooty lie, then telephoned Naomi, repeated it, and threw in a bribe for good measure.

When she got into the limo, Ned grazed her cheek with his. He'd never done that before.

The plane was waiting for them on a small runway at Newark Airport. They had to walk across a windy stretch of ground to get to it. She felt like Ingrid Bergman in *Casablanca*. Better than that, she felt like Nancy Reagan in the White House.

The pilot welcomed them aboard. The steward served them drinks and disappeared. Beyond the windows on the right side of the plane a pale winter sun melted over the horizon. Ned reached out and took her hand. "God, I'm glad you could come. You make this whole damn hassle bearable."

While Ned took care of business, a secretary took care of Hallie with politeness and without curiosity. Then another limo took them back to the plane.

There was an air of domesticity to the trip home. Ned took off his jacket to reveal a custom-made shirt with a tiny monogram and a pair of red suspenders. Hallie had been trying to get Daniel to wear suspenders for years. When Ned finished his drink, he got up to freshen it himself instead of calling the steward. Then he came and sat on the arm of her oversize, overstuffed swivel chair. The plane lurched a little. It had nothing on Hallie's stomach. Ned slid down beside her.

"I really am glad you could come," he said again and took

off his glasses. They left a small pink indentation across the bridge of his nose.

"I'm glad you asked me."

Another air pocket. The plane fell fifty feet. Hallie's heart settled in her throat. Ned's hand-stitched monogram pressed against her right breast. He touched her cheek. She smoothed the red line across the bridge of his nose. He kissed her. Hallie cataloged a piece of information. He kept his mouth closed when he talked but not when he kissed.

"Are you a member of the Five-Mile Club?" he asked.

She was having trouble following him now. "You mean, those free mileage plans the airlines are offering?"

Ned laughed and kissed her again. "Not exactly." His hand was doing extraordinary things to her thigh.

She caught on. "Oh."

He laughed again. "There's nothing like making love in a plane." He shifted position. "Though a private plane like this is a piece of cake compared to a jumbo jet. Even in first class."

She moved her hand along the back of his neck. The line of his hair was razor-sharp. "I think this chair is more of a challenge than the plane."

The hand on her thigh had progressed. He'd found the tear in her pantyhose, the chink in her armor. "There's another cabin," he said. "With a bunk. The CEO likes to nap in flight."

He stood and held out his hand. She took it. There was nothing Hallie liked better than joining an exclusive club.

Hallie was a competent woman. She was capable of handling infidelity, but she wasn't happy handling infidelity. The morning after Ned had initiated her into his club, Daniel apologized for not waiting up for her, and she almost started to cry. Instead, she went to Paul Stuart at lunch and bought him three new shirts. She debated putting monograms on them but finally decided against it. When she got home that evening, she put the box with the shirts on top of the computer. That way

Daniel would be sure to see it. At a little after eight he called and said he wouldn't be home for several hours. Hallie put the shirts back in her briefcase. She'd return them tomorrow. At a little after nine Ned called. "I thought I'd take a chance that you might answer. I hope you don't mind, but I really wanted to talk to you, and you said your husband usually works late." Hallie said she didn't mind. They talked for close to an hour. When she got off the phone, she took the shirts from her briefcase and put them back on Daniel's computer.

Ned took to calling her at odd moments from limousines and airports, the Burning Tree Golf Club outside Washington, Les Ambassadeurs in London, and the Century Club in New York. They agreed they wanted to see each other whenever they could. It was no easy feat. She had a husband, a child, and a demanding career. He had clients and invitations all over the world. Still, they managed. They met for lunch, drinks, and dinner. They also used the words as euphemisms for Ned's apartment. Hallie had never been so happy, or so frightened. This couldn't last. "Sing before breakfast and you'll cry before supper," Dottie used to say.

A month after they'd flown to North Carolina Ned sent a dozen roses to Hallie's office. "Happy Anniversary from the membership committee of the Five-Mile Club," the card read. "Your presence is requested at a meeting at the clubhouse tonight at seven."

She called Daniel and told him she had a business dinner. "Christ, Hallie, don't ever complain about my hours again."

"This is important."

"And Kate is trivial."

"Naomi's staying late tonight. Besides, I spend quality time with Kate. I spend more quality time with her than you do."

"You're her mother."

"That's an enlightened view."

"I'm not an enlightened man. I'm just an old-fashioned sexist trying to keep his head above water in a cutthroat business and wishing his wife could tear herself away from the women of America to spend a few minutes with him and his daughter every once in a while."

Hallie was late getting to Ned's apartment that evening, but she was still too early for Ned. The concierge said Mr. Sinclair wasn't in. He said it as if Hallie were wearing three-inch heels, fishnet stockings, and a crotch-high miniskirt instead of her fox coat and Tanino Crisci boots. She went around the corner to a coffee shop, nursed one cup for twenty minutes, then asked for a phone. "On the corner," the counterman said.

"There's none in here?"

"If there was one in here, lady, do you think I'd tell you to go outside? You won't freeze to death. Not in that coat." She was not having a good night.

A machine answered Ned's phone. Hallie thought of hanging up but decided he might be hiding behind it. "Are you there?" she asked. If he was, he wasn't owning up to the fact.

She walked another block. There were no coffee shops but several bars. She hated going into bars alone, even upscale ones that featured vintage wine by the glass and complimentary sushi. She chose one she'd been to for lunch several weeks earlier. A few men looked at her with mild curiosity. She didn't look back. She sat at the bar, ordered a glass of Perrier, and took a file of papers from her briefcase. After exactly half an hour had passed, she asked the bartender where the phone was. He pointed to the back.

The place wasn't as upscale as she'd thought. On one wall of the booth several names were reputed to peform a variety of unnatural acts. She dialed Ned's number. When the machine answered, she hung up. She stared at the writing on the wall. Then she went back to the bar, paid for her drink, overtipped the bartender, and went home.

When she opened the door to her apartment, the silence was broken by Byte. At least he was glad to see her. She walked down the hall to Kate's room. Naomi had put her to bed. If

Daniel had done it, Kate's hair wouldn't be braided. She walked back to the study and stood in the doorway. Daniel didn't look up from the computer.

"I'm home," she said.

"What happened to your dinner?"

"I canceled it."

"Do you think the women executives of the nation can manage without you?"

She crossed the room, stood behind his chair, and put her hands on his shoulders. He didn't shrug them off. "I'm sorry," she said.

He turned away from the screen and looked up at her. "Me too."

She bent over till her face was beside his and her arms were around his neck. "God, I love you, Daniel."

"I love you, too," he said, but his voice was matter-of-fact. "Don't ever leave me."

Hallie hadn't even had a chance to take off her coat when Ned called the following morning. "I'm sorry." He sounded sorry. He sounded, in fact, as if he were about to cry.

"I just wish you'd called." Her voice had found a perfect Greek mean between recrimination and forgiveness. She wasn't giving in to either.

"Called! I spent the whole damn night calling you. Check the Clipper Club at O'Hare if you don't believe me. I must have placed fifty calls. I kept calling your office in case you'd gone back there. I called your apartment. First I got the house-keeper, then your husband. Needless to say, I hung up. I called the concierge at my building, but he said you'd already come and gone."

She was beginning to gravitate toward forgiveness.

"Tonight," he said. "Can I see you tonight?"

She pictured Kate as she'd looked the previous evening, her fist clenched in sleep under a cheek smooth as porcelain. She recalled Daniel at his computer, as familiar and safe as the furniture. She remembered herself walking the streets. "I can't tonight."

"Tomorrow then."

"I'm supposed to have a drink with Emily tomorrow night. I'm dropping off some papers I want her to look at."

"Terrific. I'll take you both for a drink. She'll think it's accidental, and it'll be our little secret. It'll be fun."

"That's kind of a dirty trick to play on Emily."

Ned was silent for a moment, balancing some imaginary scale of justice no doubt. "Look, Hallie, I'd be only too happy to go public. You're the one who insists on secrecy. You're the one who's married."

She listened for a note of discontent, but all she heard was a voice of reason. It was a convenient trait in the lover of a married woman. It was a definite advantage in a husband, Hallie thought, though Ned had obviously given the second role no thought at all.

Ned Sinclair wasn't persistent, Emily thought. *Recurrent* was the applicable word. "We still haven't had that drink," he reminded Emily one night early in March. He stood in the door to her office, his face brown from enviable weekends in exotic places, his smile pasted on with the glue of satisfaction, his eyes, behind wire-rimmed glasses, still on that elusive drink.

"I'd love to, really, but I'm waiting for my sister."

He drifted into the office, smooth as an expensive yacht in balmy waters, and came to port on her sofa. "The executive director of AWE?"

Emily remembered that he'd met Hallie once for five minutes about six months ago. The man obviously had a social secretary where his social conscience ought to be. "That's the one."

"Terrific. Let me buy you both a drink. Maybe she can raise my consciousness. I've been told more than once that it could use some elevating." He ducked his head in a way that Emily always found embarrassing.

Emily started to refuse again but was interrupted by Hallie's arrival. Talk about fancy footwork. Fred and Ginger had nothing on these two. Ned stood. Hallie crossed the room. They clasped hands. They complimented each other's appearances. They exclaimed at the amount of time that had passed since they'd last met and confessed to a press of professional and personal demands that would break lesser mortals. The only thing they didn't do was suggest lunch soon. Ned settled for drinks immediately. Hallie accepted.

He suggested the Century Club. "Unless you think it's too stuffy." Hallie looked as if she'd been invited to bypass purgatory and go directly to heaven.

"It's restricted to women," Emily pointed out.

"Not in the evening, " Ned said.

Her point had been moral rather than practical, but she let it go. Peter always had maintained she had no backbone. She preferred to think of it as a sense of her own absurdity. In the sixties she'd sold the Dow stocks her father had left her, and now she boycotted firms that did business with South Africa, but somehow she couldn't take entering that Forty-third Street bastion of high-minded pretension and locker-room behavior as seriously.

They settled in a room on the second floor. It had an air of fusty comfort that reminded Emily of her old dormitory smoker grown to majority. She wondered what she was doing here. The club didn't want her. Ned and Hallie didn't need her. Ned appealed to Hallie to raise his consciousness, again with the embarrassing duck of head. Hallie replied that she was into mainstreaming.

"Drugs?" Emily asked.

Hallie and Ned looked at her as if they'd give her one more chance, but only one.

"Gender balancing. Desegregation," Hallie explained.

"The future lies with getting women's problems back into the mainstream."

Emily remembered that a month ago it had lain with divorce mediation and a few months before that with baby counseling. "I've seen the future," Emily said, "and it doesn't work."

"Your sister certainly can spot a trend," Ned said, ostensibly to Emily, though the comment was obviously directed at Hallie.

Emily remembered that Peter had phrased it a little differently. At least Ned was compassionate.

By the time they parted in front of the Century Club an hour and a half later Hallie had convinced Ned to write a series of columns for the AWE newsletter. They were to be on women and the law, but—and here was the breakthrough—they were to be written by a man. Mainstreaming in action!

"What do you think of him?" Hallie asked as soon as she and Emily were alone in the cab. She was tugging at a cuticle. The gesture was out of character for Hallie. Perhaps the cachet of the Century had unhinged her.

"We've been through this before. Even without Peter, I'm not interested. But if I change my mind, you'll be the first to hear. You and Laura. You know I can't keep a secret about myself."

Hallie nibbled at her cuticle. "He's never married, has he?"

"Now you're going to ask me if he's gay. Not everyone walks through life as if it were the boarding gate to Noah's Ark. Not everyone was raised by Dottie. Besides, he's not that old. At least for a man. He hasn't got a biological clock."

"Then you think he will marry, eventually?"

"Come on, Hallie. I'm not Ned Sinclair's confessor. I barely know the man. I can't even figure out why he asked me for a drink."

X

Spring came to the city with its usual excess. Like swollen brooks and surging sap, winter-bleached city dwellers burst out of their stone towers of isolation. On Fifth Avenue little old ladies in timeless suits and expensive shoes reappeared on the arms of white-uniformed black women who looked kinder than they should have under the circumstances. On Park Avenue young women carrying briefcases on their way to banks and law firms and advertising agencies walked beside Hispanic girls wheeling carriages and strollers with blond, blue-eyed children on the way to the playground. On Madison Avenue young men and women swathed in leather and ennui lined up inside restaurants for the privilege of eating outside them. The city was coming to life.

Emily began walking home from her office in the evenings. This spring there was no one to clock her in. Peter was gone. Her life was her own. But as she shed hats and boots and gloves, the sap began to surge and flow and occasionally ache.

One evening, when restlessness had carried her out of her office and halfway home before she realized she hadn't taken her briefcase, she passed a couple saying good-bye on a corner. The man headed downtown, the woman up, and Emily followed her along Madison Avenue. Her step reminded Emily of a poodle's, all prancing paws and swishing tail. In each successive window she sought her own reflection, found it, and tossed her hair in greeting. She couldn't stop smiling. That woman just got out of bed, Emily thought, and an illicit bed at that. The sap surged and ached.

On another night she stopped in Chock Full o'Nuts for a cup of coffee and found herself across the counter from a tall man with a mane of dark hair and a face so craggy and tragic it made Emily think of a graveyard. He was obviously an artist in agony. She was halfway through her coffee and a fantasy in which she patched his torn genius and restored his faith in life, love, and its carnal rewards when she noticed that beneath his once-expensive trench coat he wore no shirt. Several large and dangerous-looking medallions dangled from his naked neck. As she got up to leave, she noticed the shopping bag full of old newspapers and empty soda cans at his feet.

Emily stopped at the first corner phone and dialed Laura's number, though she knew Laura was out and the machine would answer. "I'm going mad," she said to the recording. "And one sign is that I just put a quarter into a pay phone to talk to an answering machine." She wondered if that was what Hallie meant by reaching out to life but decided not to call Hallie's machine to find out.

When she reached her apartment, her own had three messages.

"You left your office early," Laura's voice said.

"I called your office, but you'd already gone," Hallie added.

"I got your message and called you back, but you'd already left." Jake Ferris topped off the tape. "Give me a call if you have a chance."

There was no reason to return Jake's call—her message had been that his divorce was final—but she dialed his number anyway. When he answered, she congratulated him on the occasion, as she did all her clients, though each time she did she felt as if she were telling a bad and particularly tasteless joke.

"You realize what this means," he said.

"That you've broken all records for a speedy divorce in the state of New York." Jake and the second Mrs. Ferris had been both generous of spirit and decent of action. Their behavior had strengthened Emily's faith in human nature and shaken her confidence in her own moral superiority. "It also means you're a free man."

"Exactly. No longer a newly separated man. I thought you might like to help me celebrate over dinner tonight. What do you say?"

She thought of the man in Chock Full o'Nuts with character in his face and no shirt under his trench coat. She thought of the woman on Madison Avenue still steaming from her illicit bed. She said "sure."

In the shower she chastised herself silently. In front of the mirror she spoke out. "You know what they said about Louis the Eighteenth. That he'd learned nothing and forgotten nothing." The shade of Peter flickered through the bathroom. You weren't even sure who Louis the Eighteenth was until I came on the scene, precious.

Jake was just arriving at the restaurant as she got out of the cab. He kissed her hello on the cheek as he had that time he'd first come to her office about his divorce, though he'd never done it again. She wondered if he was as confident as he seemed. He said hello. The tic pulled at his lower lip. He wasn't.

He took her arm as they went into the restaurant. This was no reflex.

The bar was four deep with women in bow ties and men whose arms ended in briefcases. They all had polished skin, like babies after a bath.

"Before you say a word," Jake warned her, "the food is very, very good."

The dining room was better than the bar. Apparently all those ambitious young things were too busy networking to eat. She and Jake sat across from each other. Emily was relieved.

Banquettes were romantic only to men who'd rather grab your thigh than look in your eyes, and contortionists. They ordered drinks and got down to the nubby problem of finding if they had anything to say to each other. She hoped they wouldn't have to wing it on reawakened lust alone.

They started with current books, plays, and movies. She'd remembered how smart Jake was, but not how sentimental. He was a pushover for human suffering, the only man she knew who choked up at old newsreels and *Life* photographs.

The waiter brought the menus. Jake fished around in his pocket and came up with a pair of glasses. She was shocked. Over the months she'd always sent him papers, never given him anything to read in her office. Now the picture of him in reading glasses was as heart-wrenching as one of those old magazine photos. The boy she'd married and divorced had become a middle-aged man. She took a long swallow of her drink. She was in trouble all right.

He asked about her family. She told him more about Laura and Hallie than either professional ethics or family loyalty allowed, but she couldn't stop herself. Familiarity was masquerading as trust. They came late but inevitably to themselves. She admitted more about Peter than she'd meant to and more about herself than she should have.

"The thing I hate most," Jake said, "next to leaving Nina, is the feeling of failure." She started to say something, but he wasn't in the market for condolences. "Don't tell me I'm in good company. I've read all the articles. Hell, I've written half of them. What would the media do without divorce? Herpes and AIDS, incest and child abuse come and go, but divorce and Jackie O are eternal." She remembered now how, in the right light, his eyes turned black. "Do the statistics make you feel any better?"

"I'm a woman."

"What in hell is that supposed to mean?"

"I don't know. I always assume women take these things

more seriously. We invest more, or maybe we just expect bigger dividends."

He smiled at her, but he wasn't laughing at her. "You need more male clients. Anyway, the point is I went to the movies the other night. I don't mind going to the movies alone—"

"I remember."

His eyebrows, which made a heavy awning over his eyes, lifted in surprise.

"It never bothered me," she said. "I just remember."

"It used to drive my wife wild. Even though they weren't movies she wanted to see. Excuse me, my second wife." Now the smile was conspiratorial. "This is a damn peculiar conversation. Anyway, I was standing in line for a movie and there was a couple in front of me. You know, one of those really married couples, as Dodsworth says."

She'd forgotten the power of names and words, the obscure shared references that bind people together. Samuel Dodsworth returned and brought with him all those late-night hours they'd lain tangled in bed watching movies and unraveling differences and disagreements like an old sweater they no longer needed.

"They were in their late fifties or so," Jake went on, "very *haute* WASP—good bones, bad teeth, blood thin as dry martinis straight up. But they were holding hands. They didn't say much. You should have heard the conversation. Should they order another truckload of manure for the garden in the country? But they held hands the entire time. I was envious as hell. The longer we stood there, the worse it got, until finally I wasn't just envious, I was angry. Furious. It was the whole goddamn American dream. Something I'd been promised, then cheated out of. For years I've been telling myself that particular American dream, like all the others, doesn't exist, but there was living proof of it."

He picked up the bottle of wine and divided the last of it between her glass and his, but he didn't look at her. His lashes weren't as long as Peter's, but they were dark and thick and cast a shadow over the pronounced cheekbones.

There was a small no-man's-land of white tablecloth between his hand and hers. She considered crossing it but didn't. "I'll see your story and raise you one. I went to a concert the other night—"

"You used to hate concerts. You were always sure everyone heard more than you did."

"Someone had an extra ticket. Apparently I still don't listen very well or I wouldn't have been so easily distracted. About halfway through I noticed that the man and woman in front of me were holding hands. A strange thing in a concert. I looked around. No one else was."

"Maybe they were my couple from the movie line."

"Same description, different couple."

"How do you know?"

"When the concert was over, they stopped holding hands. She wasn't wearing a wedding band. All the other women who hadn't been holding hands were."

He started to laugh. "Did you feel better?"

"Nope. I've never cared much about marriage, but I've been known to envy passion."

He motioned to the waiter for the check.

Outside the restaurant the air was thin from the long winter but faintly sweet with spring. The lights of midtown blurred into a corona in the distance. They walked west toward Fifth, then turned north on the park side of the street.

She pointed to a cab. Jake let it pass. "I thought you liked to walk," he said.

"I do, but I'm used to walking alone."

"Solitary pleasure. Puts hair on your palms and drives you mad." He took her hand and put it in his pocket.

Fifth Avenue was quiet, the stark buildings keeping their expensive secrets on one side, the park a black and dangerous galaxy on the other.

They walked a few blocks in silence. Then Jake stopped and turned toward the park. "I bet you don't remember what happened on this spot."

"We carved our initials."

"You saw your first nighthawk."

"How could I have forgotten?"

They started walking again. "You never liked the bird walks, did you?"

"Did I ever pretend to?"

He thought about that for a moment. "Yes. The first spring I knew you I thought you were crazy about them. And it wasn't until after you'd left that I realized how much you hated them."

"Maybe you didn't want to realize."

"Or maybe it was a well-kept secret."

They covered another block in silence.

"Thanks for celebrating with me," Jake said. I believe in commemorating rites of passage."

"What did you do the night we got divorced?"

"Got drunk and read T. S. Eliot. Very classy act, or so I thought at the time. What did you do?"

"Got drunk and read Edith Wharton. Going for the high moral tone."

"A guy I know at the magazine went to bed with his ex-wife the night their divorce came through."

"You'd be surprised how many people do."

"You know," he said, and even in the dark she noticed the fragile tremor that pulled at his lower lip, "it's not too late. Wrong divorce but right characters."

She stopped and turned to him. "I thought you'd never ask."

Walking into Jake's apartment was like walking into a motel room of a national chain. She'd never been there before, but she had the feeling she had. He'd taken his interior design cues from the public library. The only things missing were the winos dozing over randomly selected volumes of Edmund Burke and *Popular Mechanics.* Hardcovers, paperbacks, oversize books, boxed editions, tired books with wrinkled spines, pristine books with dust jackets so shiny you could see your reflection in them, novels, histories, biographies, memoirs, books on politics, bird books, fishing books, and, of course the *New York Review of Books* were everywhere. Some were old friends. She recognized her own, or at least the contested volumes of Mark Sullivan's *Our Times,* the replaced volume of Auden, Peterson's *Field Guide to the Birds East of the Rockies* that she'd carried up mountains and over marshes on more forced marches than she wanted to remember, and a paperback copy of "Howl" she'd once thrown across the room at him. A good many more were strangers.

As was Jake suddenly. She took off her coat. He poured brandies. They circled like expectant fighters sizing up each other's footwork, anticipating each other's first move. The trust she'd felt in the restaurant had been fleeting as well as irrational. Nine years were a long time. She was about to go to bed with a stranger, assuming they could get from here to there. She thought of Peter. She thought of the fact that Peter had spent half his life in bed, reading, eating, drinking, correcting papers, watching a variety of blood sports on television, doing several of those things at once. Say what you wanted about the habit, and over the years she'd said a good deal, he was always there when it counted.

"You look," Jake said, leaning against his desk in a parody of ease, "as if you're about to argue your first case in front of the Supreme Court."

"I was just wondering how we get from here to there." She feinted toward the bedroom.

Jake put down his glass. The motion was smooth, all control and good form, but the gentle tremor at the side of his mouth persisted. "Child's play," he said. "For two consenting adults."

Sex with someone new was like opening up an unknown continent. A few thrills, plenty of danger, and who knew if you'd return. Sex with someone you knew was like cultivating your own garden. You could count on reliable rewards, provided you were working fertile ground. Sex with Jake resembled both. She was certain she wasn't going to run into any savagery or bizarre tribal customs, but there were still plenty of surprises. Jake had an excellent memory. And he was no slouch in the imagination department. He had the most beautiful arms and legs she'd ever seen, and almost forgotten. All those hours on the squash court obviously paid off. His timing was superb; his form, peerless. His eyes were watchful as well as beautiful, his hands subtle, his mouth devilishly clever even without words. And she didn't think once of Peter until it was all over.

She didn't miss him. She didn't even compare him to Jake. She just thought of him. And for the first time she understood the destructive power, cataclysmic as an atomic blast, of those four innocent words *What . . . are . . . you . . . thinking?* Fortunately men never asked them.

She awakened a little after four from a nasty dream in which Peter had been accusing her of infidelity with Jake. My God, had her unconscious no imagination? Couldn't it even muster a neck-and-neck race up a staircase or soaring planes and a fight over the autopilot? It was one of those rotten dreams that linger sourly into wakefulness. She turned away from it. Her hand struck unfamiliar territory. This was no electric blanket. She thought of unknown continents and the explorers who'd conquered them. De Soto hadn't been satisfied with Florida but had pushed on to the Mississippi. Lewis and Clark hadn't stopped at the Rockies or Vancouver but had forged on to the Pacific. You couldn't rest on your laurels.

"If you keep that up," Jake said, his voice in sleep as thick as cream, "you're going to get into trouble."

"That," she said, "is exactly what I had in mind."

* * *

"Where were you last night?" Laura asked the following morning.

Emily swiveled her desk chair around to face the window. The Chrysler Building was no more than a wavy streak of gray behind the soot- and rain-mottled glass. I'm thirty-five years old, and my sister still asks where I was last night. And I still answer. "With Jake Ferris. Celebrating his divorce."

"Did you have a good time?" A simple question, but every word, like the chamber of a gun, was loaded.

"I had a very good time."

"Then why do you sound so miserable?"

"Because I shouldn't have had a good time. Peter's been gone for four months. I lived with him for four years. I knew him for six."

"It's nice you found someone else so quickly."

"Nice? What's so nice about having emotional round heels?"

Hallie didn't call until lunchtime. Emily was on her way out the door. "I hear you had dinner with Jake last night."

"Laura must have sent out Indian foot runners."

"How do you feel about him?"

"We haven't posted the banns, if that's why you're calling. Christ, Hallie, it was one night."

"You're right. That was the old Hallie speaking. Or at least moving her lips so Dottie's words could come out. I've been thinking about it a lot lately."

"About what?"

"Marriage. If Daniel and I do break up, I don't think I'll ever marry again. I've got Kate. I've got a career. I've got money."

"I've got rhythm," Emily said, because she'd stopped arguing with Hallie's conversions some years ago. At various times in her life Hallie had harbored equally strong convictions about reincarnation, soybeans, and the deleterious affect of bathing on the body's chemistry and the soul's creativity.

Dottie called Emily at home that night. "How was your date with Jake?"

Forget Indian runners. Someone had sent Mailgrams. "I'm too old to have something called a date, and it was fine."

"I always knew you two would get back together."

"We aren't back together. We had dinner together."

"People remarry all the time."

"That's right, Mother, they do. They also put on down jackets, get into dinks off Catalina Island, and drown mysteriously. They do it, but I wouldn't recommend it."

When Jake called and asked Emily if she wanted to have dinner that Saturday night, she said "sure" to him and nothing to anyone else. Afterward they went back to his apartment again. She wondered whether he knew that the ghost of Peter still haunted hers the way the myth of Robert E. Lee did the South or was merely territorial.

He was up early Sunday morning. The clock on the night table said 7:30. Jake's hands were sending off other, more pressing signals. The nice thing about Sunday morning, Emily thought as she turned to him, was that you could wake each other up, go back to sleep, then wake each other up again.

"You're not going back to sleep?" he asked after they'd waked each other up thoroughly.

She moved her face till her nose was resting against his shoulder. He was a one-man argument against aftershaves and eau de anything. Maybe Hallie had had a point about body chemistry after all. She wound a leg around his. "Look, I know there's more than a whiff of déjà vu in all this, but we're not back in college, and you aren't twenty-one. You're supposed to need sleep. Give all those brave sperm in the trenches a chance to regroup their forces."

"On one of the best migrating weekends of the year? Jamaica Bay's going to be crawling with birds. You'll probably get to see a Louisiana heron."

She rolled back to her side of the bed. There was no reason not to. Jake had already taken his shoulder and the rest of him out of reach. "Only if I'm really lucky."

"Listen," he said on his way to the bathroom, "you don't have to come if you don't want to. You can go back to sleep. I'll go alone."

Emily said she wouldn't think of it. As she lay there waiting for her turn in the shower, a kernel of wisdom Hallie had winnowed from her vast store of the chaff of pop psychology came back to her. The rules of every relationship are set in the first forty-eight hours of that relationship. Like all pop psychology, it had just enough truth to scare the living daylights out of her.

XI

That year Laura and Emily went to a lot of movies, both together and separately. Laura said she was glad Ezra had taken the VCR. "Otherwise, I couldn't justify the price of a ticket. And I like going out. I also like the silver screen. Ezra prefers a small television one. It makes him feel larger than life."

When they went together, they usually met in front of the movie, but on the second Sunday after Emily's first weekend with Jake, Laura came to Emily's apartment to pick her up.

"What are those?" Laura pointed to a bowl of nuts on the coffee table.

"Cashews."

"I can see that. I mean, what are they doing there? You don't eat nuts."

"Jake is a cashew nut. I mean, he's crazy about cashews." Emily had remembered the predilection without prompting, and Jake had been pleased.

"Creeping domesticity," Laura said, but Emily could tell her sister was happy for her, too happy.

"And when Isabel comes, I buy chocolate chip cookies. It's the same thing," Emily said, though they both knew it was similar but not the same.

The following night Laura was in the kitchen, flouring the veal for the piccata, when Isabel got home. She dropped her books, perched on the stool in the corner, and began juggling the lemons Laura had left on the counter. "I won't be home for dinner tomorrow night," she said.

"My God, twenty-four-hour notice. I must be doing something right."

"You do a lot right. You're a terrific mother. Except when you make a stink because I forget to tell you I won't be home for dinner."

"That's what mothers are for. Making stinks. It's a civilizing process. Where are you going?"

"Daddy's."

Laura kept her face averted as she carried the salad bin from the refrigerator to the counter.

"You don't have to look that way about it."

"I wasn't looking any way about anything. I was trying to decide whether to put mushrooms in the salad."

"You looked the way you always do when I tell you I'm going to do something with Daddy."

The mushrooms were damp and slippery with age. Laura almost nicked her finger with the knife. She turned to face her daughter. "Look, Isabel, I know I'm unreasonable about a lot of things. I won't let you ride the New York subway system at three in the morning, and I refuse to let you pierce either ear once, let alone repeatedly, and I am entirely lacking in color sense, but you don't really think I don't want you to see your father, do you?"

Isabel dropped a lemon and murmured something. It sounded like no. Laura was sure it was no. She turned back to the salad. "What do you think? Scallions, too?"

"I'll slice them." Isabel slid off the stool and picked up the paring knife. "Daddy bought the Fassbinder. That's why he wants me to come over tomorrow night."

Laura put the butter and olive oil in the skillet and watched it begin to foam.

"It's a numbered limited edition. A collector's item." Isabel's smug tone reminded Laura of those stand-up comedians who do imitations of presidents and movie stars.

"Collectors of what? Numbered limited editions of video-tapes."

Isabel tossed the chopped scallions into the salad. "That's exactly what I mean. You've never even seen a Fassbinder film. You just put it down because of Daddy."

"I have seen a Fassbinder film. I didn't much like it, but that's not the point." Laura turned the flame down under the skillet. Where did sniping stop and self-defense begin? "I just find it a little pretentious—excuse me, peculiar—that a man who slept through *Citizen Kane*, twice, has suddenly become a collector of great films." Laura put the veal in the pan. The oil and butter foamed approval of her timing. "But I'll be curious to know what you think of the Fassbinder," she told her daughter. Put that in your VCR and run it, she warned her estranged husband. Ezra controlled the money, the property, even the timing of their divorce, but she was getting a grip on herself.

The following Sunday morning Isabel returned from her father's with several back issues of *Les Cahiers du Cinéma* and a handful of opinions on the art of the film. That afternoon Laura suggested a movie. There was a revival of *The Women* on the West Side. Afterward they splurged at a Chinese restaurant. "I'll never call you bitchy again," Isabel promised over the spring rolls.

"I appreciate that. But did you like it?"

"I loooved it," Isabel crooned.

"Emily, sweetheart," Kron began that Monday afternoon. Emily turned her chair to face the window, but it was no help. The sky was as gray and bleak as the side of a battleship. "My client isn't about to hand over a seven-room co-op on Park Avenue so Laura can turn it into a love nest."

"Love nest! For God's sake, Gary, where did you study, the Daily Tabloid School of Law?"

"What was going on there Saturday night?"

"I don't know what was going on there Saturday night, but I have a feeling you're going to tell me."

Kron's laughter reeked with prurience. Years ago Emily had divided her colleagues in matrimonial law into three categories: men who defined women as cunts with calculators; women who thought divorce was a criminal offense punishable by emasculation; and little boys who regarded their clients' goings-on as they might the contents of a candy-store window. Kron belonged to the last group.

"So Laura fools around." Emily could hear him smacking his lips. "Big deal. My sixteen-year-old kid fools around. I'm open-minded, sweetheart. These are the 1980s. Of course, some judges don't see it that way. But nobody's mentioned court—except you."

"Talk about crying wolf, Gary. Laura lives like Caesar's wife. Ezra's past is a little more checkered. You might ask him what he was doing last winter when he sent Laura to a spa and Isabel skiing with her class. But we agreed to no fault. The only one who's threatening adultery is you."

Kron said he wasn't threatening anything. He was just keeping her up-to-date on developments. Emily thanked him, hung up, and called Laura at her office. Laura's voice was muffled, as if she were a child hiding the phone beneath the bedclothes rather than a woman speaking from behind a curved Plexiglas wall.

"At the risk of sounding like the grand inquisitor, or Dottie, what did you do Saturday night?"

"I went to a party, believe it or not," Laura whispered. "Among the people I used to know there is still one couple who don't think I'm the Typhoid Mary of divorce. I was going to tell you about it tonight."

"Did you meet anyone?"

"Now you do sound like Dottie. As a matter of fact, I did."

Emily gazed out the window. The sky no longer resembled

a battleship. Now it was black as a cave. "Laura, I don't want you to get excited—"

"I barely know the man."

"That's not what I meant. I don't want you to panic, but I think Ezra is having you watched."

"What!" Her voice was no longer muffled.

"I think he's having a detective follow you and stake out the apartment." Emily told her sister about Kron's conversation.

"The man brought me home and came up for a drink. One brandy!"

"I know. Or rather I didn't know. I wouldn't care if he came up to swing from the chandelier or tie you to the bed— whatever makes you happy—but Ezra doesn't seem to feel the same way. So much for no fault."

"Ezra was doing all that and more before he even moved out." Emily heard her sister's voice and knew the Plexiglas wall was no match for it. "He took the baby tycoon away for the weekend—with Isabel!"

"And made a big point of separate rooms. Neither of you has any evidence, Laura, and I want to keep it that way. Just be careful."

"What does that mean?"

"I told Kron you live like Caesar's wife. Until this thing is over, you have to go on living like her, or a herpes carrier. Most judges are still men, and men, in case you haven't noticed, have a lingering affection for the double standard. It's worked so well for them."

Laura left her office promptly at five that night. As she came out of the building onto Fifth Avenue, she looked around at the rush-hour crowd. The crowd barely glanced back. It was self-involved, self-protective, selfish. She threaded her way through the army of high-priced running sneakers marching determinedly uptown to the beat of the same drummer; through the waves of middle-management men, washed and bleached by exhaustion, flowing downtown toward trains that would carry them to houses and yards they saw only in darkness from October to April; through the bus queues of anomalous New Yorkers who didn't live in New York at all but in the outer boroughs. Laura looked at the faces, the older ones hostile from the strain, the younger ones surly with sudden freedom, and realized that though every one of them had an opinion about the mayor and crime and crosstown traffic, not one of them had the slightest interest in her. She couldn't believe there was a private detective among them.

Louis, the doorman, greeted her with an observation on the filthy weather. Hector, the elevator man, the resident gossip columnist of the building, told her that Isabel was already home. Hector missed nothing. He'd seen the man come up for a brandy and leave after it. What else had he seen? Did Ezra's detective bribe the staff to chronicle her comings and goings, catalog her guests, and count the liquor bottles in her trash? As she stepped off the elevator, Hector wished her a pleasant evening in the same obsequious tone he used when he thanked her for his Christmas gift. The quisling.

The apartment felt violated. She walked from room to room, though she didn't know what she was looking for. She went to the living-room window and looked down at Park Avenue. When the doorman across the way glanced up, she stepped back from the window. Then she went through the rooms again, pulling down the shades. It was like closing a dead man's eyes.

She went into the kitchen to start dinner. When she opened the cabinet to take out a mixing bowl, the nest of four rattled violently in her hands.

Isabel drifted into the kitchen. "How come you pulled down all the shades?"

Laura swallowed. She felt as if her glands were swollen. "Privacy."

"You don't usually."

Laura said nothing, and Isabel walked to the kitchen window and pulled up the shade. "That was Daddy on the phone."

"How is he?" Laura listened carefully. Her voice was in control, definitely in control.

"He said to tell you not to start obsessing about your check. He'll drop it off with the doorman tomorrow."

"Thank you for the message. And just for the record, I don't obsess."

Isabel shrugged and took a radish from the salad Laura was making. "I'm just passing on Daddy's message. I don't want to get involved."

"And I don't want you to. I'm not asking you to take sides, Isabel. Mine or your father's. But I don't like being accused of incipient madness because I want to make sure there's a roof over our heads and food in our fridge."

"Daddy says you don't have to worry about all that. He says you've got this whole apartment, and he's camping out in a one-bedroom rental. He says—" She stopped.

"That I'm extravagant. That I was born with a silver spoon in my mouth and don't know the value of money."

Isabel said nothing.

"I know your father. We were married for a long time." And at various moments during that time Ezra had accused her of being born with a silver spoon in her mouth, but there'd been more pride than bitterness in the accusation, and when she'd once corrected him and said "vermeil," he'd been delighted.

Laura handed the flatware and napkins to her daughter, and Isabel took them into the dining room. "Your father's right," Laura said when Isabel came back for the plates. "We're lucky. We've never had to live on spaghetti for a week—and I'm talking about spaghetti, not pasta—and I've never seen a rat, and when you had pneumonia and chicken pox, I worried about you rather than the doctor bills. We're lucky, Isabel, but so is your father." Lucky enough to afford round-the-clock detectives, she wanted to scream, but anger was one more luxury she could no longer afford. "And I think cries of poverty have a tinny ring when they come from inside a brand-new BMW."

Sometimes Laura took a sandwich or salad and ate lunch in her office. Occasionally she went out with one or two of the girl-women. But on the day after her discussion of silver spoons with Isabel she refused an invitation to join them. It wasn't that she didn't want to spend the money—they usually went to one of the coffee shops in the neighborhood—only that she'd had enough girlish gullibility for a while. The Kristofferson look-alike had panned out, in a way. Nancy was in love. So was the look-alike—with, from the sound of it, at least half a dozen slim women over five feet six inches tall and under twenty-eight years of age. Nonetheless, Nancy bought his assurances of undying devotion as blindly as Isabel had Ezra's of poverty. The night before Laura had tried to enlighten Isabel about the facts without disillusioning her about her father, but she didn't have the energy to raise two daughters. She told Nancy she wasn't hungry and spent her lunch hour in the Fifty-seventh Street Doubleday.

She wandered through the fiction section, past shelf after shelf of books by women, for women, about women. She took several down at random, skimming the flap copy, glancing at the first paragraph, checking out the writer's biography. The author lives in California with her two children, Arizona with her son, New York with her daughter. Perhaps women who remained married didn't have the time or inclination or maybe the courage to write. She browsed through the art books, lusting after the four-color reproductions, luxuriating in the thickness of their stock, remembering the days when she'd bought them without a moment's hesitation. She gravitated to the cookbooks, but they'd lost their lure. She found herself in the

divorce corner of the self-help section, though like a suddenly
awakened sleepwalker, she didn't know how she'd got there.
She was shocked at the number and variety. Divorce, how to
cope with, survive, win, triumph over, and prevent. Divorce as
a cure, solution, panacea, sign of the times, symbol of the decline of the West. Divorce, by lawyers, accountants, psychia-
trists, psychologists, sociologists, ministers, rabbis, internists,
dietitians, astrologers, gurus, and varied and sundry celebrities.
Divorce for men, women, children, and even household pets.

It was an epidemic. Laura drew back as if she'd stumbled
into a quarantined area by accident. Then a title caught her
eye and reminded her she'd already been exposed to the disease. *Divorce: A Man's Guide to Winning It All.* She lifted the book
off the shelf. She felt as she had years ago when Dottie had forbidden her to read *Studs Lonigan* and she'd borrowed a copy
from a friend and hidden it under her bed. There were secrets
here that she wan't supposed to know. The table of contents
was naughty but not shocking. "How to Avoid Alimony—Or
Getting Blood from a Stone." "Child Support—or Indentured
Servitude." "Child Custody—or How to Keep Your Children,
Your Self-Respect, and Your Hard-Earned Cash." Laura
flipped to the chapter as automatically as she'd once turned to
the steamy passages marked by her friend, and just as those
lines had been underlined in a hot and sweaty hand, so here
italicized phrases had been called to her attention by the author. *Getting the goods on her. Cutting Mom out of the picture. Turning
the screws.* And one last caveat: *Remember, you can't afford to be soft.
You're fighting for your child, your income, and your life.* Ezra always
had had an inordinate respect for the written word.

She put the book back on the shelf feeling as unclean and
uncomfortable as she had years ago. Dottie had said then that
Studs Lonigan was a dirty book, but her childhood friend, who'd
had literary as well as sexual pretensions, had assured her it was
a truthful book. Shocked as Laura, cosseted by her lovely face,
soft cashmere sweaters, and Dottie's unyielding sexual code,

was, people really did those things. She looked at the volume she'd just replaced on the shelf. People really did those things, too.

Back in her office building she walked past the bank of elevators straight to the pay phones in the back. For the first time since she'd begun working there she realized there were no booths. Come to think of it, there were few booths left in the city. A society in which mere acquaintances asked her the details of her marital breakup and public figures fought to be the first to reveal their own alcoholism and drug abuse and their former mates' moral turpitude had no need of walled telephones. She dialed Emily's number. As she waited for the receptionist to connect her, she listened to her neighbors. A man with a display case on wheels was setting up what might have been an appointment but sounded more like an assignation. An expensively dressed woman was warning someone that she was calling from a pay phone and had no intention of being put on hold. When Laura heard Emily's voice, she held a finger to her free ear to shut out the alien sounds and reported her discovery.

"You called from a pay phone to tell me there are self-help books on divorce!"

"I called because I just realized what's going on. It's not only money. It's Isabel. Ezra wants Isabel!"

In the silence that followed, Laura heard a mechanical screech at the other end of the phone. She knew that when Emily was worrying a problem, she had a habit of turning her chair to the window, but the noise still sounded like a cry of pain.

"I suspect he does," Emily said finally. "That's why he hired the detective. That's also one of the reasons I suggested joint custody. To head him off. I'm not saying 'I told you so.' I wasn't sure what he was up to. I'm still not. Maybe he really wants custody. Maybe he just thinks it'll be cheaper. Maybe both. But it doesn't matter because he doesn't have a case.

You've stayed home with Isabel, you've raised her, and there's no way he can prove he's more fit as a parent—short of producing pictures of you doing obscene things to the entire United States Navy. So just stay calm. Correction, stay calm with Isabel. Feel free to call me and scream at any time. And incidentally, you don't have to speak to Ezra at all. That's what you have me for."

Ezra called a little after eight that night. "I'm concerned about Isabel." He was wearing his professional voice. It made up in authority what it lacked in feeling. It drove her, as he well knew, up the wall.

"So am I, Ezra. That's why I told you I thought she should see someone." Her tone gave a good imitation of his.

"Actually I don't think it's Isabel's problem."

Laura saw what was coming, but she refused to meet it halfway. She said nothing.

"Are you still there, Laura?"

"I'm still here."

"I think it's yours." So she hadn't had to meet it halfway after all. Still, she said nothing. Silence was the only weapon. She'd learned that lesson at the feet of the master. "You're putting too much pressure on her."

As in turning the screws. "I don't think we can discuss this anymore, Ezra. If you have anything to say, have your attorney call mine."

"About Isabel!" All pretense of professional distance was gone. Ezra was shocked and didn't mind showing it.

"About everything. That's what lawyers are for."

"You and I don't need attorneys about this, Laura, about Isabel. Was there ever a time when we couldn't put aside our feelings for her welfare?"

"The time I suggested she needed professional help. The time you decided to punish me by not paying her tuition. And I hate to flog a dead horse, Ezra, but the time you hustled us both out of town to make room for the baby tycoon."

"Now I see why Isabel is having trouble. You don't want to solve problems; you just want to have the last word."

"I don't want the last word, Ezra. I don't want any words with you."

Ezra slammed down the phone. In all the years Laura had known him, she'd never heard him do that. She replaced her receiver quietly.

Laura waited a full twenty-four hours to report the conversation to Emily. That was another first.

After they had got off the phone, Emily went back to her living room, where Jake was sitting with a drink and a book. No two people had ever been more fastidious about toothbrushes, keys, and the minutiae of everyday life, but it was a losing battle. Domesticity was, as Laura had noted, afoot.

"That was Laura," Emily said because their self-imposed rules prevented Jake from asking. "Ezra has escalated from money and property to Isabel. She's the new battlefield."

There were times when Jake's eyes gave away as much as they took in. Now they were flashing guilt like a neon sign. "You think he wants custody."

"I think he wants something."

"It couldn't be his daughter? He has to have ulterior motives?" The specter of male bonding reared its threatening head. Or maybe it was simply the specter of that small strawberry blond head.

Emily sat beside him on the sofa. His hand lay palm up on the cushion like a fallow field. She resisted the urge to take it. "I don't know a damn thing about kids despite all the custody agreements I've drawn up. I don't know whether they're better off staying in one apartment while their parents shuttle back and forth or shuttling back and forth between their parents. I don't know whether it's worse for them to live on a battlefield or profit from the cold war competition between the major powers. I don't know if a five-year-old boy is traumatized by the unexpected joy of besting his father in the oedipal game or if a seven-year-old girl will spend a lifetime with losers because her father abandoned her at a tender age. I don't know a damn thing about kids, but I think I know something about their parents. Men and women talk about staying together for the kids, worry about getting divorced because of the kids, argue about fair financial settlements for the kids, debate about custody of the kids, and then men and women do pretty much what they want."

"I suppose you have a point," Jake said. His voice was a flat, barren landscape that made her wonder why she'd felt obliged to make it in the first place.

XII

"I'd like to meet your daughter," Ned said. He was putting away his American Express card, and he kept his eyes lowered as if he recognized the intimacy of the request and was a little embarrassed by it. They were on the second floor of Tiffany's, where Hallie had gone with him to help choose a silver porringer for a colleague's new baby.

"I don't see how," Hallie said, though her mind had already raced ahead not only to how but to why. "She's practically at the age of reason. She's certainly at the age of conversation. 'Daddy, Daddy, guess who I had lunch with today. Mommy's lover!' "

"What if I ran into the two of you accidentally?"

Hallie had been leaning on the glass display case, but now she straightened. "I won't lie to Kate. I still have some standards, though it probably doesn't look that way to you."

A young woman with eyes like Bambi and legs to match came over and asked Ned if he needed help. He said he'd already been taken care of.

"Of course, I wouldn't be lying if all I did was introduce you."

Ned put an arm around her shoulders. "It'll be fun." He'd said the same thing about that drink with Emily. *Fun* was not the word Hallie would use in either instance.

She brooded about it all that week. She kept remembering

a friend who'd liked nothing better than getting together with her lover and unsuspecting husband. Hallie had been to one of her dinner parties. The air of dangerous titillation had been as thick as the bordelaise. All night long Hallie had had the feeling that the illicit pair were having more fun at the table than they'd ever had in bed. There was an ending to the story, too, and it wasn't a happy one. The couple had separated, but the lover had moved on. He had a taste, Hallie had heard from another friend, for married women but not for marriage.

Nonetheless, on Saturday morning Hallie dressed Kate in her jeans and the handmade Irish sweater Dottie had picked up on her way through Shannon Airport and headed for the playground in Carl Schurz Park. And sure enough, at a little after noon who should come jogging by but Ned Sinclair?

Kate wasn't suspicious. She didn't find it odd that a casual acquaintance of her mother should want to spend fifteen minutes pushing her on the swings and another ten climbing the geodesic Junglegym with her. And she saw nothing peculiar in the sight of T. Edward Sinclair, who could command a table, not to mention a phone in restaurants so exclusive they had unlisted numbers, dripping the special secret sauce of a Big Mac on his running shorts. But that night she did notice that for the first time ever her mother gave in to her pleas and read *Bread and Jam for Frances* through in its entirety a second time.

Ned was out of town all the following week. He called Hallie from his hotel rooms, other people's offices, and a variety of clubs. The connections were often bad, the noise in the background loud, the experience unfulfilling, at least for Hallie. The last call was the worst of all. The static was so thick she could barely hear him. He wanted to know if she could see him that night. She was beginning to get annoyed. Didn't he ever think ahead? "I know I didn't give you much notice," he said. "But I wanted to be sure I was going to make it this time. I'm in the air now."

She said she could get away.

It was a Thursday night. They met at a restaurant that would win four stars and accolades for its design in that Friday's *Times*. Everything was gray and mauve and stiffly textured, like the body of a dead mouse.

"Kate's beautiful," he said after they'd ordered. "She looks just like you."

Hallie could tell that pleased him. He wouldn't have exerted quite so much energy on the swings and Junglegym with a chip off the old Daniel.

"I was reading an interesting book on the plane. One of my clients just optioned it for a made-for-telly movie. It's about fathers and daughters. About the profound experience of parenting."

Hallie wondered if he too was having second thoughts about the trick they'd played on Kate. Ned sipped his chardonnay in silence. Hallie began to worry. The only time Ned was silent was in bed.

The waiter brought their dinner. Pale fish and the first fiddleheads of the season where arranged to look like an orchid. Ned stared at his plate as if he'd never seen California cuisine before. Maybe a decade of jet lag had suddenly caught up with him.

"Are you all right?" she asked.

He looked at her. His eyes were moist, as if he were about to cry. "Hallie," he said, and ducked his head, "would you ever consider leaving your husband?"

Would she ever.

A week later Daniel moved into a studio apartment a block away from the one he'd shared with Hallie. He took the separation philosophically. Obsolescence was part of his religion. Their marriage was no longer state of the art. It was like the outdated terminals and software that littered his office.

Kate was inquisitive. At least five or six times a day Hallie answered the same questions about where Daddy would go and where Mommy would live and what would happen to Kate. Twice that often she repeated the catechism of divorce. Mommy and Daddy still love Kate. Nothing can change that. But Kate was no fool. She knew a great deal was changing.

Naomi took it badly. Hallie came home one evening to find her putting clean sheets on the former marriage bed. "For richer or poorer," she chanted as she pulled the fitted fabric tight. "In sickness and health." She unfurled the top sheet as if it were a bridal canopy. "Till death do you part." She plumped the four pillows.

"Naomi!" Hallie said.

The woman turned from the bed to Hallie, her face a mask of perfect innocence. "I didn't hear you come in."

Byte had welcomed her at the door with all the secrecy of a ticker-tape parade, but Hallie wasn't going to argue. "You have a right to your opinion, Naomi. Just not in front of Kate."

Naomi's mouth opened like a wound. "I wouldn't hurt that poor orphaned child for anything."

Dottie flew north, without Herb. She stayed in Laura's guest room, formerly Ezra's consultation room, and made dinner for her daughters the first night she was there. Hallie had suggested going out, but Dottie reminded her it was not a celebration.

"It's not a wake either," Hallie answered. They were sitting around Laura's dining-room table, which Dottie had set with everyday china and silver and fresh flowers while her daughters were at work. The thought of them chained to various desks around the city tore at her conscience, her sense of justice, her heart.

"I'm doing the only sensible thing," Hallie insisted.

Dottie's eyes roved over her daughters' plates. There was no early retirement from motherhood. "I may be stupid. I didn't graduate cum laude like my daughters. I didn't even finish college. I dropped out to marry your father. But I wish someone would explain to me what is so sensible about throwing out a husband of nine years, a decent man, a good provider, the father of your child. What is so sensible about raising a daughter alone, about facing life alone? I had no choice after your father died. Laura doesn't either. I could cry every time I think of the way that man has behaved." During the past few months Ezra, the man Dottie had loved like a son, had become the name she refused to pronounce. "But you, Hallie, you're a different story. You're the one who wants the divorce. So you explain why you think life without a husband is going to be better than life with one."

Hallie's eyes, slippery as butter, slid away from her mother.

"You were too young to remember," Dottie went on. "That's the problem. You don't know what it was like after your father died. I didn't know anything. Not how to pay a bill or talk to lawyers or anything. I was raised to be a wife."

And still you went on to raise us the same way, Laura thought but didn't say. It was Hallie's turn.

"And the loneliness. What did three little girls know about the loneliness. At first people were nice. I was so young. It was such a shock. Everyone wanted to help. But that passed. People got used to the fact. Who cares about an extra woman, a woman alone? Do you remember that little Italian restaurant we used to go to?"

"Emilio's," Laura said.

"We used to go there once a week. Sometimes two or three times. After your father died, I just stopped cooking. What's the point of cooking for a woman and three children? But no matter how often we went, we always had to wait for a table. It was always 'Just a few minutes, Mrs. Brandt.' But the women who came in with men, they never had to wait for a table. You were too young to notice, but I noticed."

"I remember," Hallie said quietly. She looked like the child of Dottie's reminiscences, a child in an adult's restaurant, hungry, scared, and determined not to show it. Then the woman who could spot a trend a month off banished the child who'd been denied a seat at life's banquet. She sat up straighter. "Times have changed. These days a woman can make a life for herself, herself and her children. I go out to dinner all the time, and I never have to wait for a table. It's just a matter of knowing the maître d' and tipping him well."

Dottie glanced at Emily's plate and passed the asparagus before Emily could ask for them. "I try to make her understand about life, and she tells me how to get a good table at a restaurant," Dottie said to no one in particular.

"Maybe I'll remarry. You did. I believe in sequential marriage. When you outgrow one mate, it just makes sense to move on to another."

Emily decided not to remind Hallie that she'd sworn fealty to the single state. No one had ever accused Hallie of foolish consistency.

"You call that growth?" Dottie asked.

"I call that realizing my potential. I only have one life."

"Stop sounding like your newsletter," Dottie said, "and think about what you're doing."

"I have thought about it. My mind is made up. It's time to move on."

Without a word Dottie stood, went into the kitchen, and returned with the salad. "You're all too young to remember Dior's New Look. After the war," she said as she began serving the salad. Her daughters leaned back in their chairs. Fashion was one of Dottie's consuming interests. She wasn't finished with Hallie, but she was taking a breather, like a sherbet to clear the palate. "But Laura remembers the crinolines and waist cinchers of the fifties. And of course, you were all around for the miniskirt. When I think of the way we used to change hemlines. The designers said 'jump' and we jumped. Shortening clothes one year, throwing them out two years later. I suppose we were very frivolous women in those days. I suppose we wasted a lot of money. But I can tell you one thing." Dottie passed a plate of salad to Hallie. "We never called it progress."

* * *

Life was finally living up to Hallie's expectations. She felt like an ad in the *New Yorker* or a photograph in *Town and Country*. She was about to become one of those women she'd envied last Christmas with a perfect marriage, a vibrant sex life, and a schedule of A-list parties. She was about to marry one of those men she'd passed with a six-figure income, a working knowledge of contemporary painting, literature, and film, and a healthy respect for the art of conversation. She was about to divorce a man who was behaving as logically and well as one of his own programs.

"That's because he's consumed with guilt," she explained to Emily. They were having dinner at one of those restaurants Hallie favored where rudeness passed for exclusivity and upward mobility was a geographical direction.

"Why is he guilty? You're the one who finally decided on the divorce. And I'm assuming there are no corespondents— other than the mainframe."

The idea of confession was as enticing as the dessert tray the waiter carried by, but Hallie had willpower. The few minutes of pleasure would not be worth the consequences. Besides, they were discussing Daniel's fidelity, not hers.

"The mainframe was enough," Hallie said. "At least an affair can punch up a marriage. Kind of like bringing in new management from outside the company. Suddenly everyone tries harder. But there was no new blood in Daniel's life, just the same old machine." She thought of Daniel's return from the Las Vegas convention. After three days devoted entirely to computers he'd been glad to see her, but after three days of round-the-clock work he'd managed to express his pleasure a little like a robot. "Daniel was like Los Angeles—there was no there there."

"You mean he didn't talk?" Emily had spent a good part of the last decade explaining to a variety of women that silence was not grounds for divorce.

"I mean, he didn't do anything."

Suddenly Emily understood. There were few things the sisters didn't speak of, but sex was one of them. They talked dirty, but they didn't talk personally. Now Hallie's disparagement of Peter, and by association Emily, came clear. Emily understood it and forgave it because Hallie hadn't understood. "He knows which side his bread is buttered on," she'd said months earlier, but from the sound of it poor Hallie had never, to quote or paraphrase Bessie Smith, Alberta Hunter, and a long line of women who had sung and understood the blues, had her bread properly buttered. The realization made Emily feel undeservedly fortunate and unspeakably sad. "Buck up," she said, "Mr. Right is probably lurking just around the corner."

"I told you I'm never going to marry again. I have too much self-respect."

"No one mentioned marriage," Emily pointed out.

"Except me," Hallie said, and ducked her head girlishly. The gesture was new and very becoming.

XIII

Ezra had continued to call about matters of mutual interest, as he described them, and Laura had gone on telling him those matters were of mutual interest to their attorneys, too. She also continued to walk a fine line with Isabel. The effort was successful but exhausting. She felt like an actress in a one-woman show. At home she was always onstage. At the office she was always on display. Patients sat and stared at her with the same bored expressions they turned on the dog-eared magazines in the waiting room. She smiled at the patients and massaged the periodontists' egos and listened to the trials and tribulations of the girl-women. The Kristofferson look-alike had departed for a younger woman. Laura hadn't thought such a thing existed. She told Nancy she was well rid of him. It was like telling Isabel she'd have no appetite for dinner if she ate another cookie.

Despite her position as a surrogate mother, Laura was having second thoughts about the job. An old acquaintance, a woman recently separated from her own analyst husband, said that her attorney had forbidden her to find gainful employment until the divorce was final. Laura relayed the information to Emily. She was not impressed. "You're showing good faith. Besides, my files are full of women sitting around feeling sorry for themselves. I have one client who says she's never worked and never plans to. It's not 'her bag.' "

"I know you're right, but sometimes I get so damn discouraged. I started out with a no-fault divorce, and I've ended up with a mess that has more faults than Southern California. Other people have nice, neat, speedy divorces. Look at Jake. Look at Hallie. Daniel's acting like a prince." Laura didn't like the sound of her own voice. It was geared to childhood complaints about parental injustice. "Hallie's younger," Dottie used to explain. "You're old enough to know better."

"Hallie's marriage wasn't as good as yours, so her divorce isn't as ugly," Emily said.

"Let me think about that one for a while."

"You need a vacation."

"I also need a spring blazer and a new air conditioner in the bedroom, but if Ezra complains about groceries and maintenance, I don't think he's going to cotton to any of the rest."

The family wheels began to move. Laura needed a vacation, preferably with Isabel. Emily called Dottie. Dottie called Laura. "We have two guest rooms. And there's nothing wrong with Florida in the summer. At least everything's air-conditioned. Come as soon as Isabel gets out of school. Stay as long as you want."

"I have a job," Laura pointed out. "But I'll take you up on it for two weeks. Thanks."

Isabel was less grateful.

"It'll be about two hundred degrees and muggy. And everyone there is about two hundred years old."

"And everyone there," Laura added, "has grandchildren your age. There're bound to be other kids around."

"And two weeks locked up with Grandma and Grandpa."

"What's so bad about two weeks with Dottie and Herb?"

Isabel looked at her mother, and for the first time in weeks Laura felt the old bond of understanding. "Come on, Mom, give me a break."

Laura sat on the side of Isabel's bed. "I wish I could come

up with something more exciting. Europe, or China like Jenny's parents. But we can't afford that right now. I'm not obsessing about money, I'm just telling you how things are. We can have a perfectly good time in Florida, though. There are all those tennis courts, and we won't hang around the pool. We'll drive to the beach. A different beach every day."

"Oh, shit!" Isabel's face collapsed out of shape until it looked like a cubist rendering of misery. "I didn't mean you had to take me someplace expensive. Florida's okay. And I love Dottie and Herb. It's just that—" Isabel stopped, pulled a tissue out of the box on her night table, and blew her nose noisily. She crumpled the tissue in her hand, but she didn't go on, and she didn't stop crying.

"It's just that what?" Laura's voice was hushed, as if in prayer. Please, don't stop now.

"It's just that everything is so . . ."

"Different?"

"Shitty." Isabel's face collapsed until there was no format all, only a pale, streaky blotch of despair.

Laura put her arms around her daughter and held her while she cried. The dampness spread over her shoulder. Laura remembered the sensation. She'd carried a baby on her shoulder, sometimes crying, sometimes drooling in sleeping bliss.

"I sound like such a baby." Isabel squeezed out the words between sobs.

"You don't sound like a baby at all."

"I just don't understand why everything has to be so awful."

Laura rocked Isabel and thought of the words that had once been so powerful: Mommy will make it all right. She went on holding her daughter in silence.

A few days later Ezra called. "Hello, Laura, how are you these days?" His voice was unnaturally civil.

She remembered the book she'd picked up that day in her

naïveté. *Keep her on her toes.* She told him she was fine in a voice she'd taken to practicing at odd hours during the day.

"I hope we won't have to turn this one over to the attorneys." He laughed. She wanted to scream. "I'd like to take Isabel to Europe. The south of France, the Amalfi Coast, Spain, and Portugal. The Iberian Peninsula is dirt cheap these days," he added. "I thought we'd leave as soon as she gets out of school."

"But you always take your vacation in August. I thought it was written in stone or at least somewhere in Freud's papers."

His chuckle was indulgent. "Just one of the profession's habits. But I can get a cheaper rate if I go before the summer rush. Fortunately private schools get out before the great unwashed, and uneducated, American public."

"I'd planned to take Isabel to Florida to see her grandparents. That's dirt cheap, too. Dottie and Herb have rearranged their plans. You know they don't usually stay down there for the summer."

"Well, sure, Laura, that's all very nice. You know how fond I am of Dottie and Herb. But you can't really compare a few weeks with them to a month in Europe. You can't compare Disney World, and I mean Disney World of the mind and spirit, to the château country, Pompeii, the Prado, and the Sintra."

You couldn't, but Laura knew Ezra had for Isabel's benefit.

"Look," Ezra went on, "there's no problem."

"You mean you'll switch your vacation back to August?"

"Really, Laura," he said, and for the first time that evening his voice sounded familiar, "it's much easier for you to change your vacation. I've already canceled my patients. What I was going to say was that Isabel isn't a baby. We can let her decide where she'd rather go. The south of France, the Amalfi Coast, Spain, and Portugal"—he ran the itinerary again—"or Florida."

"It's an open-and-shut case, Ezra. I haven't raised a cretin.

Of course, Isabel would rather go to Europe. So would I. Funny that there's enough money in the Glass coffers for two to go to Europe but not three. I'm referring to myself, not the infant psychologist who, I understand, has replaced the baby tycoon. Don't get the wrong idea. I don't want to go with you. I'd just like to go."

"I'm not taking anyone except Isabel. I work hard for my money."

"I work hard, too. For a lot less money. But I don't want to go into that now. Just let me know your itinerary. I don't want to deprive Isabel of anything. I just want to know where she is at all times."

"Still trying to control everyone."

That was the cue for her big scene. First came the denials, then the screams of indignation, finally contrition. And if she played the part well enough, Ezra would give her a moderately good review. She wasn't really a domineering bitch, he'd concede, only a bit overprotective. But not tonight, not anymore. She missed her cue.

"Isabel is thirteen. I don't think there's anything neurotic about wanting to know the whereabouts of a thirteen-year-old child. And with all due respect to your professional experience and expertise, if you do, you're in the wrong business."

The following night Isabel returned from dinner at Ezra's with a handful of brochures. She spread them out on her mother's bed. Blue seas sparkled beneath sun-bleached skies, ancient columns crumbled heartbreakingly to dust, and happy tourists sat at pristine tables littered with golden bread and ruby wines and fruit and cheese the color of semiprecious stones. Laura would have ached with envy if she hadn't been aching with loss.

"I suppose you and Dottie and Herb are angry. I mean, I said I'd go there first."

"No one's angry, Isabel. We're all disappointed, but we understand."

Isabel was thirteen. She didn't want understanding; she wanted approval. They talked for hours, about cultural advantages and family responsibilities, about the way other people live and the way one ought to live, about history, art, and architecture and grandparents, respect, and consideration, about speaking French and unspoken bonds. And finally Isabel went into the kitchen and brought glasses of iced tea and the cookie jar back to Laura's bed and said through lips curved in a tragic inverted comma that if Laura thought she really ought to give up going to Europe with her father and go to Florida with her, she would. And Laura said again that the south of France and the Amalfi Coast and Spain and Portugal were advantages that should not be casually dismissed. They embraced, all four of them, Isabel and her salved conscience and Laura and her self-sacrifice.

It was not a great sacrifice. Laura didn't mind losing Isabel's company for a month. She just wished she didn't have the feeling she was losing Isabel.

Daniel's first act on moving out had been to find a woman lawyer. "Sheila Slotnick," she introduced herself to Emily over the phone. "Here in the office they call me S.S." Emily refused to consider the implications of the initials. She didn't want to go into this expecting violence, cruelty, and putsches.

As negotiations progressed, Emily found she didn't dislike dealing with S.S. as she did so many of her colleagues of both sexes, but neither did she feel any particular affinity with the woman simply because she was a woman. Confronted with an emptying nest, her thirty-fifth birthday, and her husband's success in the legal profession, S.S. had taken up law school. Upon graduation she'd gone into marital law the way women doctors go into gynecology, with a reforming zeal. But old habits died hard. She'd once put Emily on hold to take a call from her husband, whose time was billed at corporate rates. She had a habit of referring to Daniel as Mr. Fields and Hallie as Hallie, although unlike Kron, she didn't know she was doing it. She found it impossible to hide her disapproval of a woman who had tossed out a perfectly adequate husband. S.S. lent a new twist to the old problem of overidentification with the client.

By the morning after Emily's dinner with Hallie S.S.'s disapproval had turned to disgust. "We've just reviewed Hallie's budget. It's unacceptable."

Emily's sigh was silent. She'd been anticipating this moment the way a child who has managed to stay up beyond her bedtime waits to be noticed by her preoccupied parents. "But the budget was acceptable a month ago."

"That was a preliminary discussion. On considering it more closely, Mr. Fields has found Hallie's demands unconscionable."

"You mean too high?"

"I mean unconscionable," S.S. repeated, and began to run down the list of comforts Hallie neither needed nor deserved. She offered an alternative plan. S.S. wasn't cataloging expenses; she was issuing moral imperatives.

Emily called Hallie immediately. The secretary announced with a certain degree of pride that Ms. Fields—she pronounced the term of address as if she were auditioning for a bad production of Tennessee Williams—was covering a conference on how to escape from the middle class forever. Emily felt a surge of Sheila Slotnick's moral indignation. "Of course, she's covering it for the newsletter." The secretary giggled.

"You look pensive," Ned Sinclair said.

Hallie was right about him. There was something boyish about a man who could poke his head around an office door as coyly as if he were playing hide-and-seek or show off his new five-thousand-dollar watch the way a kid might a prized marble.

"I was just thinking about people who give or go to seminars on how to escape from the middle class forever."

"People have been trying to climb to the next rung ever since man invented the ladder."

"But there are logical reasons for trying to climb out of the lower class. Poverty, disease, lack of education."

Ned wagged his head as if to say "all-y-all-y-'ome-free." He was safe, and she was out, way out. "There are perfectly good reasons for climbing into the upper class too, Emily. Money. Power. Perks."

"I suppose you have a point."

"Of course, I have a point," he said as if he were surprised anyone might doubt it.

Hallie didn't return Emily's call until after six that evening. Leaving the middle class behind for good was a time-consuming task.

"What happened between you and Daniel?" Emily asked immediately. "Have you had a fight about money or Kate or something?"

"I haven't spoken to Daniel in weeks. Naomi's usually there when he picks Kate up and drops her off."

"Well, something's got to him. You haven't bought anything wild and frivolous—anything reeking of the upper class—that he might have seen around the apartment or heard about from Kate or Naomi, have you?"

"Are you kidding? I've taken vows of poverty and chastity until this thing is over." She felt a small tug at her conscience. "It's worth it to be able to break the old one of silence."

But the quips stopped when Emily reported her conversation with Sheila Slotnick. "He can't get away with this, can he?" Hallie asked.

"He can't get away with the agreement she suggested this morning, which would entitle Kate to Aid to Families with Dependent Children, but he can get away with a lot less than you expect."

Daniel's next proposal arrived by messenger the following day. It would keep Kate off the AFDC rolls, but just barely.

Emily called Sheila Slotnick immediately. "You're not serious about this!"

"Dead serious. Hallie works. She can take care of herself."

"She plans to take care of herself. We're not asking for alimony. We're asking for fair child support and equitable distribution." The last two words that had sounded so fresh and crisp when the law was passed a few years ago tasted stale in Emily's mouth, like old popcorn that was nothing but tired air.

"That's our offer," S.S. said. "Take it or leave it."

"He's gone mad," Emily reported to Hallie. "Are you sure you haven't said or done something?"

"I told you, I haven't even spoken to him in weeks."

Sitting in her office later that night, waiting for Jake and watching the dusk settle like a cloak over the Chrysler Building, Emily was still trying to figure out what Daniel was up to. She no longer expected logic or even consistency in divorce negotiations. She'd seen men turn their backs on terms they'd spent months hammering out because of a single slur to their vanity. She'd ushered seemingly polite women out of her office and had them call an hour later describing their husbands in terms only a lifetime at sea or an inadvertent insult could account for. She'd seen both husbands and wives complain for a year about how long everything was taking, then suddenly drag their feet at the first glimpse of their replacements on the horizon. Emily knew all about the Jekyll-and-Hyde behavior of the currently divorcing. And she knew one thing more: The transformation didn't occur without a potion, though it was anything but magical.

"It's our final offer," Sheila Slotnick said.

"Your final offer is barely better than your original offer, which, to use your word, Sheila, was unconscionable. The child support is less than minimal. Kate is Daniel's daughter, too."

The argument did not impress S.S., though in the past she'd made repeated references to her own children. "Take it or leave it."

"You know we can't take it."

"Then we'll see you in court," S.S. said as if she'd been waiting all her life to utter that line.

Hallie said she was ready. "I see myself in a severe black suit with a big picture hat or maybe a pillbox with a little veil to hide my brimming eyes." But her voice was thin and artificially bright, like a streak of yellow down the black picture she'd painted.

XIV

"You can't do more than you already have. At least not until Hallie's court date, which you say will take forever even to schedule." Jake's voice had a plaintive quality, like the foghorn that had been cautioning the ferry all afternoon; only Emily knew it wasn't a single foghorn but a chorus of them, a Greek chorus of apprehension. And it wasn't Hallie she was worrying about.

She looked out at the cottony mist. The ferry could be going in circles for all she knew. She glanced down at the churning black water. Her hands felt wet and cold, like a fish just landed. She put them in the pockets of her foul-weather gear. The beginning of a vacation. Great expectations.

They'd decided on it at the beginning of June. In the years since Jake and Emily had known each other, each of them had developed a variety of new habits. Emily still couldn't get over the fact that Jake drank martinis before dinner and wouldn't drink coffee after it. She was less surprised that he'd spent part of the last nine summers on Nantucket. She'd spent a good part of them there, too. They decided to go together. Jake would look at birds and catch fish and invite his muse. Emily would read on the beach and rent a Sunfish and—she had a sinking feeling—spend more time fishing and birding than she wanted to.

Another foghorn sobbed its warning. A child cried. Downwind from her at the railing a man began to throw up. She went back to the car. At least it was warm. She tilted the seat and laid her head against the backrest. Dottie had called the night before to tell her to have a good time. "Are you nervous?" she'd asked. Emily had said she was only going to Nantucket for a few weeks.

Through half-closed eyes she saw Jake pacing the deck. Now and then he stopped to look down at the water. Occasionally he rubbed his hands. He looked happy, damn near gleeful.

He came over and got into the driver's seat of the car. The wind had lighted flames of color on his cheekbones. "It'll be better when we get to the island."

"So Napoleon said on the way to Elba."

The closed windows muffled the foghorns, but Emily knew the chorus of apprehension was still there, just on the other side of the glass. It would be better on the island, Jake said. All escape routes cut off. She thought of fish and birds and, in ten days, the arrival of Jake's daughter. Emily felt in the pocket of her jacket for the ferry schedule she'd picked up that morning and managed to get a nasty paper cut for her trouble.

The ferry glided and bumped its way in. People began surging off like waves at high tide. Emily saw the man who'd thrown up. His complexion looked like a mold culture. Drivers raced their motors furiously and inched toward land in fits and starts. Jake's own foot played an impatient game with the starter. They eventually made it ashore. In the achingly cute shops, on the cobbled streets, from other cars, people stared back at Emily with a rigid suspicion that had been etched in the crowded, dirty cities they were fleeing. It took another half hour to get out of town.

Jake got lost trying to find the house, though Emily had a map spread across her knees, which she consulted regularly. At one point he snatched it out of her hands in impatience. "You never could read maps worth a damn."

"You've been here before," Emily pointed out.

Jake handed her back the map. "We've both been this way before, babe. You think that makes any difference?"

She told him if he was going to talk in aphorisms, she was going home.

The house was better than she'd expected. Jake had raved about it, but then Jake had been known to rave about the series of railroad flats and tenements he'd lived in during college summers. His memories were painted in Proustian pastels; his expectations, based on the minimum requirements of the board of health. The weathered shingled house almost lived up to one and outdid the other.

The fog lifted in time for a garish sunset. They took their drinks out to the porch, which the rental agent insisted on calling the deck. The sky was the color of watermelon. In the distance the water danced in a prism of pinks and greens and blues. A kid carrying an oversize radio approached along the dirt road. So much for the island idyll. Mozart came creeping toward them like the gathering twilight. They started to laugh. Jake stretched out in the deck chair until his bare toes touched hers. The sun disappeared behind their neighbor's house. For a few seconds the cottage looked as if it were on fire. Emily wound her bare feet around Jake's ankle. His other foot climbed her leg. His feet were elegant—that was the only word for them—with curving arches and long pale soles. His toes had reached her thigh. "Want to lie down before dinner?" he asked.

She put her hand over his foot. "I thought you said you were tired after the long drive."

He smiled. His lower lip pulled down in a soft tremor. "Why else would I want to lie down?"

The good weather held for several days. Jake saw a prairie warbler and caught three bluefish. Emily capsized the Sunfish twice. They went in for prodigious bouts of lobster, books, and each other. There were no quarrels about the toothpaste, although Jake never screwed on the cap and Emily always squeezed from the top.

One morning, when they'd been there almost a week, she said she was driving into town. Jake was out of the hammock in seconds. Emily watched her few minutes of stolen solitude disappear like the mast of her capsized Sunfish.

"Want me to drive?" he asked.

She said "sure."

The next afternoon Jake announced he was going for a walk on the beach. Emily could tell from the way he said it that he expected an answer. "Have a nice time."

He stood watching her, his elegant feet ·arched over the weathered floorboards of the porch, his hands hooked in the back pockets of his shorts. He was waiting for something.

"Write if you get work."

"Come with me."

"Too lazy."

"Be good for you." He scratched his stomach. He knew she was crazy about his stomach. She wondered if the gesture was intended as a cautionary tale. She heaved herself out of the hammock.

He'd been right, of course. The walk was good for her. Hard, arch-building sand underfoot. Lonely horizon prompting all sorts of cosmic intimations. "I love the beach at this hour," she said. All right, the observation wasn't exactly cosmic. Still, he could have answered.

"It always makes me wish I could paint."

Maybe he couldn't hear her above the sound of the waves.

She put her arm around his waist. He dropped his along her shoulders. They walked that way for a while, then fell apart. It was hard to walk in lockstep on shifting sands.

She picked up a shell and showed it to Jake. She should have held it to her ear. At least something would be speaking to her.

"What I don't understand," she said finally, "is why you were so damn eager to have me along. You obviously want to be by yourself."

Beside her his shoulders fell in an eloquent pantomime of

exhaustion. He'd explained all this before, and only a stupid or recalcitrant child would make him go over it again. "Just because I'm not talking, Emily, doesn't mean I don't know you're here." Overhead a gull, obviously a laughing gull, shrieked its ridicule.

"Sure." She began walking again, and Jake fell into step beside her.

"I figured it out," she said that night after she'd washed the few dishes and Jake had extinguished the coals in the barbecue.

"What?" he asked without looking up from his book.

"I figured out why men have to have women in attendance all the time, why they don't like to be alone, and why women need to—be alone, I mean—sometimes."

He closed the book and put it on the table but didn't look happy about the gesture. "All right, why?"

"Because half the time women aren't there for men. They're along, but they're not there, if you see what I mean."

"I don't."

"You want a warm body in the vicinity when you're birding or reading or whatever. Like a trusty hound: That way you can be alone without being by yourself."

"All right," he said. "I don't mean, all right, I agree; I mean, all right, I understand. Now what about the rest? Why do women need to be alone?"

"Because when they're with people, they're really with them. They pay attention. They worry."

"Don't forget nurture, babe."

"Okay, but you know what I mean. And it's goddamn exhausting."

"You mean, you wanted to go into town alone yesterday."

You could call Jake a lot of things—and at one point in her life she had—but stupid was not among them.

The next morning Emily said she was taking the Sunfish out and asked Jake if he wanted to come along. He said he thought he'd go fishing. He said it from behind the morning paper.

"Are you sulking?"

He put down the paper. He wasn't sulking, only being fastidious. He went fishing; she went sailing.

That afternoon they went to the beach together. Jake was so glib he might have been auditioning as a talk show host. Listen, Johnny, she wanted to say, don't overdo it. They walked out over the sandspit that appeared at low tide. He told a long, convoluted story about a magazine assignment that had taken him to the White House. It was filled with the most unforgettable characters he'd ever met. Listen, Merv, she wanted to say, relax. You've got the job.

When they returned to the blanket, Jake fell asleep. The effort had obviously exhausted him.

Emily wasn't dreading the arrival of Jake's daughter, but neither was she anticipating it with enthusiasm. She asked Jake if he thought she ought to move into the other bedroom. He asked if she was losing her mind.

"My clients are always making policy statements about not subjecting their children to a succession of lovers."

Jake looked up from the bluefish he was cleaning. His hands, his chest, and the sink were spattered with blood and gore, but his eyes were clear. "Don't look now, babe, but you're not a succession."

The second Mrs. Ferris was to deliver Nina on the way to her own rented house and illicit housemate. Emily and Jake went to meet the ferry. As the waves of passengers surged off, Jake caught sight of his daughter and former wife and squatted like a catcher who didn't entirely trust his pitcher. Nina broke away from her mother and ran straight into his arms. Emily and the second Mrs. Ferris stood around in the sun until their frozen smiles began to melt down their chins like soft ice cream. Nina pointed out that her mother and Emily were wearing the same polo shirts. The two women looked at each other. Identical golden fleece sat over each heart, like sorority pins. They belonged to the same club.

Nina liked the house and her room and the beach and the fish and the birds and everything Jake showed her. She even seemed to like Emily. They settled down for the duration.

On the first night of Nina's arrival Emily knocked over a chair in the bedroom. She hadn't wanted to disturb Jake by turning on the light. "What are you doing?" His voice was thick with sleep.

"Looking for my bathrobe."

He turned the clock on the night table to see the face. "At four in the morning?"

"I didn't think I ought to go leaping down the hall naked."

"For Christ's sake Emily, five-year-olds don't get up in the middle of the night. And if they do, they cry or call and you go into their rooms."

"Thank you, Dr. Spock." She found her robe and crept down the hall to the bathroom.

"Nina doesn't know you and I were married before you and her mother, does she?" Emily asked Jake the next morning.

"She's five years old," Jake reminded her again.

"Stop saying that. I know her age. I just don't know what it means."

The next night Nina did wake up and call for her father. Jake turned on the light to find a robe. He turned off the light when he left but didn't close the door, and Emily saw the light go on down the hall. He returned a moment later and picked up the book on his night table. "She wants me to sit with her until she falls asleep. It's a strange house and a strange room." Not to mention a strange woman, Emily thought. After Jake had gone back to Nina's room, Emily lay awake wondering what it was like to be a child in an alien world. She felt sorry for Nina. And she wasn't entirely above self-pity either. Life had been simpler last week.

The next morning Jake and Nina returned from town with a news flash. For forty dollars and a waiver of all rights to litigation, not to mention all claims to sanity, a couple of old salts would take you out in their marginally seaworthy vessel to—are you ready, Ahab?—see the whales.

"God, I wish I could go," Jake said. He sounded the way he used to so many years ago in those darkened college rooms.

"Why can't you?"

"It's too dangerous. Nina's too young. She'd be bored. And probably seasick."

The silence spread between them on the porch like water from a melting ice cube. Emily swore she wasn't going to mop it up.

"I don't suppose you and Nina would like to do something without me one day."

The puddle spread.

"You could take her to the beach or the whaling museum or something."

Emily never could stand a mess. She said "sure."

"Call me Ishmael," Jake said, and kissed her.

The next morning Emily and Nina went down to the dock to see Jake off. The *Melville*—talk about hubris—didn't look even marginally seaworthy. "Now you see why I couldn't take Nina," Jake whispered. What about you? Emily wanted to ask. What about me? she wanted to scream.

Nina didn't begin to cry till the boat had pulled out and she and Emily were back at the car. She'd kept up a brave front for Jake but crumbled when she was alone with Emily. Ah, women.

Twin rivulets of tears streamed out from under the pink plastic sunglasses. "I want to go with Daddy."

Emily took off the sunglasses and tried to wipe Nina's eyes. "Daddy will be home before you know it," she lied.

"Why can't I go with Daddy?"

"Because you wouldn't like it. We'll have more fun here."

"I would like it," Nina insisted. "I'd like it better than this."

They got into the car. Emily started to buckle Nina's seat belt. Nina pushed her hands away. It took a good five minutes

for Nina to do it herself. Emily figured they were in no hurry.
They had a long day ahead of them. She started down the
road, hugging the right side at twenty miles an hour and trying
not to think about accidents that killed or, worse still, maimed
for life.

"You drive slow," Nina said. "Not like Mommy and
Daddy."

Emily said nothing. She'd been sent on as an understudy
and knew she wasn't coming back as a star, not in this play.

"I want ice cream," Nina said.

"It isn't even nine o'clock."

"Mommy always lets me have ice cream for breakfast.
Sometimes I have ice cream a hundred times a day."

"To hell with it," Emily muttered, and took a quick left toward one of the ice-cream shops.

A car horn shattered the quiet morning air. "Hey, lady,
didn't you ever hear of a signal!"

When they reached the stand, Emily got out of the car and
went around to help Nina out on her side. Nina didn't want
any help. She climbed out of the car. She looked at the stand.
"I want to go where Daddy took me."

"This one is better."

Nina's upper lip crept down over her lower one. "I want
Daddy's ice cream."

"It's the same ice cream." Emily was pleading now.

"It's not."

Emily switched to reason. "You haven't even tried it."

Nina was her match. "I don't like the flavors." Only later
did Emily realize Nina couldn't read the flavors.

They got back in the car and drove toward town. Emily
found the shop Jake had taken Nina to the day before. They
went inside. Nina ordered a vanilla cone.

Back in the car she licked happily while ice cream dripped
down her T-shirt and onto the car seat. Emily reached over to
mop up the seat with a napkin and swerved entirely too close to

a group of kids walking along the side of the road. She pulled over, cleaned up the seat, and sat waiting for Nina to finish her cone.

They drove to the whaling museum. Emily had insisted Nina was too young for it, but Jake, a father and an authority, had predicted she'd love it. "When we walked past the other day and I said I'd take her, she got all excited."

For twenty minutes Nina left vanilla fingerprints over the glass cases, displays, and artifacts. Emily snatched her out of reach of a harpoon just in the nick of time. The guard told Nina not to touch, one more stranger telling her not to do one more thing. Nina's lower lip quivered powerfully. She sat on the floor and began to cry. A few visitors turned to stare. One woman smiled at Emily with an air of complicity. Emily glared back. They left the museum and went home.

Emily got into her bathing suit. Nina refused help getting into her own. Emily didn't argue. She sat in the kitchen drinking iced coffee and pondering the meaning of motherhood. But of course, she wasn't a mother. If she had been, Nina wouldn't be acting this way.

Nina arrived in the kitchen ready for the beach. The blue tank suit stretched over her childish stomach. The pink plastic sunglasses sat astride the small freckled nose. The strawberry blond hair made a curly halo around her head. "Your shirt's the same color as my bathing suit," Nina said. "We're twins." Emily forgave her everything.

Nina announced a desire for a peanut butter and jelly sandwich. Emily was encouraged. She'd seen Nina eat. They'd be able to kill at least half an hour. She took out the white bread she'd bought two days ago for the first time in her life and the jar of peanut butter, then went to the refrigerator for the jelly. The Tiptree orange marmalade was just waiting to trip her up, but Emily was no fool. She went straight to the grape jelly. She spread the peanut butter and jelly on the bread, covered it with another slice, cut it diagonally, and put the sandwich in front of Nina. Nina was not impressed. "It has *crusts.*" Emily got the knife and cut off the crusts. "It's too big. Mommy cuts it in smaller pieces." Emily divided it into quarters. Nina pushed the springy bread with the tips of her fingers. A stream of brown and purple oozed out onto the plate. "There's too much," Nina said. "You're not supposed to put so much in it." Emily took the plate back to the counter, opened the sandwich, and tried to scrape some of the filling off. The bread tore. Refusing even to consider Ethiopia, she threw the sandwich in the trash and made a new one. The peanut butter was a thin film, the grape jelly a gossamer layer over it. She cut off the crusts, divided it in quarters, and put it before the three-foot-six tyrant. Nina pushed the bread with her fingertips. Not a drop oozed out. She took a bite, then put the quarter back on the plate. A crescent so tiny it might have been made by a mouse destroyed the symmetry of the pieces. Nina spread out her small hands and flattened all four sections against the plate. Emily got up and poured herself more iced coffee. When she came back to the table, the sandwich, still missing only that single perfect half-moon, was plastered to the plate.

"Eat your sandwich." Emily tried to sound as if she were making a suggestion rather than a threat. "As soon as you finish it, we can go to the beach."

"I don't want it."

"But you said you wanted a peanut butter and jelly sandwich."

"The way Mommy makes it." Nina dragged out the word *Mommy* as if it were a song of mourning.

"Are you sure you don't want it?" Emily asked.

"I want one the way Mommy makes it."

Emily started to ask how Mommy made it, then caught herself. This was not Julia Child sitting across the table. "Last chance," she sang as if she were trying out for the part of Maria in *The Sound of Music.*

"I don't want it."

Emily dumped the second sandwich in the trash. "Ready for the beach?" she sang like the whole damn Trapp family. Nina's face lit up. Emily's conscience ached. This was an abandoned child, a lost waif, a product of a broken home. More to the point, this was a scared kid, not a short adult with jelly on her chin.

Emily packed up the beach blankets and towels, pails and shovels, thermoses and bottles of suntan lotion. Not since the Allies staged D-Day.

When they arrived at the beach, there was a minor skirmish over suntan oil. Nina didn't want any. Emily insisted, though she couldn't blame the kid. Oiled for action, Nina attracted sand the way a veal chop does breadcrumbs. Then things began looking up. They built a sand castle. They buried Nina in the sand. They buried Emily's legs. They went on a shell-collecting expedition. They splashed at the edge of the water. Nina was having fun. Emily was feeling virtuous. She looked at her watch. Three-thirty. They were in the home stretch.

The crisis came a little after four, when Nina's lips had turned the same blue as her bathing suit. Emily suggested that they get out of the water. To be accurate, Emily wasn't in the water, but at its edge sitting in the wet sand watching Nina. Nina demurred. Emily pulled rank. Nina retreated into deeper water. Emily called for her to come out. Nina splashed about on her fragile plastic life preserver.

"I mean it, Nina!"

Nina turned her back and went on slapping her hands against the water.

"Right this minute!"

A wave carried Nina and the tube a little farther out. Emily started after them. The shells were sharp underfoot. When the water was chest-level, she began to swim. She was not a strong swimmer, but she was competent. You couldn't graduate from Bryn Mawr if you weren't a competent swimmer. And people said an old-fashioned liberal arts education had no relevance, she thought as she paddled.

Nina went on splashing. She wasn't far out—there were plenty of swimmers beyond her—but she'd drifted to the point where the waves were breaking. A swell crested, lifting her high above Emily and dropping her momentarily on the other side. Emily cursed as Nina came into view again. A second wave lifted her against a sky as cloudless as hope. Nina laughed wildly. Another wave came rolling in. It peaked just beyond her. The white foam came crashing over her head. Emily saw a blue blur turning in the white foam, a small foot against the sky, then a yellow and white plastic tube bouncing over the wave. She lunged into it, came up with a mouthful of salt water, and lunged again. She saw a flash of blue, grabbed for it, and pulled a squirming, screaming Nina to her. The next wave rolled over them, and Emily was surprised to find she could stand. Emily dragged the kid, wet, slippery, and still howling to shore.

At the edge of the water the ground dropped away in a sharp ledge. Emily had to make two attempts to get up it. Nina was still screaming. "You shouldn't let her go out that far," a woman in a maternity bathing suit said. Emily didn't answer.

When they reached the blanket, she tried to wrap Nina in a towel, but Nina broke away and flung herself facedown on the blanket, wailing. A few people on neighboring blankets looked over sympathetically. Most glowered. Emily covered Nina with a towel. Nina kicked it off. The sobs subsided into hiccups. Nina turned her face on the blanket. One big eye stared up at Emily accusingly. She thought of the cover of her paperback copy of *Moby Dick*. The words that had been roiling below the surface all day finally erupted. "I want my Daddy," Nina screamed.

And who could blame her?

"How was your day?" Jake asked Emily after he'd put Nina to bed.

Emily considered an answer. She'd been apprehensive in the morning, furious at lunch, terrified by the end of the afternoon. Nina had been miserable all day. Emily didn't think the child had really been in danger, but she'd never been entirely sure. The only thing she knew for certain was that they'd both been out of their depth.

On the other hand, there was no need to make waves. In the excitement of welcoming the sailor home from the seas, Nina had forgotten the ordeal of waiting for him. Jake had told wonderful whale stories. He'd seen a whole school of them, mommy whales, he'd told Nina, and daddy whales, and baby whales. The world as it ought to be. Emily decided one more fish story wouldn't hurt. "Fine," she said.

The next day Emily said she'd pack a lunch for the beach. Nina asked for a peanut butter and jelly sandwich. Jake offered to make it while Emily put together their chicken salad. Nina protested. "I want it the way Emily makes it." Emily looked at her. "Please." Nina wasn't kidding. All was forgiven. Better than that, nothing had ever happened.

They walked along the beach in search of a good spot. Nina held Emily's hand all the way.

Jake and Nina built a sand castle and buried each other and collected shells. Nina brought Emily a perfect scallop shell, thin as tissue paper. She held it out in the palm of her small hand. "This is for you." Emily thanked her.

When Jake and Nina went into the water, she left her plastic lifesaver behind and clung to her father's neck. Emily watched them from the shore. It was a radiant day. The sun felt like liquid on her skin. A light breeze tripped down the beach. She had peace and quiet and a good book. Nina's shell lay beside her on the blanket. The water sparkled like newly polished glass. As each wave rolled in, Jake held Nina high above the foam. She squealed and shrieked in ecstasy. Emily went back to her book. The envy was as small and fine as the grains of sand that managed to find their way between the pages no matter how careful she was. It was also as irritating.

At the end of the week Emily took the ferry schedule from the pocket of her foul-weather gear—it was still damp from the trip out—and began stuffing soggy clothing and sandy books into her duffel. They'd agreed from the beginning that Jake should have some time alone with his daughter.

He was sitting up in the small, lumpy bed watching her pack. The early-morning sun filtering through the venetian blinds made gold stripes across his brown chest. "Sure you don't want to stay?" he asked.

"We agreed you ought to have some time alone with Nina."

"You give us plenty of time alone even when you're here."

Emily looked at him. The eyes were innocent as camera lenses. It hadn't been a crack.

He caught her free hand as she walked past the bed. "Stay for a few more days. It'll be fun."

She sat on the side of the bed. With the exception of the day he'd gone to see the whales, it had been fun, though not as much fun as the days before Nina had arrived.

"Isn't there anything I can do to convince you to stay?" A rhetorical question. He knew that what he was doing beneath her long T-shirt was the one thing that could convince her to stay.

"Quality time. I promised to give you quality time alone with Nina," she said, though she didn't say it until somewhat later.

"I don't believe in quality time. Neither do you."

"Maybe Nina does."

At the ferry she had a moment of regret. Nina clung to her hand. Jake took off his glasses to kiss her good-bye and revealed eyes like empty caves. All the way home she couldn't decide whether she was guilty or relieved. By the time she reached her apartment she decided she was both.

XV

That September, like most in New York, autumn was a state of mind. Physical discomfort continued to run riot in the city like a tropical jungle. Emily awakened each morning to the same dirty yellow sky, arrived at her office to the same limp complaints. Ezra had returned from Europe crying poverty in a variety of languages. On the other hand, Daniel's lips were sealed. Neither he nor his attorney would explain his change of heart. Hallie insisted she didn't care why Daniel was being impossible, only that he was being impossible. But the problem still gnawed at Emily. She called Hallie one night and suggested dinner. When Hallie said it was Naomi's night off and she couldn't leave Kate, Emily offered to bring supper. "From one of those takeout places. Haute Cuisine on the Hoof."

Emily found a food shop just a block away from Hallie's. A month ago it had been a dry cleaning store. The shop was crowded. Emily was out of her element. She really didn't know the difference in taste between the tortellini salad made with walnut vinegar and the one made with hazelnut vinegar. She had no desire to network over the cellophane noodles or join the mating dance taking place around the moussaka. Somehow she managed to put together a takeout dinner for three for less than seventy-five dollars and arrived at Hallie's with a full shopping bag.

Byte went wild at the aroma. They went into the kitchen, where Emily began unpacking the food while Hallie made drinks. "You have bad news for me," Hallie said. "I can tell."

"I have no news for you." Emily stopped unpacking and turned to face Hallie. "But I can't get over the feeling that there's something you're not telling me."

"There's nothing to tell," Hallie said, and went down the hall to summon Kate to dinner. The three of them sat down at the dining-room table.

Kate moved her chair close to Emily's. A visitor was exciting. Dinner was something else. Kate didn't like tortellini salad in any kind of vinegar. She didn't think much of the other selections either. She wanted a peanut butter and jelly sandwich. Emily offered to make it. Kate was delighted. Emily spread the filling thin, trimmed the crust, and cut the sandwich in quarters. Kate ate every one of them. Then she drifted off to watch a videotape of *Superman II.*

"Can she run the thing by herself?" Emily asked.

"Are you kidding? Kate taught me how to tape programs. She's her father's daughter."

"And getting back to her father, I'm not suggesting you're holding out on me, but maybe you did or said something inadvertently. Think."

"I have thought, Emily, and I haven't come up with anything."

"Then why would he change his mind so suddenly?"

"For God's sake, Daniel stops being Mr. Nice, which is something you warned me might happen, and you turn into Miss Marple."

"I'm not snooping. I'm trying to protect your interests."

Hallie pushed the tortellini around her plate. "I'm sorry. I know you are."

Emily watched her sister's face half hidden by the curtain of hair as she bent over her plate, toying with her food. "Look, Hallie, I'm speaking as your lawyer, not your sister. And at the risk of sounding like some crazed refugee from Masters and Johnson, I hear a lot of stories about sex and the lack of it in my practice. I had a client who won the lion's share of the property because she'd been generous enough to let her husband wear her lingerie during the marriage and another who queered a generous settlement from a dyed-in-the-wool liberal when she announced in front of both lawyers and a secretary that she hadn't gotten laid since Nixon resigned from office. I have also known any number of couples who returned humiliated and hungry for blood after abortive weekend trysts intended as try-outs at reconciliation."

Hallie looked up from her plate. "There have been no attempts at reconciliation. Daniel was strictly a Jockey shorts man, and he felt sorry for Nixon." She turned her attention back to her uneaten dinner. "Maybe he just found someone new, and she's worried about her future."

"Is he seeing someone? That would make sense and give us some leverage."

"How would I know? I keep telling you I don't speak to him, and if he has found someone new, he has the sense to keep her away from Kate at this point." Hallie stood, picked up her plate and Kate's, and started for the kitchen.

They cleared the table, put away the leftovers, and stacked the dishes in the dishwasher. Then Hallie went off to put Kate to bed, and Emily drifted into the living room and began browsing through the books. Her own were arranged according to an entirely idiosyncratic view of literature, history, art, and life. Hallie's were cataloged alphabetically by author. It was one way to make order, if not sense, of a library heavy in Kahlil Gibran, back-to-nature catalogs, and managerial treatises that promised to impart all the wisdom of the Harvard Business School in ninety seconds. There were also current best sellers and a variety of old friends Hallie had collected going through the same schools as Emily and taking many of the same courses. Emily came to D. H. Lawrence and remembered the boy who had cataloged Hallie and her as easily as if they were volumes of fiction. Hallie was the pretty one, Emily the smart one, he'd said. He hadn't been alone in his judgment. Hallie had never been without a boyfriend, frequently more than one. Emily looked at the copy of *Lady Chatterley's Lover* she was holding. She had little faith in human change.

Hallie came back down the hall from Kate's room. "Why are you looking at me that way?" she asked.

"You're seeing someone, aren't you?"

Hallie bent over to pick up a plastic toy in the form of an extraterrestrial being. Her hair fell in front of her face again. "What do you mean?"

"You have a boyfriend."

Hallie straightened. "At our age I wouldn't call any man, let alone a friend, a boy."

"Okay, a lover, a paramour, a significant other, a sugar daddy, if you like. I don't care what you call him, but there's someone, and for some reason you didn't want me to know. You didn't want anyone to know, but Daniel must have found out, so you'd better tell me."

Hallie shrugged. "There's nothing to tell."

"I'm not looking for prurient details, Hallie. I'm asking whom you're seeing and for how long and whether Daniel is likely to surprise us with papers suing you for divorce on grounds of adultery. And I think you'd better tell me."

Hallie bent to put the extraterrestrial on the coffee table and managed to hide behind her hair again. "Ned Sinclair," she whispered.

"Ned Sinclair," Emily almost shouted. "My Ned Sinclair!"

"You said you weren't interested in him."

"That's not what I meant. Ned Sinclair from my office. The bashful boy with cheek who's in the Social Register and into group sex."

"He's not into group sex! It was just a phase. Like my commune."

"A match made in heaven."

"I know you don't like him, but you don't even know him. He's really sweet. And considerate. He's always calling me from limos and planes and stuff. He took me to North Carolina on a company jet."

"How did he manage to miss the space shuttle?"

"And he's crazy about Kate."

"Kate! Am I the only person in New York who doesn't know?"

"No one knows. Kate just met him once. Accidentally. At least she thought it was accidentally. At the playground."

Emily put the copy of *Lady Chatterley's Lover* back in the bookcase and sat down. "But you didn't think you ought to tell your lawyer."

"Ned didn't think I should. He thought if you knew you might feel"—she ducked her head—"constrained."

"You mean, he thought I wouldn't fight as hard for you. You mean, he thinks I'm incompetent."

Hallie sat across from her sister. She picked up the rubber toy and began twisting its appendages into a grotesque shape, a more grotesque shape. "I don't see what you're so angry about."

"I'm angry about your stupidity," Emily shouted. "I'm angry about my betrayal. You lied to me. I trusted you, and you lied to me." She remembered the night at the Century Club. "You used me as a beard! I'm right, aren't I? You and Ned were gloating over your little secret the night the three of us went for drinks."

Hallie shook her head. The silky hair swung against her cheeks. "We weren't gloating."

"Which was, if I remember correctly, several weeks before Daniel moved out."

"I'm not the first woman to leave her husband for another man."

"You're the first client I ever had, not to mention the first sister, who lied to me about it. Why? Not just because you didn't want me to feel 'constrained.' "

Hallie went on torturing the small toy in her hands and said nothing.

"You lied to save face, right? Just like telling people Kate was an accident. Christ, when I think of all those diatribes about never marrying again. And all the while the executive director of that noble feminist organization the Association of Women Executives has a warm body lined up before the old one is even cold. Because the executive director of AWE, the role model for Kate and American womanhood—at least that segment of it pulling down more than twenty thousand a year—is just plain scared of living alone for a week or a month or a year. That's why you wouldn't tell me about Ned, isn't it? Because you were saving face. Clapping your little heart out, Tinker Bell, so that everyone else would believe."

"I was scared. Maybe because of Dottie, Dottie and all those nights standing in that damn Italian restaurant. Or maybe just because I'm weak. I don't know why. All I know is that for a long time I was miserable with Daniel, but I never had the nerve to leave him."

"Then Ned Sinclair came along in his white limo—or was it the company plane that did it?—and offered to take you away from all that."

"That's right, he did."

"And we think we've made progress."

"You can laugh all you want, but if it weren't for Ned, I never would have had the courage to leave."

"That's the point. And I'm not laughing."

Hallie put down the toy. She was no longer apologizing. "No, that's right. You're not laughing, just judging. You talk a good game, Emily, but at heart you're one hell of a misogynist."

"I am not!"

"You ought to hear yourself when you talk about your clients."

Emily picked up the toy off the coffee table. It was soft and ugly. "You're wrong, Hallie. Unlike some of our contemporaries, I don't believe that if you let women run the world, they'll put an end to war, but unlike Freud and certain of his cronies, I don't think women have an inferior moral sense either. I'm convinced that ethically, if not biologically, men and women are equal. But most of my friends are women, and so are most of my clients. In other words, it isn't a question of thinking less of women, only of knowing them better."

"It's a shame this vast knowledge doesn't extend to yourself."

"What do you mean?"

"I mean you spend half your life doing imitations of a doormat and the other half pretending you're a free spirit. You're either lying down or walking out." Hallie stopped suddenly. Emily stared at her. Hallie met her gaze. The only sound in the apartment was the noise of the dishwasher going through its cycles. It came to an abrupt end. The room was silent. Emily and Hallie went on staring at each other. They'd been undressing together since they were children, witnesses to each other's disfiguring birthmarks and unsightly flaws. These days they were more modest, turning their backs, clutching at towels, but there was little left to hide. Intimacy lingered, and with it acceptance, and finally forgiveness.

"I'm sorry," Hallie said. "And I'm sorry I lied to you."

Emily shrugged.

"What now?"

"I'd like a drink. A big drink. Then we get down to work. You're still my client. More to the point, you're still my sister."

Hallie went into the kitchen and came back with a scotch for Emily and a glass of wine for herself. "Do you really think Daniel will sue on grounds of adultery?"

"Not if we can reopen negotiations and head him off. I don't suppose he had a jet-propelled romance of his own."

"I told you. His only love was the mainframe."

"What about those computer conventions? Didn't he ever find anyone who was plug-compatible?"

"He was too busy working. The closest he ever got were Polaroid pictures."

"What do you mean?"

"There was a convention in Las Vegas a year or so ago. All his salesmen were screwing around like crazy, but Daniel was too busy wheeling and dealing. So one of them took some pictures of a girl he'd picked up and gave them to Daniel. I found them in his suitcase."

"Let me get this straight. Your husband comes home from a business trip with do-it-yourself dirty pictures, and you forget to mention them to your lawyer. I'm beginning to think that kid was right. You're not the smart one in the family. Do you still have them?"

"I think I can find them. Naomi packed Daniel's stuff, and I would have heard if she'd run across them. But I believe Daniel."

"That's sweet Hallie. But I doubt that anyone else will. Don't worry. I don't think we'll have to use them. I just want Daniel and S.S. to think we'll use them. I'm going to get you the kind of settlement every unfaithful wife dreams of."

"To prove something to Ned?"

"To prove something to me. And to take care of Kate's future. And because it's my job."

On the way back to her apartment, Emily thought of Hallie and Ned and Daniel and his Polaroid pictures. She'd told Hallie she was just doing her job. The words had a familiar ring. Then she remembered where she'd heard them. The Nuremberg trials.

Most metropolitan areas boast a variety of entertainments frequented by divorced men and almost unknown to their married brothers. These are not massage parlors or singles' bars, but rather kiddie events of some expense and, if the divorced fathers play their cards right, duration. Among the favorites in New York are the matinees of the local Gilbert and Sullivan company. Every Saturday and Sunday afternoon veterans of the feminist wars and heroes of the sexual revolution sit like Victorian gentlemen, explaining arcane references and archaic jokes to their children. Jake decided to take Nina and asked Emily along. He made a lunch reservation for three at Maxwell's Plum, the ice-cream parlor, decorated like a Victorian bordello, favored by all the local products of broken homes.

"I have a problem," Jake said Friday night. He was no fool. He said it just as Emily was about to doze off. She moved sleepily against him. "About tomorrow."

The problem wasn't serious. It was certainly solvable. It had something to do with a foreign bureau chief who'd breezed into town for the weekend. Jake had to see him, and time was tight. "If you take Nina to lunch, I can see him and meet you at the theater. What do you say?" Jake moved his hand strategically. Emily said "sure."

Jake said he'd put the lunch on his expense account. Lunch cost the magazine dearly. The magazine had nothing on Emily. It wasn't the disaster their day on Nantucket had been, but neither of them had much fun. Emily tried too hard. Nina didn't try at all. At least their responses were age-appropriate.

"What's wrong?" Jake asked after he'd taken Nina home that night.

Emily denied that anything was wrong and went on reading the early sections of the Sunday *Times.* Getting a running start on the paper always made her feel virtuous.

He repeated his question. She repeated her answer. He went into the kitchen to get more ice for his drink. By the time he returned she'd reached the "About Men" page in the magazine section, the worst joke the women's movement had played on journalism. This week's contributor was telling the world how hard it was to be a father and a son. It was so damn hard it had driven him to an unsuccessful suicide attempt. The piece read as if it were written in blood from his own ineffectualy opened veins.

Emily finished the magazine section. Jake finished the book review. They traded.

He stood and asked if she wanted another drink. She looked at him over the top of the paper. He shifted from one foot to the other like an impatient outfielder while he waited for her to decide. Wiry body, undergraduate khakis and oxford shirt, boyish Jake. The kid.

"I haven't spent sixteen years on various kinds of birth control to run for mother of the year at this point in my life."

The kid sat. "So that's it. All right, I'll never ask you to take Nina to lunch again."

"It isn't just lunch."

He leaned back and looked at her. His eyes were angry black smudges in his face. "Here we go. You've been makin' a list and checkin' it twice, gonna find out Jake's naughty and Emily's nice."

"You're out of season."

"Not with you, babe. Let's see, there was the day I went to see the whales and left Nina with you. Right?"

"I never complained about that."

"You never said anything, if that's what you mean. But you were storing it up. Did anyone ever tell you that you have one hell of a flair for martyrdom?"

Someone had told her, but she didn't approve of talking about old loves with current ones. "I just find it odd that in this post-*Kramer vs. Kramer* age of ours fathers are always hot for custody so long as there's a surrogate mother to take some of the heat off."

He leaned his elbows on his knees and his head on his hands. "I never sued for custody," he said as if he were making a confession.

"I'm sorry, I didn't mean that. You're a good father."

He leaned back and looked at her. His eyes were still un-readable smudges. "Okay, you're right. Nina's my daughter. My responsibility. I shouldn't ask you to take her to lunch or the beach or anywhere else. I shouldn't use you as a baby-sitter. But I want to know one thing. Why the hell can't you say no?"

"I just did."

"Before it's too late, I mean."

Jake was careful. He asked no favors. He made no assump-tions. He gave Emily options. When he took Nina to the movies, supper, or his apartment, she could join them, but she didn't have to. That went on for a few weeks. Then things re-turned to normal. Jake began assuming Emily would be there. Emily usually was. She was there the day they decided to carve a jack-o'-lantern."

"I'm going to make a jill-o'lantern," Nina said as the three of them walked from the market to Jake's apartment. Jake was carrying the pumpkin. Emily was holding Kate's hand. She squeezed it.

"I like the way your mind works," she said to Nina. "Her mother must be doing something right," she whispered to Jake.

"Maybe I'm doing something right," he said.

Emily just laughed.

They took the pumpkin into Jake's kitchen. Emily and Nina spread newspapers. Jake took a carving knife, made an imitation samurai sound that sent Nina into a spasm of giggles, and cut off the top of the pumpkin.

The phone rang, and Jake went to answer it. Emily took a spoon and gave another to Nina. They began scooping.

"This is yucky," Nina said. It was not a complaint. Emily thought of the utopian who'd proposed letting children clean up the mess of his ideal community. Nina scooped happily. Emily worked less blissfully. They finished the job.

"Now can we make the face?"

Emily looked at the smooth orange skin. She was bad with

her hands, worse with a knife. "Let's wait for your father to get off the phone."

She suggested a Hostess cupcake. Nina took the bribe. Emily watched in fascination. It was like the loaves and the fishes. The more Nina ate, the more chocolate and marshmallow proliferated on the counter in front of her.

They waited. Emily asked Nina what she was going to be for Halloween. Nina mentioned a character who could only be a trademark. Emily wondered what had happened to the innocent ghosts and hoboes of her youth.

"Where's Daddy?" Nina asked again.

It was an excellent question. Emily went inside to find out if Jake planned to spend the rest of the day on the phone.

He looked up. Emily pointed to her watch. He nodded. In the kitchen Nina screamed. Jake was off the phone and into the kitchen in seconds. Emily was right behind him. The knife Jake had used to cut off the top of the pumpkin lay on the floor. A small trickle of blood ran from Nina's finger into the chocolate marshmallow-pumpkin mess. Tears streamed down her face. Jake grabbed her and carried her into the bathroom. Emily followed. He held her hand over the sink and managed to wash away enough of the sticky mess to reveal a small but apparently deep cut. He washed it. He disinfected it. He covered it with a Band-Aid. Nina liked that part. She stopped crying. Emily went into the kitchen, picked up the knife, and began cleaning up the mess.

"Christ, Emily," Jake said from the doorway, "what kind of a moron leaves a five-year-old alone with a carving knife?"

She threw the crumbs in the trash, the sponge in the sink, and the towel in. "A moron who doesn't have children," she said, and slammed the front door behind her.

XVI

Isabel came into the kitchen and dropped her book bag on the floor and a kiss on her mother's cheek. "That smells good."

"Me or the chicken?"

"Both of you." She took a handful of peas from the pile Laura was shelling and went to work. "I charged a book to you today at the Burlington."

"Which one?"

"Something on Pompeii."

"For school?"

"For Daddy. He fell in love with Pompeii when we were there. I thought he'd like it."

"Then why didn't you charge it to him?"

"Because I wanted to buy him a present. You're the one who always says it's nice to give presents when you're inspired rather than because it's a birthday or Christmas or something."

"That's right, I do. And I think it's a nice gesture, but I think if you want to give your father a gift, *you* ought to give him a gift."

Isabel stopped shelling peas. "In other words, you want me to pay for it."

"That's what you get an allowance for. To teach you to handle money."

"Daddy paid for that handbag I brought you from Italy."

"Maybe he doesn't care if you grow up knowing how to handle money, but I do."

"Okay, okay. You don't have to make a moral crusade out of it."

"I wasn't making a moral crusade. I was making a point."

"I still think it's kind of chintzy. He spent a lot on that handbag."

Laura looked up from the peas. "He spent a lot more on that whirlwind tour of Europe. I love the bag, Isabel, but I'm not impressed by your father's conscience money."

Isabel said nothing, but she went back to helping her mother shell peas.

Isabel had returned home from Europe with an enlarged French vocabulary, a smattering of Italian, and a broadened view of Western culture, but she'd achieved her real growth since she'd got back. In three months she'd chalked up an inch and a half in height. She had nothing to wear. She made the announcement dressed in a pair of jeans that were too short and a blouse that barely buttoned. She asked Laura to go shopping with her. Laura accepted like a teenager invited to the prom.

Isabel had a list and a plan. They would start at Brooks Brothers and work their way uptown, stopping at Orvis and Saks, Kreeger and Bloomingdale's as if they were stations of the cross. It was a pilgrimage the two of them had made many times in the past.

They took a bus to Forty-fourth Street. It seemed to be peopled entirely by underaged couples in lust and lone fathers with children. A man who wore his weekend tweeds without ease clutched the hand of a small girl as if it were a briefcase. A second in jeans and T-shirt identical to his adolescent son's fired questions about life, love, and admission to an Ivy League school that no adolescent should be asked, especially on a crowded Fifth Avenue bus. A third with two small boys chattered in a voice so artificially bright it made Laura's teeth ache.

By the time they reached Fifty-ninth Street, it had driven the four-year-old to tears and his older brother into a sulk. Laura pitied the trio. Their day had started badly and was bound to turn out worse.

Isabel had picked up the same signs. As she and Laura left the bus, they exchanged glances of mutual understanding and indignation.

They began working their way through the stores in compatible accord. They agreed on oxford shirts and corduroy pants and shetland sweaters. At Kreeger Laura watched her daughter and a smooth-faced boy make a point of not watching each other and felt tender, sad, and old. At Saks they stumbled upon a mother and daughter locked in battle over a burning question of taste. Laura stepped back as if their strident voices and twisted faces were contagious.

They made slow but steady progress uptown, zigzagging their way east and west, dividing the shopping bags among four hands in an attempt to share the burden fairly. They stopped at their favorite hamburger place, then moved on to a boutique where the lighting made all the juvenile delinquent saleskids look sick and the music assaulted Laura's head like a mechanical hammer. The air was heavy with a scent reminiscent of marijuana, sex, and burning rubber. The hamburger, which had tasted delicious twenty minutes ago felt like a pool of grease in Laura's stomach. She felt old but no longer tender or sad.

"Which do you like better?" Isabel held up two skirts. One looked as if it had been designed for the moll in a thirties gangster movie. The other had a hemline that rose and fell like the stock market on a day of heavy trading. So the sartorial battle would be joined after all.

"I can't say I'm wild about either."

Disappointment tugged at Isabel's mouth.

"What I mean is, they're not my taste. Whichever you like better."

Isabel disappeared into the upright wooden crate that

served as a fitting room. Laura looked for a place to sit. It was a hopeless quest. Young people do not sit, and seated people do not buy. She folded herself into a corner where fuchsia and chartreuse walls met. The effect was not restful. She leaned her head against the wall and closed her eyes. The music thumped relentlessly through the posterboard.

Isabel emerged in one of the skirts. "I can't decide."

"Then maybe you don't like either," Laura said. Hope rose in her voice like the front of the skirt hem.

"Maybe I ought to get both."

"One or the other."

Isabel gravitated to the mirrors. She examined herself from all angles. She held the other skirt in front of her. She debated with a salesperson—Laura wasn't sure of the sex—whose eyes appeared too glazed to see Isabel or the skirts. The conference went on for some time. Laura's head throbbed in time to the music.

Isabel and the unisex clerk finally managed to come to a decision. She'd opted for the gun-moll look. Laura glanced at the price tag. It was highway robbery. She paid without a word. Falling out into the sunshine and relatively fresh air, she felt like a mauled body being tossed from a speeding car.

Their progress up Madison Avenue was slowed by the anonymous crowds, stalled by people they knew. Laura had long since stopped being surprised at what a truly small town the Upper East Side is. She rarely walked the neighborhood without meeting someone. Today they counted two groups from Isabel's school, a mother and daughter they knew from playground years, and a divorced friend to whom Laura had grown closer since her own separation.

"You didn't have to say it like that," Isabel said when they'd begun walking again after the last encounter.

"Say what like what?"

" 'She was in Europe with her father,' as if you were telling her some inside joke, some bitchy, sarcastic inside joke."

"I didn't say it that way," Laura insisted.

"Yeah. Then why did she raise her eyebrows and make that crack about what some people can afford?"

"She wasn't talking about you."

"I know she wasn't talking about me, Mother. I'm not an idiot. She was talking about Daddy. You both were. As if he were some selfish creep. As if all men were. As if you hated them."

The words pounded in Laura's head more harshly than any music. She felt sicker than she had in the store. Man hater. It was worse than any name Ezra had called her. It conjured up weak, neurotic women suffering from obscure neurasthenic disorders or strident, twisted women fighting battles that took no prisoners.

"I didn't," Laura said. "I don't. Not in the least."

Isabel kept walking. Her face was averted to look in the windows, but Laura recognized the sullen curve of cheek.

"But I really don't," Laura insisted.

"Sure."

Laura stopped walking. Isabel continued for a few steps, then stopped without turning around.

"Isabel."

"What?"

"Don't just walk away from me."

"I'm not walking away. I'm standing right here. Waiting for you."

"I'm still your mother."

"Mom." Isabel was pleading now. "Can we just forget it?"

They could, Laura decided, pretend to. She caught up with her daughter, and they began walking again. Isabel pointed out a window display in a tone that only a mother would recognize as an apology. Laura decided to accept it.

They stopped before another window. "What a cool sweater," Isabel said. "It would look really neat with my new skirt."

Isabel had a point. The sweater and skirt had come from the same wardrobe trunk. Together they would make Isabel look not like a gun moll, but like a child hooker. If the sequins and rhinestones didn't give her away, the neckline would. "Don't you think it's a little flashy?"

"I can't spend my whole life in button-down shirts and shetlands." Laura fought the urge to ask why. "I just want to look," Isabel said, and Laura followed her into the store.

The sweater fulfilled all Laura's expectations. It made Isabel look as if she were pulling down a couple of hundred a night. She would have had to make at least that much to afford it. Laura pronounced it out of the question. "It's much too expensive. The skirt was one thing, but I refuse to pay ninety-five dollars so you can look like a ten-cents-a-dance tart."

Isabel put a hand on her hipbone. "I'll pay for half of it out of my allowance."

Laura pointed out that her allowance was already garnish-eed for past debts. "Besides, it's a sinful price for a sweater for a fourteen-year-old."

"Come on, Mom, it's a sweater, not a moral issue."

"That sweater is a moral issue."

Isabel faced her reflection in the mirror. The line of her mouth was pure determination now. "I'll ask Daddy."

"No."

"What?"

"No, you won't ask Daddy. You won't play him off against me."

"I'm not playing anybody off against anybody. I just want the sweater. You never let me have anything I really want. I bet Daddy will buy it for me. Just like he bought the handbag for you. He says money's there to spend. To give pleasure. He says that's why you're so weird about it. Because you can't deal with pleasure."

"Get dressed, Isabel."

Isabel looked at her mother. The line of her mouth grew more firm. She didn't move.

"Take the sweater off and get dressed. We're going home. You and I are going to have a talk."

Neither of them spoke on the way home. When they reached the apartment, Isabel started for her room, but Laura stopped her. "Come into the study."

"I have to put this stuff away."

"Then put it away and come into the study."

Laura went to her desk and waited for her daughter. Isabel had never taken so much time or care putting things away. Finally she came and stood in the doorway. The line of her mouth, the sharp angle of her shoulders, the fists jammed into pants pockets—all screamed in silent protest at being there. Laura told her to sit down.

"I don't want to hear anything about Daddy."

"Why not? You're happy enough to listen to what Daddy has to say about me?"

Isabel sat in silence.

"Anyway, I don't want to talk to you about your father. I want to talk to you about money. That mysterious substance that gives him so much pleasure and makes me so weird."

"You don't have to be sarcastic."

Laura looked at her daughter, a mean little stranger slumped in a chair with a sullen expression on her face and a chip on her thin shoulder. "You're right, I'll try not to be sarcastic. I just want to explain a few things. I never have before because I didn't want to frighten you. The way Dottie used to frighten me."

The angry expression didn't change. Isabel's eyes remained fixed on the opposite wall. She had no interest in ancient history.

"After your grandfather died, Dottie got a little erratic about money. Weird, as you would say."

"I know what *erratic* means."

"She used to spend a lot of time at her desk—God, I can still see her sitting there in the old house—figuring accounts. One week she'd be sure we were all on the way to the poorhouse. I remember looking at those sketches of the hundred neediest cases in the newspaper at Christmastime and thinking we were next. Then she'd do an about-face and take us on some wild shopping spree or theater orgy. Cashmere sweaters. Camel's hair coats. Orchestra seats to Katharine Cornell and Lynn Fontanne and all the great ladies of the stage she thought we ought to see before they died. Once, just before she met Herb, she took us all on a cruise to the Caribbean. When we got back, she panicked. I remember asking her for money for one of those varsity sweaters with my club's name on the back. I was thirteen. She said we couldn't afford it. I'm not complaining. I saw a lot of good theater, not to mention several tropical islands. And who needs a club sweater when you've got a drawerful of cashmeres? I'm not criticizing Dottie either. She'd had no experience with money and couldn't decide whether she'd been left a fortune or a pittance. The experience was confusing, though, to put it mildly, and I didn't want to visit the same thing on you. I didn't want to make you fearful about money."

"But now you do?"

"I'm not the only bitchy one in this family, Isabel. No, now I want to make you understand a few things." Laura took a ledger out of the desk drawer. "I want to show you what your father earns and what I earn, what he pays, when he decides to pay—I'll show you those records, too—and what your school and clothes and this apartment and all the rest cost." Isabel shifted position in the worn chair. "I don't care if you're bored. It's about time you knew these particular facts of life."

If Isabel learned anything that afternoon, she kept it to herself. But she didn't sulk through dinner, and before she went off to a party, she came into Laura's room and asked how she liked the new skirt with her old gray sweater. Laura said she liked it fine.

Isabel spent Sunday afternoon with her father. Ezra called that evening. "Isabel and I had a talk today," he began.

"About the sweater?"

"What sweater?"

"Nothing. What is it you want, Ezra?"

"I told her I don't get to see as much of her as I'd like."

"You see a lot of her. As much as I do. She lives here, but she isn't here all that much of the time. It's the age. She'd rather be with her friends."

"That's healthy."

She closed her eyes. Wasn't he ever going to give up? "I didn't say it wasn't healthy. You were the one who complained about not seeing enough of her."

"I was thinking of the time she divides between us."

The book she'd seen that day in Doubleday came back to her. "Child Custody—or How to Keep Your Children, Your Self-Respect, and Your Hard-Earned Cash." She thought of telling him that this was a matter for their attorneys. She said nothing.

"Are you there, Laura?"

"Get to the point, Ezra."

"I'd like to take Isabel to California for Thanksgiving. I'm giving a paper in San Francisco, and I thought she could spend a few days there with me. She's never seen San Francisco."

"This was supposed to be my year to have Isabel for Thanksgiving."

"Well, of course, if you're more interested in punishing me than in Isabel's happiness. I thought she ought to see a little of the West Coast. In fact, I was thinking I might take her out of school for a day or two and drive north. If you have no objection, that is."

"I don't understand you, Ezra. For the last year and a half you've done nothing but cry poverty. Just last month there wasn't enough money to fix the leak in my bathroom, but now there's enough for a weeklong jaunt on the West Coast—after a month in Europe."

"You never did understand anything about money, Laura,

except how to spend it. I'm giving a paper. I can write most of the trip off."

Laura gave up. She'd fight for custody but not points. "Isabel can go if she wants. I have no objection," she lied.

Laura had a bad week. Wherever she turned, she met defeat. At the office Dr. Goodnuf turned down her request for a raise. "We don't feel it's warranted," he explained. Laura wasn't sure if he was referring to his colleagues or using the royal *we*. It didn't much matter. A friend called to say that a man Laura had had dinner with a few times had just married a twenty-three-year-old aerobic dance teacher. But most of all, she felt the loss of Isabel. "I can't compete with Ezra," she complained to Emily.

"You don't have to compete. Isabel loves you."

As Emily was always the first to admit, she knew nothing about children. "Kids are materialistic little buggers," Laura said. "And I know grown women who would sell their mothers for less than a month in Europe and a week at the Mark Hopkins."

That Thursday night Isabel returned home late from dinner with Ezra. Laura was sitting up in bed watching an old Hitchcock movie. Isabel kicked off her shoes and sat on the other side of the big bed. As the tension built, she crept closer. "Watch out!" she screamed to Cary Grant. Cary turned just in time. "Tell me how it ends," she begged her mother. Laura shook her head and laughed.

"You know great movies," Isabel said when it was over.

"I'm a buff." Laura slid her robe off one shoulder in a mock sexy pose. "In the buff. Now stop stalling and go to bed. It's a weeknight."

Isabel didn't move. The curve of her cheek was solemn but not sullen. "Daddy wants to take me to San Francisco for Thanksgiving."

"I know."

"He said after the meeting we could drive north along the coast."

"It's supposed to be beautiful."

"Haven't you ever seen it?"

"I've been to San Francisco, but we didn't have time for any more."

"I was thinking," Isabel said.

Laura was silent.

"Daddy and I went to Europe."

Laura still didn't answer.

"Well, if he can afford all these trips for him and me, why can't he afford some for you, or you and me?"

Laura's heart flipped over the way it had when Ezra had first told her he loved her. "I love you, Isabel Glass."

Isabel smiled. Laura wondered how she'd ever seen Ezra's smile in Isabel's. She had her mother's mouth and her mother's expression. "Well, why can't he?"

"Did you ask him?"

"Yup."

"What did he say?"

"That he could write off this trip. I asked him if that meant he didn't have to pay for it, but he said it was more complicated than that."

"It was considerate of you to think of it, Isabel. I'm proud of you." Laura picked up the hairbrush from her dresser and began brushing her hair.

"I'm not going."

The brush hung in midair, a small silver-backed sword over her head.

"I told him the next time I go away it ought to be with you. I told him it wasn't fair for he and I to go all those places and always leave you home."

The grammar grated on Laura's ears, but the words wrapped themselves around her heart and tied it up in a neat package. She walked to the bed and put her arms around her daughter. Isabel's hair was wiry against Laura's cheek and smelled from some herbal shampoo that gave an excellent imitation of spring. "You're quite a kid."

Isabel looked up at her mother. "Now can I have the sweater?" She started to laugh. "Come on, Mom, I was just kidding."

XVII

       Emily had slammed the door to Jake's apartment on a Sunday afternoon. Jake called her office that Friday morning. "Was that your exit line," he asked, "or do you want to have lunch?"

She said "sure."

"Sure, it was your exit line, or sure, you want to have lunch?"

"Lunch."

"Sometimes it's hard to tell with you."

They met at an old-fashioned French restaurant that had outlasted their marriage. It hung on to its faded plush banquettes and flocked wallpaper as desperately as if they were illusions. Jake was there when she arrived. He must have been waiting for a while because he had only half a martini in front of him.

"You know what you do when you enter a room?" he said as the waiter held her chair for her. "Check all the exits."

"So it's going to be one of those lunches."

"I'm sorry I called you a moron."

She shrugged. The waiter brought her a bloody mary.

"I'm sorry I called you a moron," he repeated, "but I don't think it's a reason for walking out."

She was silent. The busboy brought rolls. They stared at his hands as he put the butter, carved like seashells, on their plates.

"Remember that fight we had when we were married?" Jake asked after the busboy had retreated.

"I believe there was more than one."

"When I called you Ed."

"You also called me Lucy. Your old girlfriend."

"I was preoccupied."

"Writing the great American cover story."

He downed the remains of his drink and motioned to the waiter for another. "But when I thought about it later, the Ed slip made sense. Do you remember him at all?"

"Only that he was a little strange."

"Senior year he never bothered to unpack. Lived out of suitcases and cartons the whole time. Said he was just passing through, and it didn't pay to settle in."

"Where did all this come from?"

He stared at her. Something tugged at his lower lip, and it wasn't desire. "It's been coming."

"In other words, you set up this little reunion so you could be the one to walk out."

The waiter approached. Jake took the drink from his hand before he could put it on the table. "You'd like that, wouldn't you? It would save you the trouble. Though God knows, it ought to be second nature to you by now. Truck out the list of wrongs, speech, exit, curtain. And if I walked out, you'd be wronged and therefore in the right. Your favorite place to be. You have to be right, and you have to be safe. Or maybe they're the same thing."

She looked away from Jake. The busboy stood at his station ready to refill their water and refresh their butter and replace their ashtray. Two tables away a woman was signing the check while a man fingered his striped tie uncomfortably. From the center of the room the aroma of garlic and the words *forty percent return* drifted. Everyone else in the world was doing business or a job. Why was she wallowing in this mess? "Is there anything else you'd like to tell me while we're at it?"

"Why can't you negotiate? You do it all day in your office. You're always lecturing your clients about it. But you can't seem to pull it off after hours."

She said nothing.

"No answer?"

"You don't need me. You're doing too well on your own."

He shook his head, perhaps at the waiter approaching with the menus, perhaps at her. "That's what I mean. You never say no, and you never ask for anything. But you expect a hell of a lot. And since you aren't likely to get a hell of a lot, especially if you don't ask for it, then you're just naturally justified when one day you decide to pick up and walk out."

"So we're back to that."

"You never leave it. You've got your eye on the exit right now."

"Just what is it you want?"

"I don't want to have to be a mind reader. I want you to say no when you want to, not six months later, and yes when you want to. And I want you to stop keeping track of injustices against you in that emotional balance sheet in your head."

"Anything else?"

"I want you to stop saying 'sure.' "

"I can't make any promises."

"I'm too old to believe them anyway."

It was not a celebratory lunch. They knew each other and themselves too well to think they had anything to celebrate. When the check came, Emily reached for it, but Jake managed to outmaneuver her just as he had that time they'd had drinks a year ago. "It's my turn," she said.

He put his credit card on the check without bothering to add it up. "That's right, it is. Which means if I pay for this, you're going to be in debt to me. Do you think you can handle it?"

She almost said "sure," but that would have been a lie. "I don't know."

* * *

Though Peter had sublet an apartment in the same neighborhood, Emily had not run into him in the eleven months since they'd separated. Sometimes she thought of her years with him as a figment of her imagination, other times as one of the happiest periods of her life. But whatever her judgment, she thought of him less and less. Then, that Friday night on the way to Jake's apartment, she ran into him.

She was walking down Third Avenue and he was walking up and there was no one else within half a block of them. She saw him first. Then he noticed her. They kept walking toward each other. She recognized the long-legged stride. A scene from *High Noon* flickered through her mind.

She wondered what to do. Did they shake hands? Touch cheeks? Hurl accusations? She kept walking. She smoothed her hair. She ran her tongue over her front teeth to make sure there were no lipstick smudges. She smiled. "Hello, Peter," she said when they were a few feet apart.

He looked directly at her, then away, and kept walking. He didn't even break stride.

She stopped, turned, and stared after him. He didn't look back. They'd lived together for four years, fighting frequently, discussing rarely, swearing undying love constantly. Now he no longer recognized her. Talk about nonnegotiable.

Emily didn't mention the incident to Jake. For one thing she didn't have a chance to. Nina was there for the night. He'd warned Emily she would be. Emily had considered telling Jake she'd wait until Saturday to see him but hadn't wanted to seem ungenerous after their lunch. Besides, she liked Friday nights with Jake.

They had dinner and put Nina to sleep in the alcove Jake had turned into a second bedroom for Nina's weekends. A little later they went to bed themselves. It had been a long week. They were glad to see each other. They were so glad they didn't hear Nina open the door. Jake hadn't been entirely right on

Nantucket. Five-year-olds did occasionally wander about in the night. "Daddy," she whispered. She might as well have screamed. They sprang apart.

Jake slid out of bed, wrapping the blanket around him. Emily cowered under the sheets. By the time he returned from Nina's room Emily was out of bed and half dressed.

He sat on the side of the bed. She refused to. "I've told her to knock," he said.

"She apparently doesn't listen."

"She's only a kid."

"It's not her fault; it's yours."

"You're getting dressed?"

"I think I'd better go home."

He looked at her. "I should have known." He went on staring at her. She thought of the way Peter had looked through her a few hours earlier. She sat on the side of the bed.

"All right, I'm not going home now. But you've got to start making some changes, too. I can't do it all on my own. Or rather, I could, but I sent my martyr's robes to the cleaners. Tomorrow morning I want you to buy a lock for that door. And tomorrow afternoon I want you to put it on. If you don't, I'm not staying here with Nina anymore. I'll stay here without her. And you can stay at my place. But no more group sex with a five-year-old."

He took off the blanket and got under the covers. "Is that what's known as an ultimatum?"

"That's what's known as negotiating." She joined him under the covers. He reminded her of one of those new halogen lamps, lean, well designed, and capable of going from zero watts to five hundred at the touch of a fingertip. "Negotiating from strength."

XVIII

That Thanksgiving they gathered at Hallie's apartment, where she and Ned and Kate were camping out until the loft they'd bought to renovate was finished. They'd hired a hot young architecture group called Iguana. In place of professional cards they handed out small ceramic iguanas that could, if the need arose, be used as coke spoons. They were, Hallie said, the coming thing.

The wedding was set for Christmas, but Ned was already turning into a super surrogate daddy. He was the one who came up with the idea of childproof locks on the temperature-controlled wine cellar they were building into one wall of the loft. "Is Kate hitting the bottle again?" Emily asked.

"He's afraid she might lock herself in," Hallie said. "He's very serious about parenting."

Laura hadn't offered to make Thanksgiving dinner. She was too busy with her new job as a researcher in a government-funded study of the elderly. This time Dottie and Herb approved, and even Ezra found the work socially acceptable. All Laura said was that she liked it. "I'm not changing the world. I'm not even sure I'm doing anyone any good, but they're doing me some good. The other day I had a couple—he was eighty-seven and she was eighty-four—who spent the entire afternoon telling me about their courtship. They started talking about it in the past tense and ended up in the present. Then I had a ninety-one-year-old widow who, when we got to the sex questions, wanted to know if I thought she'd been frigid during her marriage. Can you imagine how long she's been waiting to ask that question?"

"What did you say?" Emily asked.

"Don't report me to the director. He'd fire me for losing my professional distance. I told her she sounded like a hot number to me. Her marriage was probably based on illusion. Why shouldn't her widowhood be?"

This year Ezra was not invited to the holiday celebration, though he hadn't gone to San Francisco to give his paper after all. He said he couldn't afford the trip, even as a tax write-off, now that he'd agreed to hand over the apartment plus an outrageous settlement. Emily suggested that Isabel consider a career in matrimonial law. Laura said that criminal law was more in her daughter's line, judging from her new wardrobe.

Emily brought Jake to Thanksgiving dinner. Nina was spending the holiday with her mother. Everyone said it was wonderful to have Jake among them again.

They sat down to dinner at four. Ned was at the head of the table. Naomi carried the turkey to him as if it were a homing pigeon. The first Thanksgiving she'd been with the Brandts, she'd put the bird in front of poor Mr. Brandt, who'd died two years later. For more than a decade she'd carried it to Mrs. Brandt's second husband, which was the way she always thought of Herb. Then Mrs. Brandt moved to Florida, and the girls began taking turns with the holiday. Over the years she'd carried picture-perfect fowls to Dr. Glass and Mr. Fields and, one year, a long time ago, to Mr. Ferris. She'd never carried one to that man Emily had lived with, but he'd been at the table, too.

"You're looking good," Naomi whispered to Emily later in the kitchen. "You all are. It's funny. Awhile ago I was praying for you. It seemed all I was doing back then was praying for you girls. Mrs. Glass had all that trouble, and Mrs. Fields was going to have to raise that poor child all by herself, and you just didn't have anybody at all. And here it is a few months later, and Mrs. Glass came through just fine, and Mrs. Fields found Mr. Sinclair, and you're back with Mr. Ferris."

"Naomi, you almost sound as if you believe in serial marriage."

"I believe in Our Lord and the hereafter." Naomi put the plate she'd just scraped on top of the stack on the counter. "But you got to admit it's funny."

"What's funny?"

"The way those men come and go, but you Brandt women are always here."

Emily didn't say that she was the only one of them who still carried the Brandt name. She knew what Naomi meant.

"Don't you like men, Naomi?"

"I don't have nothing against them. They are the way they are." She took the foil top off one of the pies. "At your age I liked them fine. But they're different." She took the wrap off the second pie and laughed. "I guess that's what I liked about them. But you got to admit it's sad."

"Sad?"

"I don't know what else you call it. It's like there's this big fence going right down the middle of everything. On one side you got all these people who are one way. On the other you got all these people who are a whole different way. Now they both know they're different. They both know they can't get together. But that don't stop them. They just keep on trying."

"And you think that's sad? I'd call it hopeful."

She handed one pie to Emily and picked up the other. "You can call it whatever you want," Naomi said, and started for the dining room. "It just keeps going on."